Undead and Unforgiven

Anthologies

CRAVINGS
(with Laurell K. Hamilton, Rebecca York, Eileen Wilks)

BITE
*(with Laurell K. Hamilton, Charlaine Harris,
Angela Knight, Vickie Taylor)*

KICK ASS
(with Maggie Shayne, Angela Knight, Jacey Ford)

MEN AT WORK
(with Janelle Denison, Nina Bangs)

DEAD AND LOVING IT

SURF'S UP
(with Janelle Denison, Nina Bangs)

MYSTERIA
(with P. C. Cast, Gena Showalter, Susan Grant)

OVER THE MOON
(with Angela Knight, Virginia Kantra, Sunny)

DEMON'S DELIGHT
(with Emma Holly, Vickie Taylor, Catherine Spangler)

DEAD OVER HEELS

MYSTERIA LANE
(with P. C. Cast, Gena Showalter, Susan Grant)

MYSTERIA NIGHTS
(includes Mysteria *and* Mysteria Lane, *with P. C. Cast, Susan Grant,
Gena Showalter)*

UNDERWATER LOVE
(includes Sleeping with the Fishes, Swimming Without a Net,
and Fish out of Water*)*

DYING FOR YOU

UNDEAD AND UNDERWATER

UNDEAD
AND
UNFORGIVEN

MaryJanice Davidson

BERKLEY SENSATION, NEW YORK

BERKLEY
SENSATION

An imprint of Penguin Random House LLC
375 Hudson Street, New York, New York 10014

This book is an original publication of Penguin Random House LLC.

Copyright © 2015 by MaryJanice Davidson.
Penguin supports copyright. Copyright fuels creativity, encourages diverse voices, promotes free speech, and creates a vibrant culture. Thank you for buying an authorized edition of this book and for complying with copyright laws by not reproducing, scanning, or distributing any part of it in any form without permission. You are supporting writers and allowing Penguin to continue to publish books for every reader.

BERKLEY SENSATION® and the "B" design are registered trademarks
of Penguin Random House LLC.
For more information, visit penguin.com.

Library of Congress Cataloging-in-Publication Data

Davidson, MaryJanice
Undead and unforgiven / MaryJanice Davidson.—First edition.
p. cm. — (Undead/Queen Betsy ; 14)
ISBN 978-0-425-28293-9 (hardcover)
1. Taylor, Betsy (Fictitious character)—Fiction.   2. Sinclair, Eric (Fictitious character)—Fiction.   3. Vampires—Fiction.   4. Hell—Fiction.   I. Title.
PS3604.A949U5254 2015
813'.6—dc23
2015025111

First edition: October 2015

PRINTED IN THE UNITED STATES OF AMERICA

10   9   8   7   6   5   4   3   2   1

Text design by Kristin del Rosario.

Penguin
Random
House

*For my son, William, who came up with the idea that
Hell isn't eternal punishment from which there is no parole.
"It's more like jail. Or detention! You can get out,
but you have to behave."*

*And for my daughter, Christina, who grew up despite direct
orders to the contrary. Sure, she's a legal adult and can
function quite well on her own even though in my mind
she turned five last week, but* I'm not old, dammit!

Author's Note

Cow Town in Hastings, Minnesota, is a thing. It's named for a part of the town that was once all farm-land and cow paths. We were lucky enough to live there for a few years when our children were small. Our first night in the new house we went to sleep with the gentle lowing of bovines in the background, which aggravated my city-boy husband beyond belief. "Shut up! Damned cows!" I laughed until I snored.

I have nothing against Fairview Ridges Hospital in Burnsville, Minnesota; my son was born there! It's one of the few hospitals in the Twin Cities area I'm familiar with, so I use it whenever a character needs to be hospitalized. It's why Marc worked there, Jessica had cancer there, the Antichrist volunteered there, and Tim Andersson (you'll meet him in the prologue) died there. Again: great place; they took excellent care of me, and also my baby, who was so fat and sweet tempered, the resident used to lug him around with her on rounds. (This was fine with me: More sleep, please! Also more pudding. Thank you.)

The midnight blue Armani suit Tina wears to the meeting in Hell costs $1,250 and it is glorious.

Unlike Marc, I don't have anything against Kristen Stewart. It's just I really, really liked Ravenna, the wicked queen, from *Snow White and the Huntsman.*

I had little to no interest in what Snow White was doing, but couldn't look away from the queen. (Also, I knew how it would end, so there was no *need* to root for Snow Stewart.)

Cinnamon Churros vodka is a thing. Thanks, Smirnoff!

Betsy is not alone in thinking *The Lego Movie* sucked. It did. Terrible. I've said it before, when the monstrosity known as the Transformers franchise took over, and I'm saying it again now: never see movies based on toys or games. Lego, Transformers, G.I. Joe, Battleship, Ouija, Barbie, Teenage Mutant Ninja Turtles . . . no. Stop the madness. There is one—*one*—exception: the Toy Story franchise. Hey, even a stopped clock is right twice a day.

Forepaugh's is a real restaurant in St. Paul and several people are convinced it's haunted. The food is divine, though the story behind the resident ghost is sad: she killed herself after she found out she was pregnant by her married boss. Try the deconstructed banana cream pie.

The Griggs Mansion, just up the street from Betsy's mansion, is considered to be the most haunted house in St. Paul. It has creeped any number of people out, including skeptical journalists, and I have to say, the pattern of owners has been pretty interesting. They move in, redo the place, then move out within a year or two. The last owners had to keep dropping the price to unload the thing (in 2012), because potential buyers were horrified of the thought of spending a single night there, never mind living there for a decade or so.

Sinclair's buddy Lawrence Taliaferro was a legit fella and pretty cool, too. Born in 1794, he was an army officer from Virginia who served as an Indian

officer at Fort Snelling, Minnesota, and had an interesting part to play in the Dred Scott slavery legal
battle some years later.

His job was to mediate between the traders, the
Native Americans, and the United States. Shockingly,
all three entities were seldom on the same page, but
he worked hard and did his best to look out for everyone's best interests.

The Native Americans called him "No-Sugar-in-
Your-Mouth," a reference to how he dealt fairly with
them and never made a promise he couldn't keep. He
had an almost impossible job but didn't shirk, and
for a while things were pretty peaceful. Toward the
end of his time there, he helped draft the 1837 treaty,
negotiating what he felt would be fair terms for all
involved. The U.S. government, however, decided
"signed treaty" meant "thing we don't actually have
to do" and failed to hold up their end. The Native
Americans were ruined, Taliaferro even more dis-
illusioned (like *that* was possible), and he resigned in
disgust not long after.

He probably thought, once away from Fort Snelling, that life would settle down, but that's because
he had no idea who Dred Scott was. A Virginian by
birth, Taliaferro owned a slave named Harriet Rob-
inson, who was in love with another slave, Dred Scott.
Not only did he give them permission to marry, he
officiated. (He was a justice of the peace in the terri-
tories.) *They're in love, that's great*, he probably thought.
*What's the worst that can happen? It certainly won't lead
to a landmark Supreme Court decision that hastens the
Civil War, right?*

Yeah, so. *That* happened. Dred Scott, as we know,
lost before the Supreme Court, but part of the reason
he fought for his freedom in the first place was because

Taliaferro had married him to a (later) freed black woman in a free state.

Taliaferro kind of disappears from the history books after that, which I found intriguing. And so Sinclair's bestie was born! You can learn all about him and other fascinating/sad/amazing bits of Minnesota history at Fort Snelling, which still stands today, and welcomes tourists.

Cutco knives are wicked sharp! My daughter sold them for about a year and I have to say, they're terrific. Betsy is right to be impressed at how much easier it is to decapitate someone with the right tool.

Finally, betrayal isn't cool, even if you're the Antichrist and think you're totally justified.

Jesus *lived* with us for like a week, what else do you need?

Son of Perdition. Little Horn. Most unclean!
I do miss the old names.

I am so smart! I am so smart! S-m-r-t! I mean s-m-a-r-t!

Hit me with it! Just give it to me straight. I came a long way just to see you, Mary. The least you can do is level with me. What are my chances?
Not good.
You mean, not good like one out of a hundred?
I'd say more like one out of a million.
So you're telling me there's a chance. Yeah!

Get you gone from here. Leave Delain behind, now and forever. You are cast out. *Get you gone.*

DEATH, LIFE, RITZ CRACKERS

Dying is taking forever.

This shouldn't have surprised him, but it did. Everything in Tim Andersson's life had taken forever. He'd been born three weeks late. Went through the fourth grade twice, needed six years to get his fine arts degree. Took the driver's license exam four times. Had to ask the DMV three times to change his name from Anderson to Andersson. Ditto his social security card and passport, the latter proving a waste of time as the trip to Scotland fell through at the last minute because of his shingles flare-up.

The diagnosis—lung cancer at age forty-nine—had been met with dull, hurt surprise. "I don't smoke."

"Yes, that happens sometimes."

"I've never smoked."

"Yes, I understand. It would seem from your family history you're genetically predisposed to the condition. That and your exposure to asbestos for several years, as well as secondhand smoke—"

"Yeah, I watched my parents and my grandpa die of lung cancer." In an asbestos-ridden house, apparently. Shouldn't have put off moving out of his folks' place for so long. "Which is why *I've never smoked.*" His only addiction was to Ritz crackers, and always had been. Never saltines. Ritz, with spray cheese (cheddar and bacon flavored), chased with sweet iced tea. God, he could use some now. He'd gobble a whole sleeve of crackers right now and shoot the cheese straight into his mouth.

"I'm very sorry."

Tim took a deep breath

(better enjoy doing that while you can)

and asked, "My options?"

"Few," the doctor replied with calm, kind sympathy. "But that's not to say there's no hope. Unfortunately, it's metastasized into your—"

Tim cut him off. He had nothing against the oncologist, who was only doing his job. Tim had gone to the ER two years before with a nagging cough and shortness of breath. He wouldn't have gone at all, but a coworker saw what he coughed up into the bathroom sink and that was that. The ER doc, a nice young fellow with bright green eyes named

(odd that you remember him so clearly)

Dr. Spangler, told him what he suspected and had gotten him a referral on the spot. "There's any one of a number of things it could be. Best to get a diagnosis and be sure, right? And sooner rather than later. Right?"

"Right," Tim had lied, and then had promptly put it off for years. Right around then the offending cough had cleared up, the coworker had been soothed by Tim's lie

("Saw a doctor, he said I'm fine.")

and that had been that.

Until now.

"Story of my life," he muttered to the empty room. As if it knew its cover had been blown, the cancer had picked up speed the day he'd gotten the diagnosis. So now here he was, twenty-two months later, coughing out his last breaths at Fairview Ridges in Burnsville. Burnsville! (Nothing against the pleasant Minnesota suburb; it was just, for some reason he always thought he'd die in Apple Valley, another pleasant Minnesota suburb.)

No family, not anymore. A few friends from work, but mostly Tim kept to himself. Making and then cultivating friendships took too much time and energy, and there were Ritz triple-decker sandwiches to stack and devour. *Everything* took too long. Including this: his death. The doctors had assured him they would control the pain and had been as good as their word. He had refused chemo, refused everything. They were going to move him to a hospice by the end of the week, per the instructions of his HMO. "But until then," his oncologist assured him, "we'll take good care of you."

"Eh. As it is, it'll take too long."

"What will?"

"Everything. The paperwork, the transfer. Dying. All of it. I'm slow at everything. Even this."

And he was right! And as was often the case, there was zero comfort in being right. Still, he at least had the knowledge that—

Wait.

What?

The room was getting darker. And smaller, and quieter. Which was impossible; it was noon on a Saturday, visiting hours were in full swing, his roommate was in the bathroom humming "Irreplaceable" while shaving and getting ready to go home, and the sun was shining. Dammit, he was missing a beautiful late-winter day in Minnesota. *Good* late winter, the kind with the promise of blooming flowers and green grass, not the mud and unearthed-garbage kind of winter. So why was everything . . . ?

Oh.

Oh.

This was it! He was dying, *finally*, and it was exactly as the movies had portrayed: everything was going dark and quiet. It wasn't even scary. Thinking about it had been scarier than experiencing it. He supposed he should be

grateful.

"Hi, I'm Betsy, welcome to Hell."

He blinked and looked around. He knew this place. He'd been there before, reluctantly. It was—

"Did you say welcome to Hell?"

The girl—woman, he supposed, she was probably in her twenties, and they didn't like that, being called girls—nodded. "Yep."

Only death could be both surreal and familiar at the same time. "Hell is the Mall of America?"

"Yep. Sorry." She shrugged at him. "It was all I could think of."

"What?"

"Never mind."

He took a closer look at her. Tall, slender, fair skinned, bright blue-green eyes. Sounded like a Minnesota gal, but what were the odds of that? Long legs, knee-length black linen shorts, a red short-sleeved shirt, reddish blond hair pulled into a ponytail. She was wearing a silver men's watch that was too big for her slender wrist, silver pointy-toed flats, and a *Hello My Name Is* badge over her left breast, which read *Satan 2.0.*

"So I'm dead?" He looked around. Yep, the Mall of America and no mistake. He and the strange girl—*woman*—were standing beside a large information kiosk. There were other people around, many of them in a hurry, and there was an overall feeling of tense bustling.

And it was some big costume party, too, because there was a gal dressed like Cleopatra and another one dressed like she was on her way to a ball in a green gown with a billowing skirt, and an awful lot of the men were wearing hats. And not many of them were proper baseball caps. Lots were old-fashioned hats like Lincoln wore. Women in hats, too, big fancy ones like they wore in the old days, or in London for a royal wedding. The people were all intent on *something*, because they paid him no attention at all. It took him a second to realize what they *were* paying attention to: her. His . . . guide, maybe? But no one was approaching, or even staring. They'd send skittering glances her way, like they were afraid she'd look back. Maybe not a guide. Maybe a supervisor?

He opened his mouth and was annoyed when nothing came out. Tried twice more while the gal waited patiently, and finally managed to croak out, "This is death?"

"No, this is Hell," she corrected him. "And since it's 12:08 p.m., that makes you—uh—Tom Anderson?"

Oh no! Death is just like life! "Tim Andersson, double *s*," he said in Hell, as he had hundreds of times in life.

"Dammit, I *knew* that." She stomped one of her feet, which was as startling as it was charming. "What I'd like is a clipboard with all the info on it I need for work today, all of it accurate and easy to find." Then she just stood there with her hands out, like those statues of the Virgin Mary you saw all over, often on lawns with plastic pink flamingos. Sometimes it looked like the statue was feeding the flamingos, which he always got a kick out of.

Now she was holding a clipboard.

Tim blinked, wondering if it was a hallucination. It had been that sudden—she asked for a clipboard and bink! There it was.

"And an Orange Julius," she added, and bink! Now she was slurping orange glop through a straw, her cheeks hollowing as she sucked like the drink was about to be yanked away. "I will never get used to this," she mumbled at him between sips. Then she was looking down at the clipboard. "Yep, Tim Andersson, got you right here. Sorry, I'm *so* bad with names. Okay, well, like I said, welcome to Hell. I'm not seeing a religious affiliation here—"

"Lapsed Presbyterian," he replied absently, still staring around.

"Uh-huh, so not a regular churchgoer?" At his head shake she added, "So why d'you think you're in Hell?"

Of all the things she might have asked, this had to be the most surprising. "You're Satan 2.0. Don't *you* know?"

Her brow wrinkled as she frowned. She was quite pretty, which was agreeable, and had magical powers, which he hadn't expected from a fellow Minnesotan. He was pretty sure. "You're from Minnesota, right? You sure sound like it."

"Yeah, I live in St. Paul." He barely had time to wonder at her use of the present tense—Satan lived in the state capital?—when she added, "Why did you call me Satan— oh, dammit!" She'd looked down at her name tag and ripped it off, crumpling it in her fist. "Ignore that. One of my horrible roommates stuck that on without me noticing."

"How could you not notice when someone sticks a four-inch-by-four-inch sticker to your—"

"Hey, I've got a lot of responsibilities, okay? I don't have the leisure to read my left boob every five minutes. And I *don't* know why you're here. There's tons I don't know, which is why I'm playing Welcome Wagon."

"Playing?" Say one thing: death wasn't dull. Then: "Welcome Wagon?"

She sighed, as if he was putting her to enormous trouble. "Before I died I was an office manager, but before that I was an admin assistant, and before that a receptionist. See?"

"Afraid not."

"Before you can run the place, you have to know how it works on all the other levels. But I can't work my way up here—I kind of agreed to the top job—so I'm doing a real-life version of Boss/Employee Exchange Work Day. A real-afterlife version, I mean."

"Oh."

"Tackling it any other way would be insane."

"You bet."

She beamed at him, probably mistaking his stunned agreement with actual comprehension. "And of course my roommates' response to my incredibly sensible plan is to undermine me with stickers at every turn. So why do *you* think you're in Hell?"

The subject change made him blink. Apparently he still had to do that. He was also still breathing. And . . . he slid his fingers over his wrist and picked up a pulse. Did he *have* to still do those things? Or was it just habit now?

"Mr. Andersson?"

"Sorry, sorry." He thought about asking her, but she didn't even know why he was in Hell. She might not know why he still blinked and breathed. "Got no idea. I've done some bad things—everybody has. Nothing to deserve an eternity of suffering in the Mall of America." Now, if it had been *Home Depot* . . . "But it's not like I, y'know, killed anybody or blew something up or did something really bad."

"Did you just sort of assume you'd end up here?"

He shook his head. "Mostly I assumed Heaven, I guess. But I dunno. Heaven's probably great for the first few decades, but I think it'd get boring after a while. Everything in my life was boring and/or took too long and . . . and here I am." He was getting hungry while they talked, which made him happy. Which was not how he'd expected to feel in Hell. Toward the end, he hadn't wanted anything. They'd kept IVs with fluids running into him so he wouldn't dehydrate before the cancer could finish him off. For the first time in forever, he wanted a wax paper sleeve of Ritz crackers. Maybe a beer to wash them down. *Two* beers. With spray cheese on the side.

"I know I just got here and all, but I gotta tell ya, Hell's not terrible."

"Thanks, you should definitely put that on the comment card later."

"Comment c—?"

"Listen, Tom, I'd like to put a check in some of these categories." She showed him the clipboard, on which were a number of questions with multiple answers. "So, religion? You were raised to believe you'd end up here so here you are? You lost a bet? You feel like you've left something big unfinished? I know, I know," she added when he opened his mouth to reply. "Then you'd be a ghost, right? Makes sense? Except sometimes the soul ends up here instead. We're all trying to work on figuring out why."

"You're not a ghost, though."

She shook her head, making her ponytail whip around. "Nope."

"But you're dead?"

"Yep."

"But you live in St. Paul."

"So?"

He shook his head. "Nothing unfinished. Except maybe the hospital bill."

"Says here no immediate family. Alive, I mean. So the good news is, you'll never have to cough up the dough for that gigantic bill."

"I was mostly bored. And if I troubled myself to do something, it was boring, or it took too long, or both." He looked around the mall again. "I guess I just want something to happen. Something interesting."

She grinned at him and he couldn't help smiling back. She was just the cutest thing, so studious about her clipboard while occasionally peeking down to admire her shiny shoes. "Oh, interesting we can provide. No problem. We can do interesting."

"Yeah?"

"You bet. So come with me, and I'll show you around, and we'll figure out your damnation or new job or family reunion or rebirth or whatever."

"Okay." He was amenable, because the last two minutes had already been more interesting than the last five years (doctor's visits notwithstanding). This place sure didn't seem like Hell . . . though it explained everyone wearing different clothes from different eras, and how they were scared to look at Satan 2.0. "Listen, ah—" He paused, mentally groped for her name, found it. "Listen, Betsy, is there somewhere around here I can get some Ritz crackers?"

She looked at the clipboard again, then up at him. "Oh. Jeez. Look, not to be a hard-ass, but the only crackers we have for you are saltines."

He nodded, resigned. Definitely Hell, then.

"And all cheese except spray cheese," she said, reading from the clipboard.

Dammit.

CHAPTER
ONE

"Elizabeth!"

I was doing my best to ignore the dead priest, and it wasn't going well. Had I thought he was persistent in life? Pshaw. In death he was indefatigable. That's the word, right? Indefatigable? Never gets tired? Always nagging? Huge downer on my downtime?

"We've rescheduled the meeting three times." He skidded to a halt in front of me, panting lightly.

Yeah, well, it's about to be four times.

"I'm sorry, but I just can't debate Smoothiegate even one more time. You guys are just gonna have to accept that blackberries are gross and suck it up with raspberries instead."

I got an exasperated blink. (That man can say more with his eyelids than most can with their mouths.) "Not that meeting. The, uh . . ." He trailed off, then made himself say it. "The Ten Commandments Redux."

Heh. It was a great idea, if tedious in execution, and for no other reason than Father Markus really, *really* hated the name. "It's Remix, and you know it."

"Regardless. We have to get started."

"I know." (I did know.) "And while I was researching—"

"You researched?" he said, sounding shocked. Then he instantly corrected his tone. "Of course you did. Good for you."

"Well, I had an idea for what to do with some of the souls that have been here for a while."

"Which is?"

"I have to keep working on it." I had no idea how my plan would go over: probably like an anvil. It meant big change. It meant changing the very nature of Hell. Father Markus was a good enough guy, but he was also a traditionalist. Baby steps. That was key. "I'll tell you more about it. Later."

He made a *ttkkt!* noise of disapproval. "Procrastination is another word for cowardice."

"It's really not."

He'd switched from Reminder Mode to Cajoling Mode. "Now, Betsy." Ohhh, I knew that tone. "You know the hardest part is just sitting down and getting started."

"Mmm." (No, the hardest part was keeping out of his way so I could avoid his eight zillion meetings. My own fault for being in Hell's food court again!)

Father Markus, though he'd ended up in Hell after he died, still thought of himself as a priest. You could look like anything you wanted here, but most people stuck with what they were familiar with: how they looked in life. In Father Markus's case, that meant the traditional priest garb: all in black except for the collar. He had a little bit of hair left, all white, which went around his head in a fringe, leaving the top bald and shiny. Like, really shiny. The king of the vampires once checked his reflection in it.

His hands and feet were small and sleek; he was in comfortable black shoes, dull leather Dockers. He'd lived his whole life in Minnesota and had the same flat Midwestern accent I did.

But I liked his eyes the best: small and brown, intent and expressive. They scrunched into smiling slits when he was happy, and focused like lasers when he wasn't. In life he'd been in charge of a pack of teenage vampire hunters, and since most vampires were murderous assholes, I couldn't entirely blame him for assuming *all* vampires were murderous assholes. I broke up the decapitation-happy team and Father Markus went his own way until he died. Now he was stuck working with me, in case he didn't already know he was in Hell. To his credit, he decided it was an honor, and never indicated what a pain in his ass I was. (Out loud, anyway.)

"The first meeting," he was rambling, "is always . . ."

The dullest. The lamest. The boringest. Wait. Boringest?

". . . the hardest."

"Yeah, y— Wait." I realized he'd put a hand on my elbow, and while we talked, he was gently nudging me toward the Lego store, where we held most of our meetings. "Are you steering me, you sly, nagging s.o.b.?"

"No, no. Escorting."

"Just because you're dead doesn't mean I can't kill you again." As threats went, it was about a 4.2 on the Lame-O-Meter.

"Just take a deep breath," he suggested with a small smile. "It'll be over soon."

"Totally pointless; I don't have to breathe. *You* don't have to breathe."

"It'll all be over soon, then," he said again. "I'll stick with that one."

"Every time I think that, something new and terrible happens. I get fired. I get run over. I die. Someone I live with dies. I die *again*. I become a queen. I get tricked into running Hell. I'm forced to wear humiliating name tags. I—"

"I miss the blowout sale for summer sandals. I get shriller and shriller rather than learning from my mistakes. I go all dictator-ey and banish blackberries from smoothies."

"That doesn't affect you one bit, Cathie! (A) You hated smoothies in life—"

"How has the smoothie industry tricked you into thinking pulverized fruit and yogurt and old ice cubes from the back of the freezer is a terrific plan?"

"And (2) you're always in Hell."

"Truer words," my "friend" Cathie replied. She was already building another conference room out of Lego bricks. (The one she built yesterday had too good a view of the amusement park, or, as we called it, the Vomitorium. If you hated amusement parks or were prone to severe motion sickness, and subconsciously decided you needed punishment after you died, guess where you ended up? With a permanent season ticket?)

"Almost done," she added, like I had an enduring interest in her temporary architecture. She could whip rooms up in no time. It helped that each Lego (or would that be LEGO®?) block was the size of a stereo speaker. One of the ancient ones, two feet high and a foot wide. Not one of the new ones you can't actually see. "You'll be bitching about the things you constantly bitch about in no time."

"Drop dead," I replied, which was redundant at best, lame at worst. Her evil snicker proved it was on the lame end of the meter. Cathie had faced down the serial killer who'd killed her; as a ghost, she wasn't scared by bitchy vampires even a little.

I'd never known her in life, but in death she was pretty great. When she first appeared (manifested? intruded? trespassed? stalked?) she was mega-pissed over being murdered.

So employing the "unlikely partners" trope, we'd teamed up. The end result: a dead serial killer, a vengeful ghost's revenge, and the Antichrist's temper tantrum, which resulted in a dead serial killer and a vengeful ghost's revenge.

(I'll go into the whole estranged-from-the-Antichrist thing in a bit. Really can't stand even thinking about her right now. Long story short: she's as dead to me as my dead father, who isn't dead.)

Unlike a lot of new spirits, Cathie had no problem looking different from how she looked on the day she died. As she explained, "I got foully snuffed on laundry day; I am *not* plodding through eternity in granny panties and a sweatshirt. Besides, my clothes aren't real. Probably I'm not real. So why not embrace it?" Excellent advice, and today she was in boyfriend jeans, a blue T-shirt with *If you don't sin, Jesus died for nothing* in white letters, hair in an elaborate French braid ("Finally! The trick to mastering French braids is not having a body, or hair that grows on the body!"), and battered blue loafers, *sans* socks. Why she refused to manifest nice shoes would be an eternal mystery.

"Gang's all here?" she asked, still messing with Lego pieces. She'd made the room, I slunk inside, and she was now working on the table.

"Mostly." I sighed. "We'll have enough to get through the meeting."

"Which you're seeing as a disaster for some reason."

"Kind of."

"Suck it up, buttercup."

"Y'know, you could pretend to be intimidated by me. Or even acknowledge that I'm your boss and am chock-full of sinister powers."

"Nope."

Well, good, I guess. Throughout history, most dictators became douches because they were surrounded by yes-men or, in my case, yes-roommates/ghosts/vampires/zombies. Having people around who aren't afraid of you is crucial if you want them to tell you what they really think, instead of what they think you want to hear. Though on days like this (nights? what time was it? Hell was like Vegas: no clocks), a *little* nervous deference wouldn't be the worst thing in the world . . .

I'd known running Hell wouldn't be easy, but hadn't planned on it being boring. It had everything I hated about my old office job (meetings, organization, meetings) and none of the stuff I liked about my old office job (paid vacation, holidays, all the Post-it notes I could steal).

But meetings, like the IRS and the DMV, were a necessary evil. It was a whole new ball game since I'd killed the devil, banished the Antichrist, yelled at my father for faking his death (badly), banished my not-dead father and the Antichrist, and taken over the care and feeding of Hell.

Luckily, I had something the devil never had, not in her five million years of punishing the damned and being pissed at God: friends willing to pitch in and help.

Thus: meetings. But there were smoothies, too, so it wasn't all bad.

CHAPTER
TWO

"Do we have the minutes of the meeting?"

I bit down on a groan and rested my forehead on the table (also made of Lego pieces). Then, remembering that the last time I'd done that, I'd walked around in Hell with Lego dots on my forehead *and no one told me*, I jerked upright.

"Do we even have those? Are we really trying to improve Hell by introducing more paperwork?"

"I don't know if 'improve' is the right—"

"Plus, we're not even all here yet," I pointed out. Not "I complained." Not "I bitched." No matter what Marc wanted to call it. And speaking of my personal physician/ zombie . . . "Where's Marc?"

"Here," my personal zombie/physician replied, ambling into the room. He was in (un)death as he was in life: slouchy and comfortable in a pale gray scrub shirt (it used to be green but after a zillion washings was faded and almost velvety to the touch), faded boyfriend jeans ("Ironic," he'd sigh, "since I haven't had a date in . . . when did I die again?"), dark hair in a George Clooney cut ("He's really locked into one style, isn't he?"), pale skin (not because of his zombification; he died in winter in Minnesota, when sunlight is more rumor than anything else), and smiling green eyes.

"What have I told you about wandering around Hell without an escort?" I hadn't been running the place for even a few weeks. My "run it by committee" idea was only a week old. I was still figuring out my godlike powers of the damned. And I wanted to bite the shit out of somebody— anybody, really. When had I last drunk? Argh. Worrying about Marc on top of all that? It did nothing for my temper, which these days wasn't great. "Well?"

"Nothing."

"Oh." Right. I'd been thinking he shouldn't wander, but didn't actually tell him. "Well, it's a bad idea."

"What can they do to me?" he asked, reasonably enough.

"It's Hell! Who knows? Why would you ever want to find out?"

"Because I'm bored?"

Oh. Well, good point. If anyone needed to stay stimulated, it was Marc.

"And," he continued, "Hell is really depressing."

"Well, yeah," Cathie replied.

"Lord Byron is so *boring*."

Not good. Boring was bad. Marc being bored was the part of the horror movie where they establish the characters, the dumb stuff you have to sit through while waiting for the blood to spill. And it always spilled. Inevitable like the tides, or *Transformers* sequels being terrible.

"Oh?" I asked with perfect fake composure, even as Cathie started to give him the side-eye.

"Byron's one of the greatest poets ever, maybe *the* greatest English poet—"

Oh, good. Now I wouldn't have to ask, Who's Lord Brian? The name was familiar. Kind of. Poets weren't my thing.

"—and just a complete downer. First off, not gay. Bi, definitely bi."

"Which is a problem why?" Cathie asked.

"Oh, bi artists are a dime a dozen." Marc waved a hand, dismissing every bisexual artist in the history of human events. "All my life I've been reading about his complex sexuality, but there's nothing complex about being able to pass for straight—he fathered a couple of kids. It's not nearly the struggle it is to be in the closet, not into the opposite sex, but faking well enough to make babies while trying to fit into society without losing your mind, except a lot of them did lose their minds."

"Those bisexuals," Cathie said dryly, "with their uncomplicated natures and many, many banging options."

"Oh, shut up," he snapped. "I get it: where do I get off—"
Don't giggle at "get off." Whew! Thanks, inner voice.

"—marginalizing anyone's sexuality, blah-blah. But it wasn't just that. The guy's supposed to be the first celebrity—I mean, how we understand the term today. Hordes of screaming fans; Byronmania kind of paved the way for Beatlemania. Sounds pretty interesting, right? He's probably got great stories, right?"

"I'm guessing no," I said, "on account of how annoyed you sound."

"You know what the number one thing on his mind is? Art, poetry through the ages, reminiscing about commanding a rebel army despite having no military experience, feeding your muse from Hell, maybe moving on from Hell, looking up his descendants . . . anything like that? No. The fever that killed him. That's what's on his mind *all* the *time.* He died over two hundred years ago and he's still bitching because Advil and NyQuil weren't invented in time to save his whiney ass." Marc slumped into his red Lego chair, rubbing his eyes with the heels of his hands. "Never meet your heroes. Or people you read about once and thought would be really cool to meet in real life." He raised his head and looked around at the ghost and the vampire queen surrounded by Lego furniture. "This *is* real life, right?"

"Nonsense," came a voice that managed to be soft, brisk, and polite all at once. Tina (real name: Christina Caresse Chavelle, which was *hilarious*) had popped up out of nowhere (she was like a census taker that way), representing herself and the vampire king.

You'd think the vampire queen (*moi*) could do that, but trust me: it's better for everyone that Tina handle these things. She's been doing it for decades; she'd known Sinclair since he was a li'l farmer kid with grubby knees, and had been a friend of his family for generations. She was descended from a not-witch I'd saved from being burned during the Salem witch trials in sixteen hundred whatever, because time travel.[1]

So anyway, she was used to repping my husband at meetings, smoothie oriented and otherwise. She was also used to incredibly long boring meetings. Plus, to be honest, I trusted her to be in Hell a lot more than my husband, a man I loved dearly but knew to be sneaky, manipulative, controlling, and murderous. (God, he was so dreamy!)

Since we were all new to the business side of running Hell, and thus equally clueless, Tina was using fashion to soothe us, dressing the part of Demure Majordomo in Charge of Meetings N'Stuff: a virgin wool Armani skirt suit in deepest midnight blue, with a two-button long-sleeved jacket, matching camisole underneath, black panty hose, and kitten heels the same shade of blue as the suit.

---

[1] The gory details can be found in *Undead and Unfinished*.

The deep, dark colors set off her pale (vampire) skin and enormous dark eyes to perfection, the dark hose made her look taller (a good trick, since she was almost a foot shorter than I was), and she had scraped her long, Southern-belle-ringleted blond hair into a severe bun. She was right out of the "Hot for Teacher" video and it was glorious. If she had to fight, or jog, the suit was a disastrous choice. If she had to look like she knew exactly what she was doing in a business capacity, it was brilliant.

I need a suit like that. But in red. No, black. No, red. Purple? Purple could be great . . . except I'd look like an eggplant wearing pumps. Does Sinclair think eggplants are sexy? Must research . . .

"If you want to meet some extraordinary men and women," she was telling Marc, who had instantly cheered up at the sight of her (they were pals bordering on besties), "I can introduce you to several, assuming they're here."

"Guess it depends which side they fought on," Cathie said, and since Tina had lived through the Civil War, that was a fair point.

"General Sherman?" Father Markus asked with a disapproving air. I jumped; he'd gone so long without speaking I'd forgotten he was there, even though he'd brought me to the meeting. "Jefferson Davis?"

"You knew the president of the Confederacy?" Cathie asked, sounding impressed, which was a rare and wonderful thing.

"No, that's the other Jefferson Davis; this one murdered his commanding officer and never saw a trial, much less prison." Hmm, who knew Father Markus was a Civil War buff? (It's worth noting that Tina wasn't, since that'd be like saying, "I live in Minnesota, so I am a Minnesota buff.")

"Robert Smalls? Wait, there's no way he'd be in Hell. Right?" It was a fair question, since people who had done good things all their lives were in Hell. One of many things to be discussed in (argh) today's meeting (argh-argh).

"Ooh, I got this one," Cathie enthused, warming to her subject. "This is the guy who stole a military transport, steered it past a bunch of Confederate forts, gave the ship *and* the signal codes to the Union, then went on to find and get rid of land mines he himself had been forced to plant. And he did all this while he was a slave!"

"Robert Smalls!" I cried. At last, I could contribute something to a historical conversation that didn't sound asinine. "I saw that episode of *Drunk History*!"

"Actually I was thinking of notables from the Revolutionary War," Tina corrected gently. She gave us a moment to chew that one over

(she looks so young and hot but is ancient! weird! we know this, but keep forgetting! weird!)

before adding, "Nancy Hart, for instance. Half a dozen British soldiers accused her of protecting a Whig leader (she was), and didn't believe her when she said she hadn't seen him (she was lying). At the end of the night, all those men were dead. They found the bodies—"

"Thanks, but I don't actually have to seek out sociopaths, I hang out with plenty on my own."

"Or Mary Ball Washington."

"Who?"

"Washington's wife." Duh. I managed to keep the sneer off my face, if not out of my tone.

"Washington's mother," Father Markus and Tina corrected; he colored a little and ducked his head while she kept the sneer off her face *and* out of her tone. I should learn that trick.

Tina somehow sensed my rising boredom (the way I groaned and cradled my head in my hands may have tipped her off), because she said to Marc, "You come along with me later, darling. I'll introduce you to lots of interesting people."

Marc perked right up. He'd been getting steadily more morose (moroser?) since Future Me had made him a zombie after he'd committed suicide to avoid being turned into a vampire (also by Future Me). Given that in life he'd been prone to depression, it was a concern.

I loved Marc, but unfortunately it was one concern on a laundry list of a bazillion concerns. Tina, thank God, had been spending lots of time with him lately. He had a blanket nest for her in the trunk of his car (complete with reading lights, water bottles, a cell phone, an iPad, and chargers) and often took her out (in the daytime!) for what I called errands and they called missions. Sure. A mission to Cub Foods for raspberries and yogurt. A mission to the liquor store for Cinnamon Churros vodka.

"Sorry I'm late," one of the many banes of my existence said, booting an errant Lego brick out of her path.

Father Markus warned me, "Behold, evil is going forth from nation to nation," because that was how he liked to preface nagging me about the last meeting (or the next meeting), and he was probably talking about me, but I thought of my stepmother, Antonia Taylor, known to one and all (well, me) as the Ant.

In life, we'd been deadly enemies. But in death, she had found a grudging

"You look haggard. Is plastic surgery a thing for vampires? You might want to inquire."

a very, very grudging respect for me

"Why would anyone want hair the color *and* texture of pineapple?" I batted back. "I don't know what's worse, your outfit or the fact that you're freely choosing to look like that."

as I had for her.

"And with that," Cathie said after trying, and failing, to disguise a snigger as a cough, "let's get started."

CHAPTER
THREE

"Monday's minutes," Cathie announced. *"Betsy moved* that meetings were dumb, but no one seconded it so it didn't pass."

I glared at Marc. I'd counted on him, dammit! "I'll never forgive you for letting me swing on that one," I hissed, and I got an eye roll for my trouble.

"She then remembered she's supposed to be in charge and lead the way of reform, and we settled in to get some work done, when she moved that Hell no longer be eternal punishment from which there is no escape. But rather—and this is a direct quote—it'd be more like jail. Or detention! You can get out, but you have to be sorry for what you did and behave for a really long time, and when you're out, we're still gonna keep an eye on you so don't go being an asshat or anything. Unquote."

Father Markus groaned, and not for the first time.

Who knew a representative of the Catholic Church would be so resistant to change?

"I stand by my brilliant idea," I said modestly. "Look, I always thought that was the dumbest thing. I can remember having huge problems with this in Sunday school. Presbyterian," I added before anyone could ask. I had liked Sunday school, but mostly because we got Peeps for correct answers. So . . . much . . . marshmallow . . . "We're supposed to be good so we don't go to Hell, right? So you make one mistake—depending on what religion you were raised with—and the rule is you spend a million years in Hell because you cussed out your mom while taking the Lord's name in vain as you stole your neighbor's wife and made her tell you how pretty you were?"

"Um," Marc began.

"How many broken commandments is that?"

"Four." In unison around the table.

"I think Hell should be where you learn what you screwed up, where you went wrong screwing it up, and, if you're willing, how to make amends or just be a better person. Like, if you killed someone, and you were both here in Hell, you'd have to do nice things for your murder victim until they forgave you. It could take ten years or five hundred. And then you . . . you . . ." I was gratified, and horrified, to see I had their full attention. "Well, I don't know. Get born again? Leave Hell but be a ghost? Go to Heaven?" Again, part of my idea that would change the face of Hell (assuming Hell had a face), if I could pull it off. If everyone here could help me pull it off. "That's the other thing—"

"Also from the minutes," Cathie interrupted. "Quote, So, like, are the people leaving Hell controlling where they go or are they just vanishing or is it something Satan used to do but now I have to do even though I don't know how? Oh my God, I must have been out of my mind to agree to this shit, unquote."

"None of that sounds like me," I grumbled. "Those minutes are counterfeit, I bet."

Tina kept the smile off her face, but was unable to prevent her eyes from crinkling at me. "Every last word of it sounds quite like you, dread Majesty." Sigh. No matter how often I said she could drop the "O Dread Queen" stuff anytime, she persisted. Who knew someone from the antebellum South could be so stubborn?

"One thing at a time," Father Markus said. "Else we'll get bogged down in all the problems to surmount and not how to surmount them."

I liked how he said "we." It was why I'd made the damned committee in the first place. I nodded and he continued.

"Setting aside the idea of parole from Hell—"

"Not for long, though," Marc said quickly. "I think it's a really great idea." At the surprised looks, he added, "What? I'm a gay atheist who knows how to perform abortions and is now a zombie. Hell being permanent does not work for me."

"Oh, *now* you're backing me up. When it's political and stuff."

"Well, *now* you're making sense," the Ant cut in and Marc, who had never liked her, grinned anyway.

"The seven deadly sins," Markus said loudly, cutting off my whine. "That's where we'll start. I've been interviewing quite a few souls down here—sorry, not *down* here, of course—not anywhere, is my understanding . . ."

I couldn't blame him. The Hell tropes were hard to shake. We weren't *down* anywhere; Hell wasn't a physical place you could go to, like Duluth. It was an entirely different dimension with its own rules, and hardly anyone was burning alive in a lake of fire. Okay, a few hard-core

Christians were burning alive in a lake of fire, and they ignored all my attempts to rescue them, shouting over the crackling flames that they'd earned their punishment. What could I do? They seemed fine. Well. Not *fine*. But not inclined to move, either. That was the stuff that made this job seem so overwhelming. You'd focus on one person or one punishment area and get totally overwhelmed. To think I found the vampire queen gig daunting!

". . . and most of the people here understand the concept of sin. They were unsurprised to find themselves here; they understand they sinned in life and this is their punishment in death. We've got murderers, thieves, false idolaters—"

"I don't think people should go to Hell if they don't believe in the Christian God," I interjected. "This is America, isn't it? Freedom of religion!" Oh. Wait . . .

Literal face-palms around the table, except for Tina, because at least one person in the Lego room was an adult who respected her sovereign. And, given all the religious talk, she was keeping her shivers and shudders under control. To most vampires, even hearing the word *Jesus* out loud was like a lash to the face.

"That is the entire concept Hell is based on!" Father Markus shouted, leaping to his feet. Ooh, only five minutes in and I got the eyelid twitch *and* the forehead vein. A new record! (It's not enough to set goals; you've got to reach them, dammit.) "You can't just pitch everything and start all over, you gorgeous idiot!"

"Sure I can. Wanna watch?" I hadn't moved, just stared up at him, but he must have seen something in my face because he plunked back down in his Lego chair almost as quickly as he'd leaped out of it. Good thing he'd called me gorgeous, or I'd have been *really* pissed.

"I'm sorry I raised my voice," he managed, not quite looking at me.

"No biggie. Yelling's allowed." Usually. "And you didn't let me finish. I think I have a way that'll make both of us happy. Just a reminder, though, for everyone here: I agreed to run Hell by committee for the *most* part, because it's a huge job and I trust everyone in here." Unspoken: *Even you, Ant, much as it kills me to say it.* "But I've got veto power over everything happening in this place, old rules *and* new, understand? If I don't think a certain plan is the way to go, I'm open to discussion, but the final decision is always going to be mine." This in my "how dare you try to sell me knock-off Jimmy Choos, you degenerate asshat!" tone.

"No one doubts it, Bets," Cathie said. She'd pushed the minutes aside, thank God, and had been giving Markus a thoughtful look. Now she turned her attention to me. "Y'know, we touched on this last time, too. You were going to think about a twenty-first-century version of the Ten Commandments. Maybe nothing will get changed at all," she added when Markus opened his mouth. And then, to me, "Did you? Think about it?"

"As a matter of fact." I whipped out my cell phone in triumph, called up the document I'd e-mailed myself. (Yeah, cell phones work in Hell. No, I don't know why. Take it up with AT&T.) "I went through the whole list. You guys should prepare to be impressed."

"No one is prepared," the Ant said. "At all."

"Shut up," I suggested sweetly, and began.

CHAPTER
FOUR

THE TEN COMMANDMENTS REMIX
Because It's the Twenty-first Century Already, Come On

Big Number One: Thou shalt have no other gods before God. Whether that's God, Jesus, Jehovah, Allah, Yahweh, Elohim, Hu, Ishvara, Nirankar, Shiva . . . whatever spiritual being in your life you pray to.

That means your cellulite-free thighs aren't your god. Network ratings aren't your god, a fixed mortgage rate isn't your god. Your stock portfolio isn't your god, or your stylist, or your brand-new phone. None of those stupid material things are your god. Clear? Great. Moving on.

Number Two: Thou shalt not make unto thee any graven image, or any likeness of anything that is in Heaven above, or that is in the earth beneath, or that is in the water under the earth.

See number one: no other gods before *the* God. So don't make a statue of whatever you're worshipping instead of your god. The earth is cluttered enough.

Number Three: Thou shalt not take the name of the Lord thy God in vain.

Don't throw around the big guy's name like it's meaningless. It's the opposite of meaningless. It's full of meaning! Look, I get it: we live(d) in a world where third graders drop f-bombs. I know you're gonna do it. You know you're gonna do it. I blasphemed eight times before lunch. Just . . . try not to. Or at least cut back. It's not unreasonable to show a little respect to your creator.

(I dunno, I get that God says these sins are all equally awful, but I'm having trouble punishing the guy who lived a good life but shrieked "Jesus Christ!" when his daughter came home with four piercings, with the same intensity as the serial killer who slashed his way through an Atlantic City Laundromat.)

Number Four: Remember the Sabbath day, to keep it holy.

God rested on the seventh day, and so should you. What, resting's good enough for God but you're above it? Your compost won't mulch itself? (That's what you do with compost, right? Mulch it?) There will never be a better time to micromanage your children as they clean their rooms? Ah . . . no. This commandment is like your mom's nap-time rules: you might not feel tired, but you are. So just rest already and when you get up you can have cookies.

*   *   *

Number Five: Honor thy father and thy mother.

Hey, they made you! And most of the time, after making you they took care of you: they put a roof over your
helpless, diaper-soiling head and fed you and basically gave
up a huge chunk of their lives for you (what, you thought
they loved *The Lego Movie* as much as you did? they didn't;
that movie sucked), and the least you can do is not be a shit
about it. (All right, the least you can do is nothing.) Yes,
they're annoying. Yes, they can't quite get the hang of
seeing you as an adult even if you're wearing bifocals. But
come on. They made you.

And some parents are utter shits. They just are. My
friend Jessica's, for example; her dad molested her and her
mom knew and didn't care. So "honor thy father and thy
mother" is getting a somewhat looser interpretation in
cases like that: don't kill 'em. No matter how much you
dream about it. No matter how much you're sure they've
got it coming. You think it'll fix things? It'll make your
life better? It won't. So. Come on. They made you.

Number Six: Thou shalt not kill.

Really a no-brainer on this one. There are aggravating
people in the world. (Me, for example.) There are terrible
asshats in the world. (Sometimes also me.) That has always
been true. There are people so depraved and violent and
dangerous that the world is actually better once they're
dead. But don't kill them. Not your call.

(Murder disclaimers: Self-defense is fine. War is sometimes fine. Protecting loved ones is fine. A situation that
encompasses all three is fine. In this case, "fine" means,
okay, it was wrong, but let's take a look at the extenuating

circumstances and see if we can cut you a break. Welcome to a kinder, gentler Hell!)

Number Seven: Thou shalt not commit adultery.

C'mon, it's not asking too much to expect you to keep it in your pants. You're married; that means you've acknowledged that you caught your limit. You promised each other and the priest or minister or judge or aunt who was ordained by the Internet that you wouldn't bang anyone else. So: don't bang anyone else. Easy. (Rather: *don't* be easy.) If you need it? If your life will be over if you don't fuck that particular person? Get a divorce. Then bang away, baby.

Number Eight: Thou shalt not steal.

Another no-brainer. That shit doesn't belong to you. Leave it alone. There's really no explaining to be done here, no loopholes. Murdering a serial killer is one thing, but stealing your neighbor's newspaper is something else. Plus, what were you thinking? You can read it on the Internet for free!

Number Nine: Thou shalt not bear false witness against thy neighbor.

Don't lie about him or her. Don't make up crap to get them in trouble. Yeah, they only mow their giant lawn about once a month. And their dog is constantly escaping just long enough to leave a major dump on your lawn. They call the cops every time you have a party, not because of the noise, but because they're pissed you didn't invite them. All those dead cars parked on the lawn they never mow are bringing down the value of your home. And you *know* they're the ones who fill up your recycling bins with their old newspapers.

Irrelevant. For whatever reason, that's your home. You have to take the good (the ice cream truck always starts on your block!) with the bad (the ice cream truck runs late because it has to avoid hitting the neighbor's dog). Suck it up, buttercup.

Number Ten: Thou shalt not covet thy neighbor's house, thou shalt not covet thy neighbor's wife, nor his manservant, nor his maidservant, nor his ox, nor his ass, nor anything that is thy neighbor's.

C'mon, this isn't the seventies and you're not throwing a key party. Don't be coveting: not his/her spouse, ox, *or* butt. Sometimes it's hard not to be jealous, especially when your neighbors have the bad taste to flaunt their good fortune: "Gosh, don't you think everyone should be driving electric cars? If people *really cared* about the environment, they'd find the money somehow." Yeah, yeah, go plug yourself, you smug jerk.

Just . . . try to cut them a little slack. Remember, fifty thousand years ago if you didn't play nicely with your neighbors, death came a lot quicker. These days it's not death you have to worry about so much as intense annoyance. But you never know when you'll need them. So be nice. Or at least don't be terrible.

Addendum:

"And on the eighth day the Lord said, 'Ye have done well in mine eyes; go ye forth to all the malls of the land and shoe you well with the shoes of designers. And avoid ye knockoffs, for if ye adorn thyself with such thou shalt know naught but blisters.'"

Yeah, I know: uproar. Can't blame a gal for trying.

CHAPTER
FIVE

"Okay . . . that's not . . . completely terrible." *Whoa. From* the Ant, that was high praise. "Except for the shoe addendum. That's just stupid."

"It is not! Okay, it's a little dumb. But give me a break, it took me hours to come up with all that." Well. *An* hour. Except it was more like thirty minutes. I had time to kill while waiting for Sinclair to get ready to go another round. For a dead guy, his refractory period was pretty impressive. But not, y'know, *instant*. Besides, he was getting steadily more sulky about being left at the mansion every time I went to Hell. But that was an argument for another day. Another *year*, hopefully. "But it's like Father Markus said: the basics are pretty much always the same. Don't kill, don't steal, don't be a dick. The big diff is, it's not a hard-and-fast set of rules for Christians. Don't kill and don't steal apply across religions, or lack of religion."

"I can't decide if that's brilliant or deepest blasphemy.

I'll pray on it and get back to you." He would, too. He was always tracking me down to let me know he'd prayed on something, and how the power of prayer revealed to him my general incompetence. Blech. "It's true, you've covered the basics," Markus admitted. "Though I'm not one hundred percent behind the 'murder is okay in wartime' clause."

"When *else* would murder be okay?"

"Meet the new boss," Tina murmured, "same as the old boss." At the stares, she replied, "Why are you looking at me like that? I enjoy the Who as much as the next woman."

"Except that'd be me," Cathie pointed out, "and I hate that shit. *The Simpsons* described the sixties perfectly: 'What a shrill, pointless decade.' In fact, as more and more boomers end up in Hell, I'd like to move we forbid all bands who were in the top one hundred between 1960 and 1979. For their own safety."

"I'm not the same as the old boss," I said, stung. "I'm giving Hell a much-needed and long-overdue makeover, for free, I might add, which is something the old boss either never thought of or never cared about."

"I'll guess it's the latter," Markus replied. "So then. How to get this information to the masses?"

"I dunno. Put up flyers?"

"Isn't that a little late, though?" Marc asked. He was definitely more engaged in the meeting, which was really, really, really, really good. You know that whole "zombies need braaaaains" thing? It was true. But the movies got it wrong: zombies needed stimulation, not Dr. Hannibal frying up brains in butter. Marc needed to keep busy, to keep learning, to stay focused, to be *alive*. He was a zombie, but one who had been dead maybe a minute. Still (mostly) warm, still (for most intents and purposes) alive. He doesn't need to eat or drink; he'll enjoy his Caesar haircut forever; he'll never have to worry about cancer or Alzheimer's or arthritis. But if he went too long without stimulation and got bored, or was away from me for too long, he'd start to rot.

Nobody wanted him to rot. Especially after all he'd done for us from the moment I talked him out of jumping from the rooftop, BBC Sherlock–style: embracing our vampire natures, backing us up regardless of the Big Bad du jour, risking his life, being turned into a vampire in the future and a zombie in the present . . . endless. Endless sacrifices.

So we put up with him dissecting mice on our kitchen counters and reading and writing at all hours of the night and doing Sudoku (when will that puzzle trend die?), cleaning out the attic by dumping all the old stuff into the basement, then reversing the process to clean the basement, and roaming the mansion at all hours, always looking for something to keep himself occupied. Not that I had anything against roaming; Sinclair, Tina, and I did it all the time. (We've tried to keep the lurking to a minimum.) But it was less creepy when vampires did it, which makes no sense but is true regardless.

"Right? Betsy?" I blinked and realized Marc had been waiting for an answer.

"Okay, I see what you mean. If we put up flyers—"

"We're not putting up flyers, for crying out loud," Cathie muttered, staring down at the minutes. "What year do you think it is? Why not just round up all the town criers, have *them* disseminate the info?"

"—what good does it do? The people who 'earned' Hell, for lack of a better word"—There were *kids* down here, for God's sake. No kid on the planet fucking deserved an eternity in a lake of fire and that was the fucking end of it. Although if a kid spent a century in a lake of fire, were they a kid still?—"they're stuck here now. Knowing the rules won't help them avoid Hell. It's too late. Isn't it?"

"It's still a starting point. As I said, most of them know what they did to deserve eternal damnation." Father Markus looked around the table at all of us. "But if I understand Betsy's plan correctly, they can learn what to do to earn their—I don't know how you'd say it—heavenly parole?"

"I can't decide if they go to Heaven," I said, shocked. "It's absurd enough that I've got any say at all in what goes on in Hell! That's . . . you know." I pointed at the Lego ceiling. "Up to the big guy. So to speak. Once they're paroled, they can leave here and go wherever." Which reminded me: we needed some parole officers of the damned. I might not be as hard-core as the devil was, but I'm not about to release random spirits back into the wild without a way to keep an eye on them for a while. "Tina, while I'm thinking of it, could you make a note for us to talk to some actual parole officers, pick their brains?"

"Of course." She tap-tap-tapped on her phone, which would have been impressive except I knew how much time she spent playing Cupcake Crash on the thing.

No one else had said anything, so I added, "Even if we could get the word to the living: 'Hey, here are the new and improved Ten Commandments, even though that's not for me to say—oh, who am I? Just a vampire who runs Hell on the side—anyway, I've got no authority on earth over regular people and God is probably generally disgusted with me, but just abide by the new (except not really) commandments as best you can and maybe you won't end up with an eternal season pass to the Mall of America of the damned.'"

"That . . . probably won't work," Tina said, ever the tactician. (That's what you call someone who's super tactful, right?)

"Betsy has a point about not choosing who goes to Hell," Markus said. "That's completely out of her—your—purview." He shifted his full attention to me. "All you can do is decide what to do with the souls who show up in your territory."

I shivered. My territory used to be designer shoe stores

and Orange Julius drive-thrus. Then it was the whole of the vampire nation. Now it was the endless dimension that was Hell, with all its billions of inhabitants. If I kept getting these unasked-for promotions, I'd end up running the universe if I wasn't careful. And who needed *that* headache? I now perfectly understand why God created the universe and then basically went on vacation. I could almost picture the mind-set: "Here it is, you've got free will. Enjoy and good luck." God: the first slack-ass.

"I guess it's God's purview," I said at last. "And He's welcome to it! My end's hard enough. I wonder—d'you think He knows? About Satan being dead and me being undead but nominally in charge? Of course He does," I answered myself. "He's omnipotent. Or Satan went up there to tattle on me."

"Doubtful," the Ant said. "She wouldn't set foot in Heaven for anything. They haven't spoken since the Fall."

"A long time to sulk," Cathie commented, and that made Father Markus bristle.

"It's a bit more complicated than a father-son spat over who put the ding in the bumper," he said. "Lucifer upended the world order. Even if there could be forgiveness for such an act—and of course our Father can forgive all who genuinely repent—who's to say the Morningstar would want it?"

"Clearly she *didn't* want it," Cathie replied. "Or at least, not in all the time she was running the show down here."

(Clarification: Lucifer, also known as Satan 1.0, was a fallen angel and thus, apparently, genderless. But she'd always appeared to us in the guise of Lena Olin in terrific designer suits and killer footgear, so most of us were in the habit of referring to the devil as "she." "It" was probably correct, but it sounded weird *and* mean. Though why I worried about sounding mean to the devil, of all creatures, was a mystery. You can take the Miss Congeniality out of the Miss Burnsville pageant, but you can't take the

Miss Burnsville pageant out of the Miss Congeniality. Or something.)

And all of this raised the question: where did the devil go when you killed her? Not Hell. Not Heaven. Where? Walmart? Where?

I shook my head. "I can't worry about that now. Too much other stuff on my plate."

"Majesty, if we cannot stay focused, bringing change will be that much more difficult." Tina always managed to say "focus, idiot!" without actually saying it, which I appreciated.

"Yes, focus, idiot," Cathie said. I mentioned I appreciated Tina's tact, right? Tina's lips went thin and she opened her mouth, so I jumped in. (Figuratively. Not literally.)

"I *am*, but there's so much stuff to worry about! For one thing, I'm still figuring out how my kind-of onomatopoeia works."

"Omniscience," Tina corrected gently. "Onomatopoeia is when the name of a sound is its sound, my queen."

"You lost me," Marc said, and thank goodness, because I was trying to limit my stupid questions to under a dozen an hour. So far, no good.

"Like honk or quack or sizzle," she explained, and you'd think that would have helped, but nope. "*Quack* really does sound like a duck's quack. *Splash* really does sound like a splash. Like that."

"Whatever. So my problem is figuring out the other thing you said. Omniscience. I'm stronger here than I ever have been, which, for a vampire queen, is pretty great." Queenhood, much as I liked to bitch about it, had its perks. Unlike other vampires, I could bear sunlight, could blaspheme from dawn 'til dusk, could gargle with holy water with no ill effects (except wondering how many people had had their hands in the holy water I just glugged, and then feeling ill). I could accessorize with crosses like a mideighties

Madonna and the only thing that would hurt would be knowing how tacky and mideighties Madonna it was.

In Hell, however, I was even more powerful. Which was cool, but terrible. Because . . .

"The power—Satan's abilities? Are they an executive perk, like a company car? I can use them because she isn't? They come with the job, like health bennies?"

"I think that's exactly it," the Ant said. "You can't do such things up in your precious mansion, right?" Ooh, she couldn't resist getting in a zinger. The Ant deeply coveted my Summit Avenue mansion, but was usually better at hiding it.

I took her breaking of the Tenth Commandment (People: I *just* gave you a list of things not to do!) at face value. "Right. In the 'real world,' for lack of a less lame phrase, I can only do vampire queen stuff. Down here I can do a lot more. But it's all over the place, and totally unreliable. Sometimes I can make things happen . . ." I waved my clipboard, which in addition to holding all the stats on the new arrivals also smelled like blueberries. I had made yesterday's clipboard smell like strawberries and planned to run the gamut of fruit scents before the month was out. It was important to have goals. "And sometimes not. Watch this. Rain. I want it to rain in here really hard."

Cathie and Marc let out unanimous yelps of alarm, but even as they scrambled to take shelter beneath the Lego table, nothing happened.

"Oh, God, what does it rain in Hell?" Marc shrieked from the floor. "Acid? Blood? Clumps of pubic hair?"

"Right now it's not raining anything, even though I ordered it to rain in here. My point! Why do some commands work and some don't? Oh, come out from under there," I added impatiently.

Only Father Markus had kept his shit together and remained seated. "Frustrating," was his only comment, and was that a smile?

"Ya think? Quit grinning at me, you're awful." He shrugged it off, which was fine because I hadn't meant it.

"Since it didn't rain pubic hair," Marc said, climbing out from under the table and collapsing back into his chair, "I think it's as good a time to adjourn as any."

Not much had been accomplished, but Father Markus seconded it almost before Marc had finished the sentence and, like that, I was paroled from another meeting. Yippee! I was like a kid let out of school! Except I was a kid (one of the youngest in the room, never mind the whole of Hell) let out of the bureaucracy of Hell, which was even better.

"Same time tomorrow?"

Oh, blech.

CHAPTER
SIX

"Excuse me, Mrs. Sinclair?"

Like an idiot I looked around for whomever she was talking to. Then I realized: "Oh. Me. It's me? Yes." *Mrs. Sinclair. Mrs. Eric Sinclair. Mrs. Sink Lair. Mr. and Mrs. Sink Lair?*

When I was little I was nervous about trying a kiwifruit. Fuzzy brown skin, green inside with icky-looking black seeds, it was some sort of fruit/Tribble hybrid and I had no interest in sticking it in my mouth. Nothing that looked that weird could be yummy.

But my mother hectored me until I bit into it. It was perfectly ripe, if not entirely sweet, with an odd texture that wasn't unpleasant, just strange to me. It took me a few seconds to decide if it was vile or delicious; I eventually settled on delicious, but only when I was in the mood for one. That was how it felt now, hearing someone call me Mrs. Sinclair, which was my legal name even if I never, ever used it.

It was not that I didn't love Eric Sinclair. It was beyond love; I'd die for him and kill for him (and had). But our relationship was at once like and unlike any union between lovers. We were in love, yes. But we had a business relationship, too; we were co-monarchs . . . except not really. As the foretold vampire queen, I outranked the king. Tina had explained it to me: Sinclair was a king consort, I was a queen regnant. I reigned in my own right; Sinclair, to be blunt, was just along for the ride.

Like most lovers (but not many business partners), I had no secrets from him, and he didn't have very many from me (given his exquisite skills in the bedroom, there were some things I didn't want to know . . . hearing your lover's bang résumé wasn't at all romantic). And though we'd touched and kissed and caressed every inch of each other, I almost always called him Sinclair, and he always called me Elizabeth. It sounded formal (in his case) and flippant (in mine) to everyone else; to us, it was like a stolen kiss.

We also shared everything . . . kind of. I let Sinclair handle the tedious side of monarching—the petitions, the management of our property, the newsletter (hey, we were a modern vampire monarchy), while I handled the fun stuff, and Hell.

I was very specific about Hell: it was mine. Yes, I formed a committee to help me, but at the end of the day (and the beginning, for that matter) I was in charge. I wasn't a co-anything in Hell, and although that was the way I wanted it, I wasn't entirely sure why.

Sinclair and I trusted each other—except he knew I was a procrastinating shoe lover with a horror of paper-work and any kind of bureaucracy, and would do my best to wiggle out of anything that hinted it might not be one hundred percent fun. And I knew he was loyal only to me . . . but always kept an eye on his own bottom line.

I had yet to let him have much to do with Hell. I'd brought him here once, but hadn't done so again. Unlike the vampire monarchy, there wasn't a foretold partner who would pop out of nowhere to help me. I had killed the devil and then taken the Antichrist's birthright. If I couldn't hold it on my own, I had no right to be here.

At least, I was pretty sure that was my reasoning. Bottom line, I was worried about giving him any real power. This was the man who had tricked me into making him king, after all. I loved him, but never forgot who he was.

All that to say I loved kiwis, sometimes, and my husband, all the time, but was wary of both.

"Mrs. Sinclair? Ma'am?"

"Right, right. Sorry. I was thinking about kisses and kiwis."

"As you will." I got a good look at the older woman who had hailed me from the direction of the Lego room. She was short, with a sort of hat/bonnet hybrid on her head, a long-sleeved blouse and floor-length skirt in sober gray and cream, with an equally sober darker gray shawl wrapped around her shoulders. The clothes were modern, if not trendy. And she looked vaguely familiar, though I was sure I hadn't seen her before. "My pardon for disturbing your thoughts of fruit and bussing."

Eh? Oh, who cares. "What can I do for you?"

"My name is Mary Ball Washington." She paused, expectant. When all I did was blink at her, she adjusted her shawl a bit higher and looked crushed. "Oh. I thought . . . I thought you might know me."

"I'm new here, I'm still learning everyone's names." *The billions of names, cripes, give me a break, lady!*

"Oh, not know me personally, but rather know my

purpose. My old friend Christina Caresse Chavelle—" My giggle stopped her. "Pardon?"

"Nothing." Tina's real name, heh. I knew I was an immature asshat but every time I heard it, I pictured a romance novel cover from the eighties, complete with shirtless muscular tanned hero and the heaving bosom of a heroine whose name was probably something like Christina Caresse Chavelle. "You were saying?"

"Miss Chavelle asked me to escort your friend Dr. Spangler about. She wishes me to introduce him to 'interesting people.'" She paused, then added, "I know several interesting people."

"Huh?"

"Dr. Marc Spangler." She paused, doubtless trying to gauge the depth of my ignorance. "The sodomite."

"Jesus, don't call him that!"

She flinched away from me. "I— Forgive me. You seemed to have trouble placing— I mean, I thought that—"

"He's not in Hell because he's gay, y'know. He's in Hell because he's my friend!" Hmm. Better rephrase. "I mean, he's a volunteer. And it's nobody's business who he's attracted to."

"Oh, I quite agree. A friend of mine was only interested in adhesive love—"

"Ad—" I made my mouth snap shut. Then made it open again. "Sorry, go on." *Adhesive love. Jesus God.*

"But he was a good man for all that," she hastened to assure me, like I'd assumed otherwise. "He was a good Christian; he loved God. He would have taken the vows but he wanted children. He prayed for the devil's feelings to leave him . . ."

"Devil's feelings," I managed with a straight face, "are the worst."

". . . to let him be with a woman as he wanted to be with a man. We both prayed," she finished sadly, then peeked up at me. "It didn't work. And now that I've been around for a bit, I've begun to understand why. Some things cannot be helped. I meant no disrespect to your queer fellow."

I mentally groaned. But she was already skittish and old. So I let it go. "That's great, now we know who everybody's talking about. But what does Tina getting you to give Marc the Cool People Tour have to do with me?"

"Oh. Well." Mary Ball Washington floundered for a moment. (*Flounder*, not *founder*. They're not interchangeable. Major pet peeves: *towards* instead of *toward*, *amongst* instead of *among*, and *founder* instead of *flounder*. Nobody was filling with water and sinking. Mary Ball Washington was verbally thrashing. Not sinking.) "As your underlings—"

"For your own safety, never call them that within earshot. Well, Dr. Spangler, anyway." Tina probably wouldn't care. I'd even heard her refer to herself as a minion once. I dunno, she might've lost a bet.

"—it is a courtesy to bring such things to your attention, lest you wonder if she's usurping your lawful authority."

"Time for a new rule, Mary Ball Washington. I don't have to know every little thing my underli— No, not that . . ."

"Lackeys?"

"No! My—my fellow committee members! I don't need to sign off on everything they're doing." Especially something silly like Tina asking a local to give Marc a tour. Exactly the sort of thing I trusted Tina with while also not giving a shit about.

Cripes, Satan, micromanage much? I knew Cathie and the Ant tried to head off a lot of these types of—petitioners, would they be? I made a mental note to be especially nice to Cathie, and a little nice to the Ant. "It's why I have a committee. Because the new boss isn't the same as the old boss, no matter what the Who said."

She dropped her head so quickly I heard her neck creak

a little. "Of course, Mrs. Sinclair. My apologies for over-stepping again."

"No, no. It's good that you brought it up; it's something that everyone in Hell needs to know. It's gotta be understood that anyone on the committee is acting with my total permission." My fervid, thankful, grateful permission. "I'll bring it up tomorrow at the next meeting. I guess that's gonna mean more flyers."

She'd been standing with her face at an angle. Now she faced me straight on and the feeling that she looked familiar got stronger. Something about the hair . . . and the dour smile . . . "Your pardon, ma'am?"

I had a vision of her picturing literal flyers: souls soaring about Hell bellowing out the news of the day. Fun, but ultimately impractical. "Nothing. Have you been here awhile? In Hell?"

"Oh yes. Since 1789."

"Yeah?" I gestured to her outfit. "But you're letting yourself look different?" That explained the modern materials, but the old-fashioned look. And the shawl. "Good for you."

"I died in my . . ." She glanced around, then leaned in and whispered, "Night attire. I was delighted when I realized I could wear whatever I wished. It only took me seventy years to master."

Hmm. Was it like any skill, then? Some people just had a knack for driving, for picking up foreign languages, for gardening. Did some people have a knack for the whole "my flesh was only a vessel, my spirit roams as I will it" thing, while for others it took longer? Should we be teaching classes in this stuff? Something else for tomorrow's (groan) meeting.

"You've been here awhile . . ." Minnesota politeness had me ready to add *I know it's none of my business, but . . .* so I squashed it. Anything anyone did here was now officially my business. I didn't have to apologize for asking questions. "What'd you do?"

"I blasphemed. And . . ." She took a breath, let it out. "I was not as good a mother as I could have been to my George."

"What, you beat him?" Ugh, she didn't kill him, did she? She looked harmless but willful, like a church organist who ran everything behind the scenes, and she smelled like old cookies and powder. Which didn't mean shit; if I'd learned anything since dying the first time, I'd learned that looking harmless was no guarantee of *being* harmless.

"Of course I beat him! It was my duty, for does it not say, 'He that spareth his rod hateth his son: but he that loveth him chasteneth him betimes'?"

What am I, a game show contestant? "Probably."

"In point of fact I fear I didn't beat him enough. 'Twas only me, you know; my husband passed on when I was thirty-five, and left me with five children to raise and a plantation to run. I wasn't—there wasn't—there wasn't as much time for frivolity and tenderness. I had to be mother and father to him. I was . . ." She paused, visibly struggling for the words to explain to the newer, dimmer Satan. ". . . determined to have my way. In all things."

"Okay. Well. Single motherhood is a bitch. My mom was one. But if all single mothers are doomed to Hell, I'd think it'd be a lot more crowded here."

"No, no . . . I'm here because I blasphemed. And when my George was led astray by evil companions, I blamed God the Father and not my own weakness. It cost me my son."

"Did he die?"

"Well, yes." She regarded me with a puzzled smile. "It's been centuries."

"Right, right. I mean, did he die because of anything you did?"

"He died because I didn't do *enough*. I must have told him a hundred times a hundred times—"

"So, a thousand times?" *Why not just say that?*

"—not to go straight to dinner after chores. He was out in dreadful weather for hours inspecting the grounds, got miserably soaked, and then had dinner in his wet clothes! Death was inevitable! And it was my fault! And his."

"So, while you're sorry you weren't nicer to him in general, you're also sorry you didn't nag him more?"

"Exactly. He was only sixty-seven. He had years left!"

"Uh . . ." This was awful, but it reminded me of the uproar when Joan Rivers died. Okay, the clinic was definitely negligent, but she was eighty-one. So while it was sad to hear she died, all the "gone too soon!" and "she had years left!" and "she could have been saved and gone on for years!" stuff didn't exactly ring true. Because: eighty-one.

Meanwhile, Mary Ball Washington was still bitching about her dead kid whom she'd successfully raised on her own and who'd gone on to live a long time.

"Showing up at Congress in a war uniform, really! Disrespectful *and* inappropriate. It was those fellows he knew from the war, you know—much of his nonsense can be placed at their door. Encouraging him to take chances; he was lucky he wasn't killed in the Seven Years' War. Or the Braddock disaster of '55!"

"Sounds stressful," I agreed, then snuck a peek at my watch. Then remembered that since cell phones, nobody wore watches anymore. "Really stressful." *This. This is why I should stop engaging with people in Hell.*

"Was he brave?"

"I didn't ask—"

"Of course. Impetuous, rash? Of course! Some would say that his time in His Majesty's army allowed him to study their methods, and it did—it made him a much more dangerous traitor to King George III!"

"Um. What?"

"Who knew the Stamp Act of 1765 would lead to my son betraying his king and the eventual deaths of tens of thousands? George Mason should have persuaded my boy to fall in line. The one good thing that man did was refuse to sign the Constitution. John Adams, Alexander Hamilton, von Steuben . . . troublemakers, every one. It's obvious. My poor son was misled by evil companions."

Finally, the penny dropped. "Are you talking about George Washington, the first president?"

"Yes, of course."

"The evil companions . . . those would be the guys who basically fought for and created the greatest country in the world?" (I'm a patriot. Sue me.)

"Rebelling against their lawful king!" came the indignant reply.

"The money!"

"I beg your pardon?"

"Nothing." Every time I'd taken out my wallet, I'd seen the male version of this woman. No wonder she looked familiar. "Look, I'm sorry he gave you grief with the whole overthrowing British tyranny and all, but as a loud, proud American, I have to tell you, I think it all turned out for the best."

"Rebels and traitors," she sniffed. "I couldn't hold up my head in church for years."

Cripes, this woman could have been a professional buzzkill. "Well, yeah. Back then I'm sure it was a pretty big scandal." Now that I was giving it some thought, I could see her side of it. After all, some could argue Hell's rightful king had been overthrown by an annoying, vulgar American with no right to the crown and no idea what to do with it once the dim idiot had her paws on it.

It was fair to say I'd never thought about the Revolution from the perspective of a mom who was fine with being a British subject and annoyed her kid wouldn't get with the program. As kids, we're fed the version "the king sucked, so we kicked him out, God bless 'merica!" and not the one that went "if we'd lost, the names Washington and Jefferson and Adams would be synonymous with Hitler and Goebbels."

"Listen, Mrs. Washington, history's written by the winners. In this case: us. So your kid's rebellion is generally considered pretty terrific. There are schools named after your son, and highways and cities. They named the capital after him, and a state. They carved his face into a mountain! You have bragging rights most moms can only dream of!"

An affronted sniff was my only answer. If she held grudges this long, no wonder she was in Hell. One of those souls who, even if I told her she could go, would stay, would insist she was exactly where she was supposed to be, forever and ever, amen.

I tried one more time: "You know he's on all the money, right?"

"I hated that portrait."

I had to stop; the grumpy Dame Washington was making me want to snort in the worst way. Luckily I spotted the sodom—Marc running out of the Lego room, and no wonder: Cathie was dismantling it as quickly as she'd put it together. The woman should have been an architect. Or a demolition engineer.

"Marc, c'mere, I want to introduce you to somebody." He trotted right over, smiling a greeting as Dame Washington gave him a regal nod. When I tried to nod like that, I looked like I was fighting a nap. Must be a generational thing. Or a Colonial American thing. "This is May Bell Washington; Tina asked her to introduce you to interesting people."

His friendly green eyes got big. "George Washington's mother, hi!"

"You know who this is?" How was that possible? She didn't have a show on cable and wasn't on social media, two vehicles that let Marc instantly recognize almost any celebrity in the world.

"And it's Mary Ball, Betsy. Jeesh. Get with the pro-gram." To her: "There's a monument *and* a hospital named after you. It's so nice to meet you!"

She cleared her throat and—whoa. Was that a blush on her wrinkly cheeks? "Foolish aggrandizing. And the pleasure is mine, Dr. Spangler. I thank you for not hold-ing my son's crimes against me."

"Crimes? Right, right, you were a loyalist . . . okay, back then, yeah. But don't you see? You made him the man he is! Was. Where do you think he got that whole 'lead by example' thing? From you! Why do you think he called out Britain for their dick moves with the Stamp Act and the Townshend Acts?"

This whole conversation is proof that I didn't have to be here for any of it. Ugh, he's still going on. What'd this Townshend guy ever do to him?

"Who taught him to stick up for the little guy? You! You're a huge reason why America's been kicking ass since before there was an America."

Definitely a blush. I could see her revising her opinion on Marc in particular and sodomites in general. "Oh, well," she managed, then giggled. Giggled! So very, very, very weird to see a female version of the guy on the one-dollar bill giggling with a gay zombie. "I could only do my best and God's will, like any woman."

"What, you're a Revolutionary War buff now?" I wasn't feeling pissy because they were ignoring me. I wasn't! I had honest curiosity about whether or not Marc was a Revolu-tionary War buff.

"I minored in eighteenth-century American history," was his absent reply as he extended an elbow for Dame Washington to clutch with her gnarled fingers. "Madam, I can't wait to meet people *you* think are interesting."

She chortled in response and began to lead him away, which simultaneously relieved and irked me. "Okay, well, see you later!" I said loudly. "And we've established I don't need to be present for this kind of stuff, right?"

Dame Washington stopped dead (not really), turned, gifted me with a warm, slightly yellowed smile (were *her* teeth wooden, too?). "Thank you so much, Mrs. Sinclair, for allowing this." She dipped her head in a respectful nod, the twenty-first-century version of a curtsy, I figured. "If I can assist any other committee members, or you, in any way, I hope you'll call on me."

"Mrs. Sinclair! Oh, that's wonderful!" Marc's delighted shriek drowned out my muffled groan. "Oh, that's worth any amount of tedium. I'm going to use that *constantly*. I'm buying her *so much stuff* with her name on it."

"No need!" I called loudly, to their rapidly retreating backs. Sinclair had paid off all Marc's student loans, so the son of a bitch had actual disposable income he could piss away on stuff I didn't want. It wasn't an idle threat!

"Engraved stationery is always a thoughtful and practical gift for a lady," Dame Washington suggested, because my life wasn't weird and stressful enough. "Or monogrammed handkerchiefs."

"No, really! I'm all set, guys. Got everything I need and then some."

"Engraved everything! Monogrammed everything!" Marc replied grandly as they went far, far away. Or so I hoped. "Towels, toilet paper, iPhone cases, luggage tags!"

Engraved stationery and monogrammed toilet paper. Jesus wept. Or maybe that was only me.

CHAPTER
SEVEN

I did the Being Seen thing for a while, on Sinclair's advice
("The denizens of Hell should know their new queen, though if any should be bold enough to attempt familiarities with your delectable self, I insist on the privilege of making them suffer for it."

"Aww, you're so cute. You're like an undead Fred Flintstone.")

and it wasn't terrible. I strolled around with my hands clasped behind my back, trying to look unconcerned and, I dunno, regal or evil or regally evil and like someone whose delectable self was never to be messed with.

Most of them were too shy or terrified to talk to me, or even meet my gaze, but I caught a lot of glances out of the corner of my eye, usually from people using the corners of *their* eyes. I ended up in one of Hell's food courts, stepped up to the Orange Julius counter, and ordered a medium orange. (Anything in an Orange Julius

that wasn't orange or Julius wasn't an Orange Julius.
Strawberry Banana Julius just sounds dumb.)

"Um . . . ma'am . . . you must know . . ." The girl behind
the counter, who looked like a young lunch lady crossed with
the wardrobe from *Flashdance* (leg warmers! baah-ha-ha!),
made a vague gesture behind her at the big shiny Julius
dispenser. "It's not going to . . . I mean, it might look like
what you ordered, but I wouldn't drink it."

"It'll work for me," I said, and she nodded so hard I was
afraid she'd brain herself on something. She turned, grabbed
a cup and straw, fiddled with the machine, and ta-dah! She
handed it to me with a shaking hand, and I took a sip.
Excellent. A very good year. "What's your name?"

"Jennifer Palmer?" This while fiddling with her side
ponytail. No one should bring attention to a side ponytail.

"Well, thanks, Jennifer."

"Oh!" She was young—late teens, maybe—with bitten
nails, a *Frankie Says Relax* T-shirt, acid-washed jeans, and
of course a hairnet, required by all who worked the food
courts. It wasn't that Hell cared if hair got in the food.
It's that people detested wearing hairnets. "You're—you're
welcome, ma'am?"

"Can I ask you something?"

"Um." She looked around, but suddenly every single
person in the food court was busy looking busy and not
so much as glancing at either of us. "Sure? I guess?"

Ugh, I hated the "even though this is a declarative
sentence I'm saying it like a question?" thing. But she was
already a bit of a nervous wreck, so I let it pass. "Is this
your punishment?"

She blinked. "Yes."

"Working a food court for eternity."

"Uh-huh."

"How long's it been?" I could have conjured up a clipboard laden with all the pertinent info, but was curious

to hear what she had to say. A clipboard could give me the facts, but not the person behind them.

"Uh . . ." Lots of blinking now. I could almost read her mind: *Where is she going with this? Oh fuck, am I in* more *trouble now? I tried to warn her about the Orange Julius!* "Thirty-one years."

"If you didn't have to be here, where would you go?"

"I—" Another glance around, but nope. No help from anywhere. And I wasn't budging. "I don't know."

"Well, think about it." I sucked up Julius and waited. I was as patient as a mannequin: unmoving, blank faced, and dressed in trendy clothes. Finally . . .

"I guess I'd go home. Tell them I'm sorry, tell them the whole story. My folks are still alive, my sister, and *he* is, too."

"Oh yeah?"

"The fire was an accident, but they thought it was on purpose." Definitely warming to her subject, no pun intended. The side ponytail bounced as she gestured. "I couldn't tell anybody . . . I mean, Tammy *died*." Bounce. "All because I wasn't paying attention, y'know?" I didn't, but nodded anyway. "They thought it was on purpose and I couldn't— Someone went to prison for it. I could've said something. I didn't. I was," she summed up, shaking her head so the bouncing turned to swaying, "chickenshit."

"And not surprised to find yourself in Hell."

"Suicides go to Hell," was the flat response. As if catching her mood, the ponytail went still. "So no. I wasn't surprised."

"Okay."

"Can I ask you something?"

"Sure."

"Why didn't you know that?"

"I could've gotten the info. I wanted to hear what you have to say."

"Oh." She paused. Swallowed. Then, in a small voice, and with a smaller smile: "Thanks."

"Sure." Aww. She was sweet, for an accidental murderous arsonist who watched an innocent man go to prison while never saying a word for fear of incriminating herself. And it wasn't her fault she died on a terrible hair day. Oh. Wait. It was. Well, no one was perfect.

"Hey, Betsy!" Ah, here came Marc the sodom— God, I *wish* I could get that out of my head. Damn you to Hell, Marya Bill Washington! Again! "Been looking for you." He was trotting past the tables of the damned, the only one in the place who was smiling. "Okay, how cool was Mary Ball?"

"Chums now, huh?"

"She's got sooo much dirt on people here!" He was so gleeful, he was practically rubbing his hands together. But not bored—and that was the main thing. "You wouldn't believe— I'll tell you later. Hey." To Jennifer, who blinked back. "She introduced me to a whole . . ."

My phone buzzed against my hip and I pulled it free, nodded at Marc to continue, saw I had a text from Sinclair.

I miss you.

I want you.

Come.

". . . cut both their heads off and they *still* found him not guilty! Hey. Are you all right?"

"Fine." I gulped. My sluggish, undead blood was doing its best to travel south and that one word was all I could manage. "Nnk."

"What was that?"

Oh, that would be me, swallowing an invisible lump conjured by instant horniness.

Marc brightened. "Oooh, did Sinclair send you another sexy texty? He's such a suave son of a bitch." This in a tone of fond admiration.

"First, never call it that again on pain of me kicking you in the shins until you cry. And yes. Hey!" I batted his hand away, but not before he got a quick peek at my phone. "Boundaries!"

"Nobody does that imperious-alpha-male thing better," Marc said, shaking his head. "Gotta give it to him, you lucky skank."

"That's just it!" I cried. Marc had hit on one of my favorite things about the essence of Sinclair. "He's not even trying to be sexy! *He's just sexy!* It just happens! Don't call me skank."

"I can't believe you allow texts but not text terminology," Marc grumbled. "Do you know how much of my time I waste spelling out 'laughing out loud'?"

"Do I care?" Texting back: *On my way!* I'd held out against texting as long as I could; it was laziness personified by way of technology, except in a bad way. But dammit, it was just so convenient. Especially here. But I still hated emojis and text gibberish (LOL, JK, STFU, ISHO, ES, EB, INSTBH,[2] etc.) and I forbade them.

"At least reconsider your hashtag decree—"

"There will never be hashtags or Twitter in Hell!" I shrieked. I heard a muffled *crack!* and realized I'd tightened my grip on my phone a bit too hard. Dammit! Fourth one this month. Tina kept a box of brand-new phones at the mansion, and thank goodness. "Never, never, never!"

Jennifer opened her mouth, but the thunder of a hundred chairs being shoved back while almost everyone galloped for the exits on either end of the food court drowned out whatever she was going to say.

"Never," I said again, trying to moderate my shrillness.

---

[2] Laughing Out Loud, Just Kidding, Shut the Fuck Up, I'm So Hung Over, Everything Sucks, Everything Blows, I'm Not Supposed to Be Here.

"For what it's worth, you just depressed the hell out of the gals who died in that bachelorette bus crash three days ago," Marc said, nodding over my shoulder. I looked and, yep, there was much wailing and gnashing of teeth even as people surged past us.

"Hey, it's Hell," I snapped at them. "What'd you expect?" To Marc: "I'm going. Let's gather up the gang." I never left any of them in Hell when I wasn't there. We were all too new to this. I didn't *think* anybody would mess with them when I was out—assuming anyone here would even know I was or wasn't in Hell—but wasn't willing to risk their safety to find out. As often as Satan had appeared to me in the "real" world, I knew she'd probably had some sort of "back in ten minutes!" setup here. Unless she could be in two places at once. Which would be just like that annoying bitch.

To Jennifer, now cowering behind the counter: "Good talk, thanks. Hope it works out for you." She cocked her head, puzzled, but I was already leaving.

Marc fell into step beside me as we headed past the Dairy Queen that was always out of everything chocolate, the Great Steak company that was always out of buns for the sandwiches and lemons for the lemonade, and the Panda Express entrees that always smelled wonderful but tasted like sautéed shit.

"I think you're overlooking all the people who would find hashtags kind of torturous."

"Yeah, like me. Come on, let's hit the bricks."

"#whateveryousay."

"Cut it out."

"#notalldamned."

"Marc!" I yelled, and if anything, the stampede sped up. Hate to be on the other end of the mall when they got there.

CHAPTER
EIGHT

I was still figuring out the whole "now that you're in charge of Hell you can teleport to and from there even though you were an ordinary human for most of your life" thing. (It sounds totally made up, right? Right.)

But for whatever illogical reason, it was true. To focus my will, my subconscious obligingly produced Dorothy's silver slippers from *The Wonderful Wizard of Oz*.[3] When I'm wearing them, I just think about Hell and I'm there. Or vice versa. (It sounds easy. It's not.)

But the ability was dependent on my mood and my intent. It had taken me five minutes to will myself into Hell for the meeting today, because I just wasn't keen on

---

[3] They were only ruby in the movie because MGM wanted to show off its new Technicolor technology. The more you know!

going. But now I really wanted to go home. And I really wanted to fuck the king of the vampires.

And like that: I was there. Even better: Sinclair was, too. He was better than there; his six-feet-many-inches frame was stretched out in the middle of our emperor bed, the dark sheets a deep contrast to his pale skin (he'd hated losing his farmer's tan when he died). He had one hand behind his head, the other on his cock, and he beckoned me closer without moving, which was a wonderful trick. (*He might be hypnotizing me with his dick. If so, I genuinely can't think of an objection.*)

"I'm back!" I cried unnecessarily. I was already starting to tug at my clothes, stupid clothes, stupid stupid *stupid* clothes, there should be a law, I would *make* a law, Sinclair should only be naked and I should make a law about stupid—

"Wait!"

Eh? Annoyed, I rounded on the voice. "Marc! Can't you see we'd like some privacy?"

"You teleported us in here with you, shithead!" Marc kept trying not to stare at Sinclair lolling nudely

(*nudely!*)

and failing. "Bad enough you're the luckiest shoe addict on the continent, you have to flaunt your no-doubt epic sex life, too?"

"I'm fond of you, Marc," came Sinclair's voice in a sort of rolling deep purr that made me want to bite him *everywhere*, "but I won't share Elizabeth—"

Marc was peeking at him through his fingers. "She's not exactly my—"

"—and she won't share me. Run along, there's a good fellow."

"I'd like to! But your skank wife is between me and the door!"

"Not for long." I took a big step and bounded onto the

bed with Sinclair, hitting the mattress hard enough to jar his hand loose from his cock. That was fine, he could touch me instead. Screw raindrops and roses and whiskers on kittens; a naked Sinclair was one of *my* favorite things.

"Oh, Eric, really," Tina said, sounding like a fond elderly spinster aunt. Which she was, come to think of it. It's just, she was hot, also.

"You're still here, too? What the hell, you guys?" I bitched. "Go the fuck away, I mean it!"

"You brought us here."

Tina took Marc's hand and they walked to the door. "Never mind, Marc."

"Never mind? But—they—she—ugh—"

"Do you want to watch season three of *Sherlock* again?"

"Uh-huh."

"You love 'The Empty Hearse.'"

"I do. How come a dead woman from the antebellum South is the only one in this house who understands me?"

"Out!" Sinclair and I roared in unison.

"We're going, shut up. Tina, honest question: flushing my eyes with bleach won't cause permanent damage, right?" Marc was walking so fast he was now leading them both (I'd never realized how big our bedroom was before), and Tina tripped a little to keep her balance. "If I only do it for five minutes or so?"

The door slammed on her answer. "Ugh, sorry," I said. What little clothing I still had on was getting rapidly ruined as I yanked and tugged. "They really don't get boundaries."

"So inappropriate," Sinclair agreed, dark eyes gleaming. His brunet hair was cut short and neat, and he had what appeared at first glance to be eight miles of limbs. His broad shoulders were sleekly muscled—he'd been a farmer's son in life, before a vampire destroyed his family—and tapered to a narrow waist and tight abdomen. You know how people joke about bouncing quarters off abs? You could bounce a rock so high off his you'd be in real danger of losing an eye. "And though I derive much pleasure from disrobing you myself, watching you shred your clothing in a frantic bid to get naked for me is easily as erotic."

". . . stupid . . . buttons . . . passing a law banning them . . ."

"As you wish, my own, so long as you don't—ah." I'd yanked too hard and started to tumble off our bed; Sinclair's hand shot out, grabbed my wrist, and hauled me on top of him.

"Oh," I said. I smiled down at him. "This works."

He grinned back, showing teeth. "Show me."

I did. For a lovely long time. Reason #27 not to let Sinclair have the run of Hell: if the vampire king was there, it wasn't really Hell.

At least, not to me.

CHAPTER
NINE

"Hell pretty much runs itself," I told him, panting. *Silly,* really—we didn't need to take more than two or three breaths a minute. But energetic marital banging had rocketed my pulse to at least ten bpm. I'd literally run a mile (stupid fleet-footed serial rapist!) and not had my heart pound this hard. "Half the time I'm overwhelmed, and the other half I wonder why I'm even there."

"And this surprises you?" Sinclair was leaning on one elbow, gently stroking my belly with his other hand. He'd missed a drop of blood—we often fed on each other during sex, making an incredible circuit of feeding-orgasm-feeding-orgasm-ohGodpleasedon'tstop-feeding. I reached up, thumbed it off the corner of his upper lip, licked my thumb. He kissed my thumb on the retreat and added, "It's a system that has been in place for countless millennia. They've had ample time to work the kinks out, so to speak."

"Yeah. Good point." But I wasn't thinking about Hell just then. His mouth on my thumb reminded me of his mouth being everywhere just a few minutes ago. I've never seen this put quite so bluntly in any women's magazine, but I loved fucking my husband. Loved it like cake. Loved it like shoes.

I loved him on me and in me and behind me. I loved getting on my knees for him. I loved when he knelt, too. I loved riding him. Sometimes no matter how good he was making me feel, I just had to shove his hands aside and climb on top of him. The different angle was delightful, and that was the least of it. I loved his hands on my hips, gripping so tightly I'd bruise for a week if I were alive. I loved swooping down for teasing kisses that steadily deepened.

But best of all I loved watching him shake apart beneath me. Seeing him lose his mind, unable to say clever, cutting things, and just groan my name. Watching his eyes roll back as he lost even that small verbal ability, feeling his brain essentially white out and go off-line
(!!)
was as big a high as the blood.

"Elizabeth? Are you with me?"

"Kind of," I muttered.

He snickered. "I'll need at least ten minutes, my own."

"Boo."

"And while we wait, we can continue the discussion. Are you worried your new role essentially makes you a figurehead?"

"I wish," I snorted. "I would *love* to be a figurehead. No, it's that on one hand, I see lots of things that could be changed, but on the other, how do I know more than Satan? She was a lot of things, but stupid wasn't one of them. So I'm scared to make too many changes, y'know?"

"At least, not right away," Sinclair suggested.

"But there are kids there! In Hell! I mean, some of

them aren't technically kids anymore, but they're still running around in their old-timey braids and long dresses and saying things like 'forsooth' while some asshole whips them until their backs are all bloody. It freaks me right the fuck out."

He looked at me, unblinking, for a few seconds, and I barely caught his stray thought

(but not my darling sister)

it was so quick and quiet and I'm not sure he was quite conscious of it. "She's not there," I said before I overthought it. Or underthought it. "Your sister. Of course she's not there. She never did one thing to deserve Hell and if there was a terrible mistake and she *was* in Hell I'd save her. I would. I'd do that. Sure I'd do that."

He'd started frowning halfway through my save-the-sister babble, then his expression lightened and his hand cupped my cheek. "Of course you would, my own. And my stray thought did not do her credit . . . or you."

Being able to read the vampire king's mind was pretty great . . . usually. Sometimes it was weird, often it was sexy, and occasionally it was really, really uncomfortable. Like the time I lost my damned mind and tried a whale tail with a red thong and jeans I should have tossed five years ago—whale tails had gone past trendy, past irony, past the backlash, and were now just hopelessly outdated; what had I been *thinking*? His reaction

(by all the saints in Heaven she looks ridiculous)

wasn't at all what I was going for.

Wardrobe malfunctions aside, I wouldn't give up our connection for anything. Another reason I cordially loathed Hell: I couldn't hear Sinclair's thoughts there, and he couldn't hear mine. Thus, I allowed texting in Hell. And, weirdly, so did AT&T.

I knew, even though the thought wasn't at the front of his mind, that he was wondering why I hadn't invited him back to Hell since that first visit, so I kept talking about his family and the steps I'd taken to make sure they weren't being tortured. *Sure, I'm blocking you from this huge new part of my life, but I've kept an eye out for my in-laws, too!*

"I asked my magical clipboard if your parents were there, and they aren't, either. None of the people you asked about are there. So they've been reincarnated or they're in Heaven or something."

"Almost a pity," he murmured, lying flat so I could snuggle my head into his shoulder. I could kiss the hollows in that man's shoulder and collarbone all day and all night. "What a way to impress them!"

I giggled. "Hiya, Mom and Pop. So, in the decades you've been dead I've become the vampire king and I'm married to the HBIC in Hell."

"Don't be ridiculous. I would never refer to them as Mom and Pop."

"Whatever you say, honey-bunny."

"And I forbid the use of that nickname."

"You bet, snuggly-wuggly." Over his groan, I added, "And something in the cool-but-weird category, Marc made a new pal this time. George Washington's mom! Who holds grudges for centuries, apparently. But he definitely wasn't bored."

"Excellent." Sinclair liked Marc, but at the same time was a little freaked-out by the trials and tribulations of living with a zombie. And we *all* liked for Marc not to be bored. "Well worth the trip for that alone."

"Mmm." I looked at the ceiling for a few seconds, thinking. "Y'know, I have to say I get why Satan was such a huge bitch. The Hell gig is a headache on the best of days, and if you do it right, nobody gives a shit. It's gotta be like running the DMV."

"Perhaps worse. You aren't compensated for running the netherworld."

"Maybe Satan wasn't so awful." I thought that over for another two seconds. "Nope. Still hate her."

"Perhaps I could come with you next time. You dislike acknowledging it, but I'm quite a bit older than you and certainly have more experience in management."

I held back a snort with difficulty. Management. Sure. If that was how he wanted to refer to keeping the former king of the vampires off his ass by wielding the cruel fist of a tyrant, that was fine. Whatever, pal. "Someone has to stay here and be a vampire monarch," I said. "And I acknowledge your creepy ancientness all the time, you fogey." I did, when I wasn't trying not to think about it too hard. My husband was eligible for social security, and had been for decades. I regularly boinked an octogenarian. By contrast, I was barely a triplegenarian! (That's the word, right? Triplegenarian?) "So what'd I miss this time? How long were we gone?" There was a pause and I left off the shoulder snuggling to sit up. "What? What's wrong?"

"Nothing is *wrong*, exactly," he soothed, which made me groan in despair. Sinclair had a high tolerance for *wrong*. The mansion could be in ashes and he'd classify it as "well, we had a bit of a setback this morning." Know how I knew this? Because before we were married, he lived in a mansion, and it ended up in ashes. And he was as perturbed as I am when we're out of ice. (It's easy to get ice. So I find a lack of ice to be mildly annoying, but not much else.)

"What, what? How long was I gone? What happened? Is it terrible? It's terrible, isn't it?"

"Not . . . exactly. You were gone just over two weeks." (!!!!!!!!!!!!!!!!!!!!!!!!!!!!!!!!!!!!!)

Sinclair put a hand to his forehead. "Ouch." Like me, he cherished our telepathic bloodsucking bond . . . most of the time.

"Christ, when am I going to get the hang of this?" I just about screamed. Thing #842 I hated about Hell: time moved differently there. If I had to guess, I would have thought we were there maybe half a day, long enough for the meeting and for me to chat with some locals, slurp down an Orange Julius, and listen to George Washington's mom bitch about her rotten kid who founded a country while disobeying her. Instead, half the month had gone by.

"Why didn't you tell me?"

"Ah . . ."

"Right. We both needed all the sex." Good God, I didn't think Sinclair and I had gone without a marital boink for more than seventy-three hours since . . . I had to take a second and think about it. Ah! Since I accidentally fucked him upside down in the deep end of a swimming pool, simultaneously marrying him and making him king of the vampires. (Long story. Weird week.[4] Also, vampires don't need church services to be married, for obvious reasons.)

"But why didn't you ask me to come back sooner?"

He remained silent, and I realized it was a dumb question (even for me). I knew why. It was a point of pride: *I shall support my wife in the job I did not want her to take and wish she did not have, the thing she won't share with me, and I will do this by refusing to give in to lonely horniness and beg her to come back. I'll do that for a day. Three days. Five. A week. A week and a half. Two weeks . . . now where did I put my phone?*

Goddammit.

I slumped back into the pillows. "Fine, fine. Better tell me the bad news. Did Jessica's babies disappear and take longer than usual to reappear?"

"No."

"Did my mom break up with her boyfriend?"

"No."

---

[4] It was! Details can be found in *Undead and Unwed*.

"Are you sure? Please tell me she broke up with the guy who looks like a giant baby . . . That big round head, I can't *not* stare at it when I visit . . ."

"Nothing like that," he soothed.

"Well, good."

"But the Antichrist has been trying to out vampires to the world, and it looks like she may well be succeeding."

"*What?*"

He looked at me, and I swear there was more than a note of reproach in his tone as he added, "I didn't call you back to me *just* to have sex, you know."

Silly me.

CHAPTER TEN

Marc and I crossed paths as we were both lunging for the keyboard in the kitchen. Tina had (stupidly) tried to implement hanging keys in order of status. Jessica and Dick (his name used to be Nick, but that's a whole other thing[5]) abruptly lost their minds and threatened to threaten to sue ("I don't actually want to sue, but I might promise to sue!") over what they saw as discrimination against the living.

So then she suggested we hang keys in alphabetical order by owner. ("Boo! That means the cop goes first!" "What, it's my fault my mother married a Berry?")

So then she tried alphabetical by car, but since Sinclair had two Audis, a Bentley, and a Corvette, that was promptly shouted down as well.

And then Tina noticed that in the three days she'd spent

---

[5] *Undead and Unwary.*

trying to come up with a system that wouldn't make us all want to kill each other, we were all just hanging our keys on whatever hooks were empty, and nobody had trouble finding theirs, even when in a rush. I mean, I lived with millionaires, but even they could drive only so many cars. The board had plenty of hooks.

So Marc and I were both scrambling for the keyboard. "My passive-aggressive sister is trying to out vampires to the world!"

"I missed two *Game of Thrones* and one *It's Always Sunny*, and I'm two weeks behind on *People*, *Entertainment Weekly*, and *Time*!"

"And we were gone two weeks!"

"No one watered my cactus! Which is good, actually. Betsy. Seriously." He blocked my retreat to the mudroom door. "You gotta get the time thing figured out."

"No shit!" I realized I was clutching my keys in a white-knuckled fist and eased up. Those electronic keys were insanely easy to crack. "I'm open to suggestions."

"You need a row of clocks, like they have in car rental places or brokerage firms. They all tell the time for a different city."

"When were you in a brokerage—"

"I watched *The Wolf of Wall Street*. You know what I'm talking about—they'll have a clock up for Tokyo time and one for New York time and one for, I dunno, L.A. and one for Hong Kong and one for Ann Arbor and one for Houston and one for Bismarck."

"Bismarck? Really?"

"You need one that will always tell you what time it is at the mansion."

Well. That was actually a pretty good idea, assuming my powers in Hell would work like that. Whenever I wanted to know something, my magical clipboard usually obliged. Maybe I could put a magical clock in, too. It was no surprise that there were no clocks in Hell; time meant different things to the souls there, and a fixed clock always set to, I dunno, central standard time wouldn't be much help. Maybe not a row of clocks, but maybe a wristwatch that always told me what I needed to know? "Okay, that's not bad," I admitted. "Remind me next time we're there."

He nodded and scooted aside so I could pass. "Gotta go."

"Yeah, me, too."

"Sinclair didn't tell you until after the sex, did he?"

"Oh, shut up."

"Hey, the guy went two weeks without nooky. I'm surprised he remembered his own name, all that backup."

"Vampires don't get— Oh my God, I'm not discussing this with you."

"You kind of are," he said with a grin that was half apologetic, half wiseass. No, wait. All wiseass.

"Oh, shut up."

"Have pity on the man!" my least favorite zombie hollered after me as I hurried through the mudroom. "Take pity on his penis!" Because the neighbors don't have enough to gossip about.

In my rush to get gone, I nearly fell over something and knew without looking what it was. I seized the pitchfork, yanked the door to the side yard open, ignored the puppies' yelps of welcome, and tossed it into the garden with the others.

"Stop giving me these things!" I shrieked back at the house in general. Prank-hungry bastards. Twice in a month, really? Bad enough they were defacing name tags and planting them on me, but to leave pitchforks lying around? Where does someone even buy a pitchfork? "Really? Don't you have anything better to do?"

From all parts of the house, simultaneous replies came back: "No!"

Well, that was just a lie.

CHAPTER
ELEVEN

I had the Antichrist cornered like the sun-kissed rat she
was. "Aha! I thought I'd find you here!"

Eventually. First I'd tried her apartment in Burnsville,
then Fairview Ridges where she volunteered, and then
Hastings Family Service where she *also* volunteered. Then
I stopped at Caribou for a large hot chocolate (I was back
in the real world now, and so was my unholy vampire
thirst of the damned . . . what little I'd taken from Sinclair wouldn't hold me for long), then the United Way.

Then I looked at my phone again, observed it was Sunday morning (the clanging church bells and gaggles of
families dressed in their Sunday best should have tipped
me off), and found her at First Presbyterian in Hastings.

I had thrown the incredibly heavy door open (it took some
effort—argh, so windy!—even with vampire strength—how
did the Sunday school kids manage?) and pointed my cup

of hot chocolate at her, bellowing to the startled churchgoers that, aha, I thought I'd find her there, eventually.

"Betsy!" the Antichrist hissed, setting down a coffee-pot. "This is fellowship!"

She made it sound like a place, rather than something they were doing. Unless fellowship meant "behold the ritual of the serving of the coffee and of the nondairy creamer, for yea, some churchgoers shalt be lactose intolerant."

Maybe it was the name of the room. Church—the service—was clearly over; the place was packed but every-one was eating. And it was the food moms and dads and grandmas had brought to church: pans of brownies, plates of cookies, some blondies that didn't get gobbled as quickly as the brownies (when will people just accept that blondies will never trump brownies? ooh, memo to me: people in Hell should get blondies when they order brownies), a pyramid of Rice Krispies bars, fruit plates, Kool-Aid for the kiddos, coffee for the adults, and bowls of peanuts for whomever. Somebody always brought pea-nuts; it was weird.

I'd been raised Presbyterian by a mother with agnostic leanings and a father who tried to spend every Sunday he could out of town "on business." When my mother started getting suspicious, he converted to Judaism so he could ostensibly worship on Saturdays (often in hotel rooms).

But once Mom saw I had the basics down ("A talking snake tricked a rib lady into eating bad fruit and that's why women need epidurals for labor and it's also why the world is jam-packed with sinners, but the baby born of a virgin who later came back as the Holiest of Zombies fixed it so anyone, no matter how skanky, can get to Heaven if they know the secret passwords.") we hardly went anymore. Ironically, I had prayed to God a lot more after my death than before. I wondered if that was true of everyone or just vampires. It was really something to consider when you thought about it, a complicated—

"Ow!"

"Come on." My sister had bequeathed the Ritual of Coffee and Nondairy Creamer to a scowling old man who looked like Mr. Burns after he'd been embalmed, then she'd crossed the room and sunk her fingers into my arm like it was Play-Doh and her nails were nails. "We can talk upstairs."

Upstairs was the nave, where the lectures/sermons were heard. It was gorgeous, as I found most churches to be (I had a thing for stained-glass windows; they really classed up a joint). The ceiling was quite high, at least two stories, so every footstep and whisper echoed, and the place smelled old and clean, like a library when someone had cleaned the shelves with Pine-Sol just a few hours earlier. The only person who hadn't bolted for fellowship to nom-nom-nom some brownies was an elderly lady with stacks of programs, which she was sorting at a small table at the rear of the room. What was it with church programs and how there are always at least a hundred left? Gotta give the church props for optimism. She nodded at the Antichrist, who smiled back, then returned to her sorting.

We went to the front, just a few feet from the altar, and my butt had barely settled on the pew before she rounded on me.

"What do you think you're doing, coming here of all places and at all times? This is very inappropriate!" This from the woman who had killed, and/or tried to kill, almost every vampire she'd ever met (including me), as well as the occasional serial killer.

"There are, what? At least five hundred churches in Minnesota?"

"Thousands," was the dry response.

"So why does whatever it is you're up to—"

"Repenting sin and asking for forgiveness?"

"And for brownies, yeah. So why do you have to do that here? Heck, Hastings has a dozen churches, but why this town and this church?"

"Because your husband contaminated this church with his filth."

"Are you talking about his money, or did he whiz in the corner during prayer circle?"

"Don't make fun." Her mouth turned down and for a few seconds she looked like the sad kid picked last for kickball. Dammit! I didn't have time to feel sorry for the Antichrist!

"Okay, okay. Just . . . help me understand your thought process. So because Sinclair—whom you've never liked, but that's okay, he's not on Team Antichrist, either—has started going to this church again, his *dead family's church*, suddenly you need to be here, too?"

"No one forced him to become a vampire," she snapped back. "Quite the opposite: he demanded Tina turn him."

"Yeah, to avenge his *dead family*."

She waved that away. Poof, buh-bye, Sinclair's dead family, we've got more important things to obsess over. "The fact that you've found some undead loophole so he could return doesn't mean he should be here."

Well, that was fair. It *was* a loophole. Before I'd killed her, Satan had granted me a wish (that was when I started to suspect it wasn't so much that I'd killed her as she'd let herself die). I'd been tempted to go with *what's the secret ingredient that makes Orange Juliuses so delish?* but came to my senses and went with *let Sinclair live in the light again*.

But! "You're wrong about the second one. He's got every right to be here, more than any of us. His grandfather rebuilt this church way back when . . . when there was a fire? Or something? There's probably *Sinclair rules!* from a hundred years ago scratched on a wall or under a pew around here."

"Lord, I hope not," she muttered. Couldn't tell if she was blaspheming or actually praying. "This church is where your husband and I talked, and it's where I got my Great Idea." Great Idea. You could hear the caps.[6]

"Uh-huh." I'd been here five minutes and still hadn't gotten to the crux of it. I knew why. I didn't really want to know what Laura Goodman was up to. At all. "So, speaking of great ideas that probably aren't, what's this about you trying to out vam—"

"I'll definitively prove there *is* a God!"

"—pires to the— What?"

She nodded at me with a big smile that wasn't scary at all. "I'm going to prove there's a God. Prove it to the world."

I just sat there and tried to let that seep into my brain. It was so far from what Sinclair and I had assumed she was up to, but I couldn't tell if that was good or bad.

There she sat, my half sister, Laura Goodman (subtle, fates or God or whoever), dressed in her Sunday best (she had a horror of people who wore jeans to church): a high-necked pink blouse, a rose-colored knee-length skirt, cream-colored tights, chunky black loafers. Chunky loafers were what women wore in the winter when the weather wasn't bad enough for boots or good enough for pumps. Laura's were especially hideous, like lumps of tires fashioned into a vague shoe shape. We had a few things in common; our fashion sense wasn't one of them.

Besides, she was so irritatingly, thoroughly gorgeous, she could have been wearing newspapers. Light blond hair halfway down her back, perfect fair complexion with a natural rosy blush, big blue eyes that went poison green when she was angry, or murderous, or murderously angry.

---

[6] All the plotting and general sneakiness—and more!—can be found in *Undead and Undermined*.

Nobody ever looked at Laura Goodman and thought, *Spawn of Satan? Oh, sure. Knew it the minute I laid eyes on her.*

I stopped pondering her annoying good looks and managed, "Could you say that again, please?"

"You cheated me of my birthright."

"No, no, the other thing." So not in the mood for the "Satan and I tricked you into running Hell but now I want to bitch about the consequences" chat. I'd warned her at the time that getting your own way was often as much a curse as it was a blessing. See: Sinclair's life, death, and afterlife; also mine, the Ant finally landing my father, and anyone who voted for Hitler back in the day.

"This *is* the other thing," she corrected. "You want the background, don't you?"

Not really.

"I can't do what I was born to do—"

"Be effortlessly gorgeous while sitting in judgment on pretty much everybody as you ignore your own sins?"

Her lips thinned but she continued. "But I can do this. I can bring faith to the world."

"How?"

"Any way I can." She leaned forward, warming to her subject. Leaning away from her would probably be interpreted as unfriendly. Maybe I could pretend I didn't want to catch her cold. If she had one. And if I could still catch colds. "Lectures, videos, websites. I already started a few while I was waiting for you to get back." Was there a tiny hint of reproach in her tone? No. I decided there wasn't, because if there was, I'd have to slap the shit out of her with a hymnal. "So I've been preparing the ground, so to speak, talking about our adventures and Hell and such while waiting for you."

"That's why Sinclair thinks the plan is to show the world vampires exist," I said, thinking out loud.

She shrugged. "Yes, I imagine his undead spies keep

him well-informed." When I raised my eyebrows she added, "Yes, he called me a couple of times, but I'm not obligated to explain myself to him." Adding in a mutter, "I don't know how he keeps getting my number . . ."

"So he was tipped off after he heard about the 'Betsy and Laura: Time-Travelin' Cuties' show." God, Marc would have a field day with this . . .

"What, every other sinner can have a YouTube channel but I can't?"

"Um . . ." *Stay focused.* I was already envisioning the conversation my husband and I would have: *Good news! She's not outing vamps. There's a teeny bit of bad news, though. Why don't you lie down while I tell you about her Great Idea . . .*

Meanwhile she was obliviously babbling. "I'd be different from the regular preachers . . . they're talking about faith, which is all well and good for someone who isn't *us*. I can offer proof. Look what just you and I have seen in . . . what? Less than four years? I always believed in Him, and I think you did, too—your mother failed you in your teenage years but she did make sure you went to Sunday school long enough to—"

"Do not say one
(church you're in church)
dang word against my mother."

Laura cut herself off and even flushed a little. "You're right. That was inappropriate. I like your mom."

"I know you do." I had to shake my head at my little sister's many dichotomies. Skirts in church and brownies in the basement when not plotting to dump Hell on the vampire queen and murdering random serial killers. Genuinely fond of my mom—she called her Dr. Taylor and occasionally stopped in just to chat or to play with our half brother, BabyJon—but wouldn't shed a tear at my funeral. Blithely ready to shove God onto the world whether the world wants it or not, but gets embarrassed when called out for being rude.

"You were telling me," I prompted without grimacing or clutching my temples, "about your Great Idea." God, now *I* was using the caps. At least it wasn't pronounced in all caps, like when fifty-somethings or thirteen-somethings got on social media for the first time and felt every post had to be a scream.

"Okay, so you always believed in Him, but before your— uh, unfortunate death—it was strictly faith. And I had faith without proof until my thirteenth birthday, when Mother appeared and explained my destiny. Then I knew. And we can help everyone know. We've time traveled; we've seen Hell; my mother was the devil; you're the *new* devil! We know the Bible's right, we can tell people! We can save everybody!"[7]

"Why . . . why would we do that?" Was she talking about us going on some sort of . . . lecture circuit of the damned? Would we be copresenters, or would it be her show and I'd be trotted out like the miniature elephant in *Jurassic Park*: *Look what we made! Give us money and we'll make more!* (The book, not the movie. I loved that stupid dwarf elephant. The scientists should have skipped the dinosaurs and just engineered a huge park of thousands of dwarf elephants. If they escaped, it'd be annoying but also adorable.) "Laura?"

"Why *wouldn't* we do that?" she replied, puzzled. She was leaning toward me, our hands were almost touching, she was as friendly and excited as I'd seen her in weeks. Our last meeting

("*I'll take over your job, your destiny, the one you tricked me into and lied to get out of. But there are strings, Laura. You don't get to dump this on me and walk away without*

---

[7] It's true! It can all be found in *Undead and Unfinished*.

*major strings. I'm giving you the same deal I gave our dad:
we're family or we're not. This isn't something you can
change your mind about later. And you can't half-and-half
it, either. No flitting down to Hell to check on me, or catch
up on family gossip . . . If you're giving up your birthright
and dumping your responsibility on me, then do it, and do
it all the way.*

*"You're done, you're out. Hell's not your inheritance any-
more, it's not yours in any way anymore and that means
everything that comes with it. You don't get to jettison the
responsibility but keep the perks . . . If I see you in Hell, I'm
going to assume you're dead.")*

hadn't been so pleasant. Was she—was she trying to
forge a new relationship with me? Was setting up the
"We Can Prove God Exists" lecture series her way of
reconciling herself to what she'd lost? Was she regretting
her choices less than a month after she had made them,
or was this the plan all along?

"I've barely started, and I wanted to tell you right
away—"

Really?

"—but you've been gone."

"Wow."

"I know!"

"You actually managed to make me being *in Hell*,
doing *your job*, sound like a character flaw, or like I was
rude to keep your Great Idea waiting. I can't even figure
out the time thing between dimensions—"

"Conjure up a row of clocks, like in a brokerage firm."

"—when I was—well, yes, that was Marc's suggestion
and it'll probably work, but it's not like I was off having
fun!" Although listening to Dame Washington bitch
about her kid *had* been pretty entertaining . . . and piss-
ing off all the teens and twenty-somethings with my No

Tweets rule (and confusing everyone else over fifty: "What's tweets?") had also been fun . . .

I forced a calming breath (focus!) and decided to go with the least complicated objection first.

"Never mind where I was or for how long or why I had to be there in the first place. I'm here now, right? And the thing is, about your Great Idea, our word isn't proof." I said it as nicely as I could, and not just because showing the world our trials and tribulations had zero appeal. In a future that will never come to pass, I ruled the world. And it was a huuuge downer. What little I'd seen of the other, ancient, grumpy, zombie-raising, Sinclair-killing me had been more than enough. I wouldn't revisit it. And since I could time travel from Hell, I meant that figuratively *and* literally. There was no way to prove the good (Heaven is a real possibility!) without dredging up the bad (vampires take over the world!). "People don't know who we are, and they shouldn't, Laura."

She ignored this, so the bright-eyed enthusiasm continued unabated. "There are enough of us who know the truth; if we combine forces we can reach millions!"

Sure, but so could Taylor Swift, and any Kardashian. In this day and age, reaching millions wasn't unheard of . . . and oh boy, I hoped that wasn't her point. That if ordinary mortals

(sometimes I miss being an ordinary mortal)

could make their presence known with just a video or a silly trick on YouTube, if the "Leave Britney *alone*!" guy and the ice bucket challenge could go global, the Antichrist and the queen of the vampires could, too.

"Once we convince the rest of the world, things would change overnight! No more wars, no more murders."

Oh boy. She was only a few years younger than me and I felt every day of those years now. "People not knowing if there's a God is not what causes murders and wars," I said carefully, because she was glowing like a zealot-turned-lightbulb. "At least, not all the time. Anymore. General dickishness causes wars. Money causes wars." I recalled one of my favorite lines from *Gone with the Wind*: *All wars are in reality money squabbles.* "I promise you, Laura. I promise. There will always be war and murder because there will always be assholes. They are not an endangered species. Even if every single person on the planet converted to Christianity, there'd still be crime."

She waved away war and murder and crime with a small, long-fingered hand. "We can quibble about the details later. Say you'll help me with this."

"You mean in addition to being the queen of the vampires—"

"Sinclair is perfectly capable of overseeing the vampire nation."

"—and running Hell—"

"You've made a committee, and even if you hadn't, Hell will run itself if you leave it alone."

I— Wow. Okay. Wow.

"What's the pitch, exactly? Assuming you could prove God's existence? We somehow prove it and hey presto, everyone in the world becomes a Christian?"

"Sure."

When I was little I'd wait for the bus with a bunch of neighborhood kids. And after the first big frost, we'd kill time by easing across puddles that looked frozen, but weren't—or at least, not all the way through. We'd inch across, freezing and giggling at every *crack!* Best case, you made it across and the kids gave you props. Worst case, you broke the ice and soaked your shoes, which was unpleasant but not fatal.

Well, I felt like I was inching across a puddle that was bottomless. Like if I put a foot wrong I'd fall down so deep no one would ever find me. It *looked* safe enough . . . but probably wasn't . . . and if I put one foot wrong . . .

"Hell being a thing doesn't mean every other religion is wrong."

Laura just looked at me.

I sighed. "I get it. You've decided Hell being a thing *does* mean every other religion is wrong."

"We know the devil is real, ergo God is real, ergo Jesus is real." At my expression, she plowed ahead with, "It's *not* arrogance. I'm not saying it's what I think. It's what we know."

"But that doesn't mean other things *aren't* real. You're like someone who's red/green color-blind and thinks that just because you can't see them it means red and green don't exist."

"Your analogies are starting to suck less," she said grudgingly.

"Thank you!" Ugh, I was always so pleased when she complimented me. It was the dark side of being Miss Congeniality, the thing they don't tell you at the pageant rehearsals. "Listen, Hell and the devil being real doesn't disprove Allah and Buddha and, uh, Mohammed and Zeus and, uh—" Why hadn't I taken a single religious studies course before I flunked out of the U of M?

She shrugged off Buddha and Mohammed and Zeus. "They can't prove *their* religious icons are real. That's the difference."

"But what's the point of— Oh." I saw it. Finally. "Aw, jeez. This is about you bringing gobs of unfaithful into the flock. So if you get to Heaven—"

"When."

Oh, Christ. "Fine, when you get there, you can tell your pal Jesus that you heroically avoided running Hell— through lies and trickery, but who cares about the details, right?—and that you disapproved of your sinful vampire sister but managed to recruit her into helping you bring millions into the fold so where's your Christian Gold Star already."

Her pretty mouth (how does she not have chapped lips in a Minnesota winter?) went thin. "It's a far better use of your time than lolling around your mansion slurping smoothies and accepting blood orange offerings."

"First off, I don't loll." I was pretty sure. That meant lying around, right? Lolling around? I rubbed my temples. *Don't beat the Antichrist to death with a hymnal. That would be deeply uncool.* "Second, if vampires want to stop by and bring me fruit and promise not to be assholes, what's the problem? It's a lot more than the previous vampire monarch did. His big contribution was starving newborn vamps until they went insane and making older vamps do all his murder-ey dirty work." Ugh, I hadn't thought of Nostril, or Noseo,[8] in years. Nobody talked about the undead-and-now-dead-forever wretch; he wasn't missed by anyone. New as we were to the monarch thing, Sinclair and I were still loads better at it on our worst day than Nostril was on his best. Was it weird when vampires showed up at the mansion to hand me a bag of citrus and pledge eternal bloodsucking devotion and seemed relieved when all I made them do was promise not to be asshats? Yes. Was it a bad thing? Hell no! (Or just no.)

I scooted back a bit on the pew, away from her, and I wasn't aware I was doing it until I noticed I'd put another foot between us. "Y'know the difference between you and me, Laura? Other than the fact that you've never had a pimple? I never sat in judgment on you. You and our father like to bitch about the embarrassment of having a vampire in the family; how d'you think I felt when I found out my

---

[8] Nostro, in *Undead and Unwed*.

long-lost sister wasn't just prettier and smarter than me, but was the Antichrist? And what did I do? Huh? Whine? Yes. Feel incredibly insecure? Of course. Show you the door? *No.* Tell you that you were bound to turn evil because that's what happens in every single book or movie about the Antichrist? No."

"That's not—"

"Now let's talk about what I *did* do. Did I welcome you into my home? Yes. After you tried to kill me? Yes! You tried to commit fratricide, and I could have killed you for it but didn't, but *I'm* the Hell-bound bitch?"

"Sororicide. Fratricide is killing your brother. And we're not discussing your nature," she added, but she had the grace to look uncomfortable. "This is about the great thing we can do together."

"Ohhh." I saw it then. Her actual plan, and the plan beneath, the thing driving her to recruit zillions for the Lord's force, the thing she might not be consciously aware of. "So your life's purpose *wasn't* to take over for Satan. And me giving you the boot from Hell—and by extension taking away all your supernatural abilities—that's all fine because *really* your purpose was always to bring peace on earth good-will toward men by proving the existence of God. It's not you flailing around for something meaningful to do because you didn't think past getting out of your birthright."

"I hated my powers," she said to the pew in front of us. "They were proof of my sin, my dark nature. But . . . I liked them, too. And now I miss them."

"Tough shit." I couldn't muster even a shred of sympathy. She'd been able to teleport to and from Hell, and she could focus her will, which was considerable, to make weapons of hellfire—swords and knives and, on one memorable occasion, arrows—that had no effect on "normal" people but were devastating to the supernatural. They made her remarkably skilled at killing vampires. "Like a hot knife through butter" didn't begin to cover it. "If you're waiting for me to go all 'there, there' for you, I hope you packed a lunch, because we'll be here for a while."

"You owe me!" she cried, and the hell of it was, she really believed that. I was the big bad vampire queen who cheated her out of what she wanted to give away.

"I don't owe you a goddamned thing," I snapped back. Her mouth popped open and I kept on. "I know we're in church! I think God would give me a pass on this one!" I was on my feet without remembering standing. "We're done. So sorry to keep you waiting while I was learning your job. I'm going now."

She sniffed. (I'd have snorted; did she have to be more graceful in *everything* she did?) Mumbled something that sounded like, "Typical," but I wasn't going to rise to the bait. (This time. Probably.) I heard her stand and follow me down the aisle like we were the Taylor sisters hanging out after church, just a couple of sisters disagreeing over matters that weren't life and death, instead of the Antichrist and the vampire queen arguing about the best way to prove God was real, or not, in order to demand the conversion of millions, or not.

The worst part? I still wanted her to like me. She was the only sister I was ever going to have, and I admired her when I wasn't thinking about puncturing her eyeballs with my stilettos. She was sneaky but brave, judgmental but unwavering, beautiful but bitchy when crossed. I'd been impressed and jealous since the moment we met. She was her mother's dreadful daughter in every way . . . and our father's . . .

. . . and I still wanted her to like me.

CHAPTER
TWELVE

*"And you might tell the vampire king that First Presbyte-*rian doesn't need any more of his blood money!"

I stopped on the sidewalk and turned to see the Antichrist framed in the doorway, holding the heavy door open with an effort (did they *want* to make it difficult to get in, or leave?). We had both marched through the church, past the few remaining churchgoers, tight-lipped and glaring at the carpet. All the brownies had been snarfed. (Plenty of peanuts left, though.) I'd thought we were done. But, as I often am, I was wrong.

"Churches always need more blood money!" I shouted back. I winced and lowered my voice. "I mean, regular money of the nonbloodstained variety. And frankly, Sinclair's got dibs on this place. His grandpa rebuilt it; *you're* just the Antichrist-come-lately."

The devil's daughter glared from the shelter of Sinclair's grandpa's church (there was probably a metaphor in there somewhere). "They wouldn't be so pleased to see him if they knew what he was!"

"Like I give a shit! Like *he* does! Tell anyone you want who he is, who any of us are, and enjoy the three-day psych hold that results. You really don't get it, do you? No matter how many ways I try to explain it. You've made up your mind about him and that's it, right?" Guess it was true, some in-laws were just doomed to never get along.

Laura took a few steps toward me, letting the door swing closed with a heavy *chunk!* that probably rattled the stained glass. "What's to get? He's trying to buy his way into Heaven. It's disgusting."

I burst out laughing. Not to be mean—well, out-and-out laughing in her face *was* mean, but it wasn't anything I thought about doing and then did just to be mean, if you see the difference. It just proved that all she saw was the surface stuff—and that was true of herself, too.

"Uh, news flash—"

"What are you, fifteen?"

"—Sinclair does *not* expect to go to Heaven. He could recarpet the place in thousand-dollar bills and he wouldn't expect ever to shake hands with St. Peter. And this is what I mean when I keep telling you how you don't get it."

She folded her arms and shivered a little; I realized she must have left her coat inside. Good. Hope someone stole it; how'd that be for delicious irony? Me, I was always cold, even in August, and I'd never taken mine off. Thanks, Gore-Tex! Suck it, Antichrist! "Explain it to me."

Why? To what effect? Would it change anything? Would it solve anything?

Fuck it. "The worst thing to happen to you was finding out who your mom was. That was it. Your adopted folks are still alive; they never stopped loving you; you've never lost a friend or a loved one. You've got a job you like—" Er, right? I knew she'd dropped out of the U (one of the few things we had in common), but her many part-time volunteering jobs had, over the course of the last year, turned into a couple of full-time ones. "You're a welcome contributor wherever you volunteer; you've got family you like—your mom and dad—and family you don't, like me and Sinclair."

Her lovely nostrils flared. "Sinclair is *not*—"

"And that's fine. It's good, even! You won't believe me, but I'm glad nothing too terrible has ever happened to you. Comparatively speaking. Meanwhile, one fucked-up vampire killed my husband's whole family and he gave his life to avenge them. He grew up on a farm; he loved the outdoors. And he turned his back on everything to make their killer pay, knowing he'd never see any of them again in life or the afterlife. And now, after almost a century, he can be outside again. He didn't look for it, he never expected it, he was glad to be in love and not alone, and then suddenly he could bear the light. Not just sunshine. God's love."

She opened her mouth but I cut her off. "And who are you to decide Sinclair's not worthy of any of it? God doesn't seem to think so. If the big guy had a problem with Satan granting my wish, He sure never stepped in to put a stop to it. Like it or not, Sinclair's now a creature of the day *and* the night."

For a minute I wondered why I was bothering. Was she listening? Did she even care? But never let it be said she was clueless because no one took the time to explain. She was still there, at least. Still listening.

"I don't expect you to acknowledge it, Laura, and I sure as shit don't think you'll understand it, but Sinclair's free in a way he hasn't been since he was a teenager. Anyone else would be happy for him. But not the Antichrist. All you see is an evil vampire using the church for some nefarious end. He could cure cancer and you'll always see the bad, and none of the good."

She was affecting boredom now, staring over my shoulder like this was all so tedious. And maybe it was. When I was in church, I was usually being lectured, not the one doing the lecturing. And is there anything more yawn inducing than hearing someone go on and on about how super terrific their sweetie is?

"Yeah, yeah, fine, hearing someone babble about how wonderful the love of their life is can be so dull. Bottom line, you'll never understand the true bond between . . . What? What are you grinning about?"

"Your sneaky wretch of a husband."

"You didn't listen to a word I said! You've filed him under Evil Brother-in-Law, and no matter what he does, that's how you'll always see him."

"I think he's a sneaky wretch because he's a sneaky wretch."

"I'm doing you the favor of your life and not mentioning any of this to him—"

She grinned, her gaze finally coming back to me. "I think you should mention all of it. Right now."

Dammit.

"He's across the street, isn't he?"

The Antichrist didn't answer, just giggled into her palm.

Dammit!

I whirled and there he was, sliding out of the driver's side of his silver Lamborghini, my least favorite of his cars because it looked like a giant electric shaver on wheels, and walking across the street to join us. In the backseat I saw two small, sleek black heads: he'd brought the puppies, too. My humiliation was complete.

"I can't believe you and the puppies have been stalking me!"

He stopped short and had the nerve to give me a reproachful look. "I would never." He sounded deeply serious and deeply pissed, which made me feel (deeply) guilty.

"Oh. Sorry."

"There's no need to stalk you. All your cars are bugged."

"Nnngghh." Rage stroke. Inevitable after the drawn-out come-to-Jesus meeting with Laura. I knew he bugged my car once in a while, usually when the Big Bad of the month had yet to be defeated/killed/banished. But as a general rule? All the damn time? *Ho hum, I'm bored and thirsty, let's see where Betsy drove today . . .*

"And possibly your phones."

"Sinclair! I'm the queen regent. You're the consort! I should be bugging *you*."

"Regnant, darling." He was beside me on the sidewalk now, wearing one of his dark designer suits, a tailored navy shirt, a silk navy tie with little red skulls (a Christmas gift from me), and his deep gray Belstaff coat, which I definitely didn't buy for him because it's what Benedict Cumberbatch wore on *Sherlock*. He raked Laura with a cool, unfriendly gaze, then gave his attention to me. "I should adore it if you bugged me."

"Well, I won't," I said, instantly abandoning that plan. "Not if you want me to. The point is that it should be something you *don't* like. And we are not done talking about this! Except we are, right now, just for a little while, because Laura and I— Oh, what? *What?*" Laura was looking over my shoulder again and, as God was my witness (and He was, probably, since we were hanging out in one of His houses), I was afraid to look. I heard car doors slamming, saw Sinclair's refusal to turn around—whatever it was, he knew exactly what was happening, or knew it would plunge him into more trouble, or both. He was playing stoic, hoping it'd be like playing safe. His refusal to budge told me everything.

Before I turned around, I said, "Stop following me, you bums!"

"We aren't." And here was Marc, loping up the sidewalk, and Jessica, crossing the street from where she'd just parked her own tidy red Ford Escape. She paused long enough to wave to the puppies, then continued toward me. "Sinclair has your car bugged. We just have to hit the right app in our phones and we know where you are."

"Son of a bitch! Wait—we?"

"Greetings, dread queen!" Tina's voice peeped out from Marc's phone; he was holding it like Kirk held his communicator in the classic Star Trek movies, in his palm, faceup. "If you require assistance, we stand ready to assist you!"

From Marc's trunk. Sure. "Everything's under— Jess, what are you even doing out?" Jessica wasn't a zombie, a vampire, a cop, a werewolf, or the Antichrist. She tolerated all that shit, but managed to keep out of most of the supernatural frays that had surrounded me since I woke up dead in too much makeup and my stepmother's tacky shoes.

My oldest and best friend just grinned at me, looking more emaciated than usual (which was a frightening thought, since on her heaviest days she weighed about as much as a broom). "I've got newborn twins," she said, like that would explain everything. And it did. "Any chance to get out of the house, right? Dick doesn't go back to work for a couple more days; he practically booted me out the door."

"You *all* know my car has been—"

"And phones," Marc added, then flinched when his phone spat warning static, Tina's preferred method of expressing displeasure. "Um, or so I heard."

"—are bugged?"

"Also your laptop, your favorite pair of Beverly Feldmans, and the good smoothie blender."

I reeled. Mentally, not physically. *So. Much. To. Address. Here.* "The blender?"

Jessica shrugged and yawned. The babies had been sleeping a bit more lately; she no longer looked embalmed, and the reddish undertones in her mahogany skin made her look lovely, not ill. She was even wearing a clean shirt! Her deep black hair was yanked back into its usual screaming-tight ponytail, making her eyebrows arch and giving her a look of perpetual surprise. She swore it never gave her headaches, and that she couldn't think if her hair was in her face. "Hey, you're always threatening to steal the good blender so you can creep off to make smoothies and not share them. If you weren't such a selfish jerk, he wouldn't have to resort to this shit."

"Sinclair is not the aggrieved party here!"

"He kind of is, though," Marc added, because he was a zombie and zombies don't fear death. "I mean, look at it from his perspective. You're always dashing off, there's usually a bad guy lying in wait somewhere ready to kill some or all of us . . ." He trailed off when he heard my teeth grinding together.

"All respect to the king, I don't know that I agree," Marc's phone pointed out. "The queen has had much to grieve her of late, and I—"

"Okay, no. No, I'm not doing this. You guys can stay here and debate it, I'm out. There's a Caribou Coffee around here and it's calling my name. Do not follow me there! Laura, you're crazy and your plan is insane also. Nice to see you again, good-bye. No!" I snapped as Sinclair stepped toward me. "We'll discuss boundaries and bugging vehicles and phones and blenders upon my return. You're all on my list!"

"The list," Marc's phone said dolefully. "A terrible place."

"It's not so bad," Marc said cheerfully. "I was on it for a week after I stored some dead mice in an old shoe box."

"A Beverly Feldman shoe box! Just the *boxes* are works of art, never mind the—never mind. All of you, just—shoo."

"Shoe?" Jessica asked slyly, but I didn't take the bait. And if I stuck around much longer, I wouldn't be able to stay mad. I marched across the street and, like I needed more proof I was going soft, stopped long enough to open Sinclair's rear door and pet Fur and Burr, Sinclair's black Lab puppies, who greeted me as they always did: with seizures of joy and tail wagging and licking and shrill puppy barks. Dogs *loved* my undead ass. It was one of those things that was slooowly growing on me. And I was finding the more I was around the *same* dogs, the less they needed to flock to me. A year ago, a stroll through the neighborhood meant a swarm of local dogs escaping from leashes and yards and basements to hunt me down and try to slobber me to death. Now when I was out and about, they knew I was in their territory and loved it, but didn't feel the need to escape and ruin my shoes to *prove* they loved it.

I carefully pushed Fur and Burr back so when I shut the door I didn't catch an errant paw or tail, then went to my car, determinedly not looking back at any of the sneaky bums. Yeah, they were aggravating and treated me like a blundering idiot sometimes (which was only fair, since I was one), and teased me and followed me because they were bored and because I might be in trouble, but they were *mine*.

And that was something else the Antichrist didn't get.

CHAPTER
THIRTEEN

A day later, I was on my way back to Hell. Not out of any sense of duty or desire to get better at my job, but to punish my sneaky gorgeous Belstaff-wearing tricky-dick husband. Hell: if I wouldn't run it out of obligation, I'd run it out of spite. "I'll be back in a few hours," I informed him, hands on my hips as I glared down at him

(how can anyone look so edible all the time?)

and deliberately did not return his sleepy smile. It was midafternoon and I would have loved to linger for a nap. But I had responsibilities, dammit, and I was still a little irked. I'd insisted the bugs from my car, the blender, and my shoes

(my shoes!)

be removed. The phones I decided to be okay with. Hey, we lived dangerous lives. And these days, cell phones were pretty much tracking devices anyway. Anyone who thought different hadn't been paying attention the last ten years. "Or a few days, if I can't get the time thing figured out."

"You might try a bank of clocks, all showing whatever time you need," he suggested—was *everyone* going to have the same good idea that had never occurred to me?

"Don't teach your grandma to chew cheese," I sneered, trying for tough and, given his giggle (a giggle!), failing.

"You do come up with the most charming country colloquialisms, darling."

I made a mental note to look up "colloquialisms." "You're the country kid, not me," I reminded him. "And you leave my collo—colloqu—you leave it to me. And don't smirk, you infuriating bastard."

Too late. "Darling, you forgot to add 'let that be a lesson to you.' And I must warn you, if what just happened is supposed to be negative reinforcement, you're doing it wrong."

"I am not! Never mind. I'm off to try the clock thing." I paused, then swooped to press a quick kiss to his mouth. "I'll really, really try not to be gone two weeks this time. I know you must've hated it." Have I mentioned it was sometimes very, very difficult to stay mad at Eric Sinclair? There he was, all nude and lonesome looking and nude and gorgeous. "You didn't have to wait so long before texting me to come home."

"Why do texts work in Hell?" he asked, honestly puzzled.

"Right? A mystery for the ages. I can't think about it, it makes me really afraid of AT&T. Like, Comcast-afraid." Everyone in the house feared the amoral tyrants that were Comcast/Xfinity. "But listen, I'm telling you now, my intention is to be in Hell no more than ten or twelve hours. If days start slipping by and you don't—"

"Hear any shrill whining announcing your return, and/ or experience your displeasure when you inevitably discover we're out of ice?"

"I'm not shrill," I whined then kissed him again,

because what the hell. "And for God's sake, stock up on ice while I'm gone. Okay." Another *smek!*—this one on the nose. "See you soon."

"Beloved." His hand shot out. He could have ground every bone in my wrist to splinters, but his grip was gentle. Like a small boa constrictor that liked you.

I sighed and gently pulled free. "Sinclair, just stop. I've got to go, and no, you can't come, we've been over this, you've got to stay here and king."

"We have never 'been over' it. You studiously avoid the subject." While I tried to think of a retort he arched a dark brow. "And I had no idea 'king' was a verb."

"Well, it is now. So just stop with all the trying to delay me—"

"Elizabeth."

"—I don't want to go, either, but—okay, I'm kind of curious to see how the clock thing goes, and I've been thinking about what to do about the girl doing time in Hell's Orange Julius—"

Elizabeth!

"Ow! Don't do that inside my head unless someone's setting you on fire."

Look at yourself.

I did. Then I was silent for a couple of seconds. Then: *I should probably get dressed before I go.*

"Far be it from me to tell you how to do your job," he replied, and do I have to tell you he said it with a sizeable smirk? I could almost see the thought balloon: *Won't bring me back to Hell because she fears control; can't remember to get dressed for work.*

"I had none of these problems when I was alive." I sighed. There'd been the occasional hungover Monday, but occasionally forgoing a bra because trying to hook the clasp made your brain hurt wasn't the same as forgetting you were naked.

Grumbling, I nipped into the bathroom, did a quick-yet-thorough wash, and a couple of minutes later was slipping into clean underwear, a knee-length khaki skirt, and a deep red sweater. You wouldn't think so, but parts of Hell are surprisingly chilly. And appropriate footgear, of course.

"All right, I'm leaving again. Again." I kissed him (again) and headed for the door (again). "And thanks for the 'always be dressed when you're going to Hell' tip."

"Anytime. Er, not to aggravate you further—I live in fear of your divine wrath—I believe you're forgetting—"

I turned. "I am? What?"

He gave me a lingering once-over from ankles to forehead, then showed the smile I lived for (and killed for). "Never mind. It seems I was mistaken."

"Sure, like that ever happens. Okay, it does, but you usually don't admit it."

"I am in a postcoital coma, one brought about by the most charming and delightful woman in the history of man. I'll admit anything you wish."

"Damn, can I get that in writing? And how come there's never a notary around when you need one?"

"Tina is a notary."

"Of course she is. Fuck my life."

"That's the spirit, O dread queen."

"I hate you so much."

"Oh yes." Another smile. "And I you. From the moment we met."

Man, it was hard to stay mad at that guy!

CHAPTER
FOURTEEN

Before I left, I went down a flight of stairs and tapped on Marc's door. I'd expected to find him holed up with a dozen teeny mouse corpses or working on the new Sudoku book or pitching a Rubik's Cube out his window (he liked retro puzzles, but not that one). Instead he was watching TV in his room. Odd, because Marc believed watching TV was a spectator sport, or at least a couples activity. I took one look and mentally groaned.

Quick! Be quick!

He looked away from the television and gave me a distracted smile. "What's cookin', good-lookin'?"

"I'm going to Hell to try the time thing. Wanna come?"

"Hell yes. Heh. See what I did there?"

"Yes, I'm definitely not tired of that joke yet." I was rarely in Marc's room, partly because I respected his privacy, but mostly because it was where he'd killed himself.

Tina had bought him a new bed (he'd told me suicides always made sure they were as comfortable as possible before ending it, so not only had he killed himself in his own room, but he'd been snuggled securely in bed while he died) over his halfhearted protests.[9] "It's not like I pissed myself when I died," he'd tried to explain while Jess burst into tears and I ground my teeth so hard I felt my jaw try to pop out of place. "I went to the bathroom before I OD'd. I'm not a savage."

We didn't care: new bed. New bedding. ("You threw out my Twister bedsheets? I've had those since med school!") New clothes. And extra bookshelves. Before he died, he'd had two shelves stacked mostly with *NEJM* and *JAMA*,[10] everything George R. R. Martin and Stephen King had written, the Narnia collection ("C. S. Lewis killed *everyone* in the last book but people bitch about G.R.R.M.?"), and X-Men graphic novels. He still had all those, but now he had five more shelves and they groaned with puzzle books, *Gray's Anatomy* (he didn't have his predeath dexterity and was scared of losing any predeath knowledge as well), and horrible jigsaw puzzles (a five-hundred-piece double-sided Dalmatians puzzle, a thousand-piece pencil collage—the horror and eyestrain were relentless).

But he stood firm on the "don't you want a different room?" issue: "Not only can I not hear Betsy and Sinclair's Sex Olympics from here, it's got a west-facing window. I hate trying to sleep with the sun in my face. Even before I died. Plus the bathroom's just across the hall. I might not need to piss or shit, but I still like showers."

---

[9] All the awful happened in *Undead and Undermined*. (Hint: it worked out in the end.)
[10] *New England Journal of Medicine* and *Journal of the American Medical Association*.

All that went through my head while he grabbed the remote and shut off the TV, looking like he wanted to throw something. Possibly out the nearest window, which had only recently been fixed after he'd tossed the Rubik's Cube through it. Usually breaking furniture was strictly a Betsy-and-Sinclair thing. And it was usually our bed. We were on the ninth—tenth?—headboard.

"Yeah, I'd love to get out of here."

"Great!" *Go, go, go! Don't give him time to—*

"This fucking movie."

I swallowed another groan. Deflect, avoid, or embrace? *Hell with it. See what I did there?* "Why do you watch it every time it's on if you hate it so much? And don't say it's hate-watching, because that's a different thing."

"Oh, please," he scoffed, "tell the gay man about hate-watching." But his retort was amiable enough. He'd gotten up off his bed, stripped off his T-shirt, rummaged in his closet, and pulled on a clean scrub shirt, leaving the jeans and loafers. He raked his fingers through his short black hair, squinted at a mirror, then shrugged as if to say: *Good enough.* And it was. Marc was a remarkably handsome zombie.

"It's such bullshit. *Snow White and the Huntsman* demands we jettison belief in the first five minutes. Hair black as night, skin white as snow, lips red as blood . . . hah! It's Kristen Stewart! Should have been hair brown as a dead branch, skin pale as someone who never goes outside, lips thin as paper."

"She's pretty enough. I don't think anyone could have competed with Charlize Theron." What was wrong with my life when I was moved to stick up for Kristen Stewart, of all things? Fame and wealth beyond anyone's wildest dreams, but she never smiled and didn't seem to own a brush. But all that aside, the poor thing never had a chance. Because *Charlize Theron*! "Also, I might have been rooting for Ravenna," I admitted. It was true. Charlize forever, Kristen Grumpypants never.

"Everyone rooted for Ravenna," Marc assured me in an "also, fire is hot and water is wet" tone. I realized my mistake almost at once and prayed that was the end of it, but Marc had latched on to one of his favorite grievances. "Though it's creepy to watch it now, all those annoying close-ups on Kristen Stewart."

"She *was* the star," I mumbled. *Why? Why? Why even open his door? Why didn't I run? Why didn't I knock him unconscious and then run?*

"And smooching the director, Rupert Sanders! Who was married, thank you very much, to the eternally fine Liberty fucking Ross!"

"I don't think that's her middle na—"

"Thank Christ they didn't let him direct the sequel!"

"Marc, it was years ago. Time to let it—"

"Who picks Kristen Stewart's flat butt and lack of tits and utter inability to smile over Liberty fucking Ross?"

Rupert Sanders, apparently.

"If I had someone like that, I'd *never* throw them over for a sullen teenager."

And there it was.

"No, of course not," I said, tugging at his hand until we were heading out the door and down the back stairs to the kitchen. "You'd be the best husband ever. Whoever you picked would be so lucky."

He barked a laugh. "Yes, and they're lining up, aren't they? C'mon, Betsy. It was hard enough to get a date when I was a live, cute doctor. Now? Christ. Fuck getting a date, I'd settle for getting laid. No pun intended."

"Oh. You can . . . uh . . . you . . ." I made a vague gesture in the general direction of his crotch. Sinclair could get hard, of course, which made *no* sense. It was one of the things Marc found so interesting about our "condition." Vampires shouldn't be a thing. There was just no way. And yet we lived (kinda) and laughed and banged and drank. And could do so indefinitely, provided we got regular "live" blood and nobody cut off our heads. It was pretty ridiculous, really.

"Everything still works," was the dry reply. "Believe me, I know."

"Well." At his expectant look, I gave him an apologetic shrug. "That's all I've got."

"You're a well-meaning moron, Betsy." He pulled me into a hug and I got a noseful of his shampoo (*Head & Shoulders* . . . wait, zombies got dandruff? Or was it just familiar?) and soap (*St. Ives apricot scrub* . . . wait, zombies had clogged pores?). "I love you and I'm lucky to have you for a friend."

"Well, thanks." Yes, he definitely needed to get laid. I'd already known he loved me, but getting maudlin and handsy while obsessively washing with apricot scrub and bitching about Kristen Stewart wasn't like him at all. "Back atcha."

"Can I ask you something?"

Uh-oh. That never prefaced something good. This was a guy who had no problem greeting me with, "Those flip-flops make you look fat."

"Suuuure . . ." Drawn out because I was trying to think what would be so awkward that Marc of all people hesitated to bring it up.

"Why aren't you letting Sinclair help you with Hell?"

I looked at him and felt my eyes narrow. "Did Sinclair ask you to ask?"

"What? No! C'mon, no." He shook his head at me. "What are we, in high school? Besides, that's not his—"

"Did Tina?"

"No! C'mon. Well, yes. But it's not like she made me

ask . . ." He cleared his throat. "We've all been wondering. Why wouldn't you put him on the committee? Tina was really surprised when you asked her but not him." He paused, then emphasized, "*Really* surprised."

"It's hard to explain."

"Because it's a vampire thing?"

"Nooo . . ."

"Because it's a queen thing?"

"Because I don't really understand myself. I just—can't do it. Every time I think about it, I just shut down inside. I don't know why. And you know me, you know I've got no problem ditching crap on other people."

"Some crap," he corrected. "You take the serious stuff seriously. Y'know, after you put on a show about how put-upon you are."

"It's not a show; I'm very put-upon, and—you know what? Go to Hell. And I'll come with you."

And on that note, we hit the kitchen, saw it was empty (a rarity!), and I thought about us being in Hell.

And then we were.

CHAPTER
FIFTEEN

"The bitch is back," the Ant said, which was as warm a greeting as I'd ever gotten from my stepmother.

"Don't try to sweet-talk me. What'd I miss?"

"Eleven thousand new souls have shown up, Father Markus has begrudgingly signed off on your new and improved Ten Commandments, and the She-Wolves of France are requesting a meeting with you—"

???

"I knew you'd say that," the Ant grumbled.

"I didn't say anything!"

"You looked pretty blank," Marc said in what he doubtless thought was a helpful tone.

"Several of the souls my daughter let loose a few months ago have come back and requested reinstatement—"

"We do that? Reinstate people?"

"I guess that's up to you," the Ant replied carefully.

Well. That was some good news. When I still thought

Laura and I would both run Hell, I'd been a little, um, hard to pin down. Oh, those carefree days of yesteryear when my biggest problem was Jessica's weird babies! And by *yesteryear* I meant less than a month ago.

Anyway, one of the ways she got me to quit stalling and go to Hell already was by telling me souls were "escaping." What she *meant* was, "I'm letting them out to get your lazy ass into Hell." Tracking them down and hauling them back was one of the eight zillion things on my list. But apparently life in the real world wasn't what they thought it would be.

"I want to talk to them. The ones who came back." The Ant nodded; I think she'd anticipated my request. "What else?"

"A few other administrative details Cathie, Father Markus, and I are dealing with. A copy of Father Markus's sermon for your approval." I waved that away; it wasn't for me to tell an ordained priest that his sermons weren't churchy enough. Even when he'd been running a group of vampire executioners who were trying to kill me, he'd always prayed fair. And in death he'd been beyond helpful. "And Miss Cindy Tinsman would like a meeting, if it's not too much trouble. Her words, not mine; I'm assuming anything that takes you away from the Macy's sample sale is too much trouble."

"Couldn't resist that one, huh?"

"No," was the smug reply.

"FYI, the only upcoming event at Macy's I'm interested in is the Mother's Day Fashion Show. I'm technically a mom now. Well, a big sister/mom hybrid."

Then I could have bitten my tongue. On purpose, I mean. The reason I was a big sister/mom hybrid was because the Ant had died in a car accident and my dad—presumed to have perished with her in a ball of blazing hair spray and spray tan—had faked his death.

Since then, my half brother, BabyJon, had alternated staying at the mansion with all of us and staying with my mother—of all people! She'd gone from wanting nothing to do with the spawn of the Ant to loving BabyJon and doting on him like any fond grandma. Part of it was the kid himself; BabyJon was one of those placid, happy babies who was a good eater and a better sleeper. The kind of baby who, when other people saw him, thought, *That doesn't look so hard. We should have a baby!* Then they ended up with a colic monster.

But part of BabyJon's appeal, I think, was my mom's realization that her vampire daughter was never going to have a baby of her own, that BabyJon was her one and only shot at being a grandmother. Me, I wasn't complaining. I hadn't thought I'd be lucky enough to get BabyJon, and I'd resigned myself to not having children of my own within a week of waking up (un)dead.

"Um." Marc was looking at his shoes while I fumbled through an apologetic offer; no help there. "If you wanted to—uh—I wouldn't bring BabyJon here—"

"Jesus Christ!" the Ant practically screamed, as agitated as I'd seen her since she died. "I would damned well hope not!"

Yikes! "Right, right, we're on the same page. But, uh, if you wanted to come back with me and see him—"

"I'm dead."

"Yeah, well, so am I. So's Marc. It doesn't mean you can't—"

"I'm dead," she said again, but gentled her tone. She was looking at her feet, too. I resisted the urge to do the same. "Let me stay dead. To him."

"Okay. Well. If you ever change your—"

"What should I tell Cindy Tinsman?"

"Eh?"

"The girl who wasted ten minutes of my time beating

around the bush before finally asking for a meeting with you if it's not too much trouble."

Cindy Tinsman. That sounded vaguely familiar. Marc's eyes had gone big, so I assumed she was familiar in a negative context.

"Timid girl, about five foot two, black hair, brown eyes, sixteen, died five weeks ago, lifelong Catholic, Inver Grove Heights native," the Ant prompted. "Neighbor? Maybe you're friends with her parents? Or know her through your—through the first—through Dr. Taylor?"

Heh. Even after this many years, the Ant could hardly bear to say my mother's name. Normally I'd have stuck it right to her, but she was—groan—valuable to me these days. And she'd been a real champ when her rotten daughter stuck me with Hell.

"Tinsman . . . nooo . . ." Shit.

"You might have cut off her head. About five or so weeks ago," Marc prompted.

"You're gonna have to narrow that— Oh. Oh! Oh." I returned Marc's grimace. "*That* Cindy Tinsman. Oh, shit."

"Yep."

"I'll see her right now."

"You will?" The Ant and Marc said this in unison, then sort of halfheartedly snarled at each other. Marc disliked my stepmother on my behalf, and she thought gays were icky.

"It's just," he continued, "you really wanted to try the clock—"

"Right! Right. Listen, I was gone for two weeks last time."

The Ant nodded. Her pineapple hair didn't move a centimeter. Hell was resistant to grotesque amounts of hair spray product, right? Wait, it was imaginary hair spray, so probably not too dangerous . . .

Focus!

"You don't seem surprised."

"Well, no. How would time passing on earth affect me, exactly? Why would I need to know that?"

"Okay, fair question," I admitted. "Only, I didn't *want* to be gone from the real world for two weeks. I don't know why time has to be so screwy in Hell anyway; it's a real pain in my ass."

"Yes, you do know." She said this with total confidence, like she hadn't disparaged my intelligence many many many many many many many times over the years. So this would not be a good time to look blank.

"Yes, I do know," I parroted. Think! The Ant was waiting, and Marc looked expectant, like he thought I could actually figure this out. That made him as big an idiot as I was. For God's sake, I'd been gone a day and eleven thousand people had shown up! She-Wolves wanted a meeting and the cheerleader I'd beheaded was looking for me. I'd need to clone myself about a hundred times to have time for all the

time for all

time for

Oh.

"Because there's only one of me and there's billions of them and if time moved at regular speed here it'd be impossible for any one person to get anything done even if they're the devil!" I shrieked in one long triumphant babble. Whew! Good thing I didn't need to gasp for a new breath. I almost did, purely out of force of habit.

"Toldja you knew," the Ant said, sounding more smug than usual. Because only my terrible stepmother would take credit for knowing I was smart enough to figure something out.

"Can she affect time the other way?" Marc asked her. "Can she be here for two weeks and then fix it so only a day went by back home?"

He got a slow blink from my stepmother for his trouble.

I had the impression the answer was yes. It'd need practice, like pretty much everything did when it came to supernatural nonsense.

"Okay, so, I need a bank of clocks—my phone's from the real world, so even though I can send and get texts here on it, I can't *do* anything to it to make it more supernatural." I'd tried, thinking it'd be a great phone-clipboard combo. It stubbornly remained an iPhone. Argh, stupid supernatural "rules" that were as weird as they were arbitrary! "So a bank of clocks—where? My office, I guess." Do I have to go into how much I hated having an office in Hell? No? Excellent. "And I'll just have to keep constantly checking them—what a pain in my ass!—but it shouldn't be too hard because I can at least—oh, look, now I have a wristwatch."

The three of us stared at it. Perfectly plain small wristwatch with a rose gold band and a black clock face on which I could clearly make out the little golden hands: 4:25. Small and out of the way, it was exactly the sort of pretty and practical watch I'd have picked for myself at a high-end department store.

"Well, then. That settles that." Wristwatch! Why hadn't I thought of it? From Marc's chagrined expression, I could tell he was thinking the same. "Time for a test time." Wait. That hadn't come out right. No time for a redo, either: if I didn't stay focused, the fifteen thousand other demands on my time would drown my brain and I'd forget all about the time issue until I popped home only to find I'd been gone three centuries.

I closed my eyes. "Okay, this might take a minute." Or longer if that distracting delicious smell didn't fade. Fresh, ripe fruit . . . strawberries? Here? Who was being punished by the scent of strawberries?

I opened my eyes. I was in my bedroom. Our bedroom. And Sinclair was, incomprehensibly, slurping a smoothie while messing with his phone.

CHAPTER
SIXTEEN

"Aha!" I hollered, pointing in triumph. "Caught you!"

He nearly spilled the thing all over himself, which would have been awesome. "You—er—" He looked down at the solid proof of his betrayal. "Ah . . . I'm multitasking?"

"You're cheating is what you're doing!" Oh, the triumph was as sweet as the smoothie he wasn't supposed to be drinking in our room because *he made that fucking rule ages ago.*

"You made me take the transponder off the blender, then neglected to put the blender back in the kitchen." He said this while having the nerve to sound put-upon. "But this is interesting. You only just left."

"Yeah, that's right, left and came right back only to find you— Hey! It worked!" I looked down at my pretty Hell watch only to see it wasn't there. So, like my clipboard, and Mussolini, it had to stay in Hell.

"Wait, if I just left, where'd you get the fruit? And the

ice?" I gasped at further evidence of his shadiness. "The champagne fridge!" Sinclair liked to occasionally use me as a champagne flute, dribbling the ice-cold Bollinger on me and then licking and sucking it off. He always kept a couple of bottles chilling in the unobtrusive fridge in the corner of the room. It sounded like it'd be unpleasant, all sticky and chilly and damp and annoying. It wasn't. At all. Oofta, just thinking about his steady hands and his mouth, *that mouth*, and—no. No!

I wrenched my horny brain back to the matter at hand. "How could you drag the champagne fridge into this, you heartless, fruit-hoarding, smoothie-swilling, Bollinger-slurping bastard?"

"I regret nothing," he retorted and took a defiant slug, one that would have rendered an ordinary mortal catatonic with brain freeze. He was going for regal and disdainful, so was probably unaware of his smoothie 'stache. "And seeing you suddenly pop in like that was most unsettling. But in the very best of ways, my own."

"You just lost room fridge privileges, mister." Wait. Why was I cutting off my nose to spite my sex life? Better to make him share the spoils. "Never mind, I realize now that while I was gone for two weeks you moved fruit and ice up here to feel closer to me, so I forgive you. But make enough for me next time and for God's sake don't tell any of the others! Their shrill bitching will *ruin* smoothie sexy-times for us."

He put his hand over his heart (the one not clutching his glass). "I just fell in love with you all over again."

"Maybe you could also fall in love with the idea of putting pants on." If I wasn't there to appreciate it, I disapproved of Sinclair flaunting his flauntables. Who knew who could stumble in and ogle what was mine, mine, mine?

"'Make sure that your heartfelt thanksgiving is more consistent than your nagging needs, and your passionate

apology more fervent than your unhealthy justifications.'
Israelmore Ayivor."

"Yeah, I'll get right on that. Okay, time to get back
and see how long I was busting your balls."

"An eternity?"

"Shut *up.*" Didn't even close my eyes that time. Just
wished myself back. And there they were, my stepmother
and my zombie, right where I'd left them: the seating area
outside the Lego store.

CHAPTER
SEVENTEEN

They stared at me, expectant. "So . . ." Marc prompted.

"Worked! I'd only been gone for a couple of minutes, just like here."

"Excellent," the Ant said with a grudging nod of almost-but-not-quite approval. "Now we can—"

"And Sinclair's been keeping ice and fruit in our room! He was sucking down a smoothie in our bed!"

"He defiled the champagne fridge to break a rule *he* made?"

"Right?" I cried, thrilled to be vindicated.

"Do you two mind?" the Ant asked. "Betsy, I'm sorry you caught your husband cheating on you with a blender; somehow you'll have to find the strength to move on. Marc, stop encouraging her. Can't you take any part of this seriously?"

"I *am* taking this seriously. Surely you noticed I was wearing my business shoes," I said, pointing to my black patent loafers. Too late I remembered I was wearing my red knee-high gladiator sandals. (Valeria, an actual former gladiator I met on my third day running Hell, burst out laughing when I told her what they were. Did you know there were female gladiators? I didn't know there were female gladiators. They're kind of mean, too.)

"Holy shit," Marc exclaimed, staring, "I didn't even notice!"

"What? She doesn't know?" The Ant turned to me. "Don't tell me you haven't noticed this."

"Noticed what? You know, you're being kind of negative. Even for you."

"Uh . . . Betsy." Marc pointed. "You might want to look down. I mean *really* look."

I did. And smiled. Valeria was wrong, dammit! This was the perfect footgear for kicking ass in Hell. Or anywhere else, for that matter. "Nothing you can say will make me repudiate these shoes."

"So you *haven't* noticed you're not wearing your magical silver slippers?"

"Of course not; they never would have gone with— Oh." I chewed on that for a second. "Well, the Ant did say it was all me, it was never the shoes."

"Probably hated saying something even remotely positive."

"I'm standing right here," she reminded me. "I know what I said. I'm amazed *you* know what I said. You knew they were just symbolic manifestations to help you focus your concentration."

"I know," I said and didn't sound even a tiny bit grumpy. She wasn't the boss of me. I was the boss of me! And occasionally Sinclair. And BabyJon, when he was cutting another tooth. I was starting to think the kid was part piranha. Actually, given who his biological mother was, he *was*. Heh.

"It's a little scary," Marc said. "Even for us."

"I know! Now I won't have to coordinate outfits to my footgear. It opens up a dizzying array of options."

"I meant *you*, you adorable asshat."

Over the Ant's snicker, I began, "This thing where you say something nice and immediately follow with something mean is kind of—"

He ignored me, because I am cursed with terrible friends. "A month ago you couldn't teleport anywhere. You were out-and-out *stranded* in Hell, thanks to the Antichrist ding-dong-ditching you.[11] But now everything's different. You're picking this up so fast, but you've been a vampire for a few years now and you still lisp when your fangs come out."

"Hey, *you* try speaking coherently when it feels like your mouth has suddenly filled with needles."

"Dear God." From the Ant, who looked revolted. "I never thought of it that way."

"Trust me, it sucks. Sinclair told me I'd eventually— Sinclair! That's what he meant," I said, the thought zipping through my brain and out my mouth before I could think about it. "He saw I was leaving without them. I was all ready to go after our—uh—afternoon—um."

Marc smirked. "Bangfest? Booty hoedown?"

"Dear *God*." The Ant managed to look still more horrified, which all by itself made the whole trip worth it.

"Right, so I was dressed and ready to go and he stopped me to say something. And then he changed his mind. And when I came right back, he wasn't surprised. I mean, he was, because—"

"*Bus*-ted!"

"Right, but he wasn't surprised I'd come back on my own."

---

[11] Laura did the dirty deed in *Undead and Unstable*.

"No?"

"No." It should have been comforting, but it made me feel bad. And a little scared. I was getting stronger by the month and he was paying me the compliment of assuming I could improve and grow in my new role, was openly and privately proud of me, proud to be my husband and my king. Me, I hadn't dared bring him back to Hell after the first quick visit.

"Cindy Tinsman," the Ant said, dragging us back to the topic at hand. I think it was the topic at hand, at least once the time thing sorted itself out. I looked down: Yep. The Hell watch was back.

"Yeah, thanks." I raised my voice a bit. "I want Cindy Tinsman. Right now."

"Um . . . hi?"

We all looked. And I knew her on sight—I was so much better with faces than names. I could remember our phone number from the house I lived in as a kid, but not the name of the mailman who came to our house almost every day. (Frank, I want to say? Bill? Karen? He or she had pretty muscular legs, whoever they were.) Sinclair said it was because my face perception was higher than my name retention, and that it was true of everybody, but especially me. It was a nice way of telling me I was an idiot.

"Ohhhh, Cindy," I said, going from triumphant to sad in half a second. "*Man*, am I sorry to see you here."

"Me, too," she said and burst into tears. She rushed at me and the Ant went tense, but then she was clinging to me and crying on my shoulder. "I'm sorry I'm so so sorry you were right please I'm so sorry."

"Stop that!" the Ant snapped. "That's the Lord—well, Lady—of Hell you're slobbering on, get your hands off her right now!"

"Nope," Marc said, and he grabbed the Ant's arm. From her wince, I was guessing he'd gotten in a good pinch before starting to escort her away. He excelled at those underarm-flab pinches; they stung like crazy.

"Marc, this kind of familiarity can't be allowed—"

"Wow, I had no idea you even knew my name. And no one's in charge of maintaining Betsy's dignity, remember? She established that in the very first meeting."

"It'd be an impossible task anyway," my beloved stepmother snapped back.

"Yeah, I'm not touching that one. Besides, you gotta hear the backstory on this."

"There's no need to yank. Fine. And ouch, you ridiculous pervert." She rubbed her arm, but didn't pull out of his grip. "But I warn you, I've heard every sob story there is."

"Not this one."

Meanwhile, Cindy was still crying all over me, and I felt really, really bad about cutting her head off five or so weeks ago.

CHAPTER
EIGHTEEN

"What's up? What's going on?" I'd popped into the Peach Parlor, the small room just off the front hall that boasted peach wallpaper, carpeting, and furniture, thusly named because we were all low on imagination. "Is it a new Big Bad? Is it an old Big Bad? Or are we finally having that vodka intervention for Tina?"

"Never mind my vodka," Tina warned through a smile.

"Where is everybody?"

"I shall endeavor not to take offense at that."

I waved that away. "Aw, you know what I mean."

"His Majesty will be through the door momentarily

(I shall be with you momentarily, my own.)

and this is official vampire king and queen business, and no concern of the others."

"The others" would take exception, especially Marc, but in my ancient wisdom (I'd be hitting thirty-five pretty soon) I was learning to pick my squabbles. (Marc in a snit wasn't exactly a battle. More like a nine-hour headache.)

Just then we heard the front door open and in bounded the king of the vampires, carrying two bulging bags of— Aw, no.

"Another flea market? Seriously? This obsession with other people's junk is getting grosser by the week."

"One man's trash, and all that, my love." He dropped the bags without ceremony—it was never about the stuff, just the trip to buy the stuff—and came into the parlor, bending to give me a hearty smack on the mouth. "Missed you, wife. You would have liked it."

"That's a lie and you know it. Only people furnishing their first apartment and retirees enjoy flea markets. I told you after the last one I was flea'd out, and I'm sticking to that. Those outdoor markets are like crack to you. Don't make me cut up your credit cards! And your cash."

It was all for show; I got almost as big a kick out of Sinclair enjoying the warmth of sunshine without the accompanying warmth of going up in flames.

"Tina."

"Majesty."

"Is this the four o'clock you were telling me about? The young lady and her uncle?"

"Yes."

"You were downright coy about it," he continued, and Tina smiled and winked at me. Eh? Coy? What?

"I think it might be a pleasant surprise, Majesty."

"Really? For him, or for all of us? Fill me in," I ordered, because I should at least *look* like I knew what was going on when the meeting started.

"Fill you in again, did you mean?" Tina asked with honeyed sweetness.

"Do you know what happens to a bottle of vodka when you throw it down the basement stairs?"

"I'll be good," she said quickly.

"You'd better, or the Cucumber vodka gets it." But the doorbell rang just then

(donnnnngggg GONNNNNGGGGGG)

so that was the end of extortion time. Too bad.

"Did we pay extra for the doorbell to sound so ominous?"

"Not at all, my own. I believe it came with the house."

"Well, hooray for added bonuses."

"Redundant, my dear."

"Aw, shaddup." He made a grab for me but, wise to his wicked ways, I managed to avoid it, and his deep chuckle practically made the room vibrate.

Before things could get interesting, and naked, Tina escorted our visitors into the room, but before I could do more than give them a quick once-over, Sinclair was crossing the room and exclaiming with real warmth, "Lawrence, hello!"

The vampire who'd come in with the cheerleader didn't immediately extend his hand; instead he tilted his head down and dropped his gaze in a subtle bow of deference. Sinclair waved that away (I'd *never* seen him do that with any vampires besides Tina and me) and they shook hands. Then Sinclair turned to me. "My queen, permit me to introduce to you an old friend, Lawrence Taliaferro. Lawrence, this is Elizabeth."

"Betsy," I said, like I always do. (Only Sinclair calls me Elizabeth. And my mom when I'm in big trouble.)

I got the elegant head-bow treatment and then shook his cool, long-fingered hand. Lawrence was a couple inches shorter than me at about five foot ten, with brown hair swept back from his forehead and dark, deep-set eyes. He had a lush mouth and high cheekbones and appeared to be dressed for a funeral in a sober black suit, crisp white shirt, and brown paisley tie. His coat sleeves were cut long, brushing almost to his knuckles, and he had new black dress shoes shined to a high gloss. Etienne Aigner, I decided after a peek. Very nice.

He could have been as old as he looked—late thirties— or five centuries beyond that. I couldn't tell at first sight, not the way Sinclair and Tina could. They could just sort of get a sense of a vamp's age, but not me. Of course, if they looked barely drinking age but started ranting about the fascism of the Prohibition years, that was usually a pretty good tip that they were eligible for AARP membership. But vampires weren't always so obliging about revealing their long years, and it was one of the few things Tina and Sinclair could do that I couldn't. Not everything about being the queen was something that was automatically easy. It was kind of comforting.

"This is my young companion—"

Young companion? Okay, he's old.

"—Cindy Tinsman." His tone was formal and there was a faint hint of a Southern accent. He beckoned the girl forward and she came, sticking close to his side. She looked intimidated but wildly excited, her pretty tip-tilted dark eyes gleaming as she took everything in. Her hair was razor straight, her bangs so perfectly trimmed you could use them as a ruler. She had shaved part of the left side of her head

(when will that awful trend die? curse you, Miley Cyrus!)

and let the other side swing to about shoulder level. She was in jeans, sneakers, a sweater, and a Simley Spartans high school jacket with a cheering letter.

"Friends with the family?" Sinclair asked, nodding at her.

"Her great-great-grandfather saved my life. I keep an eye on his descendants for him."

Now see, *this* was the cool thing about some vampires. The good ones used their powers for—well—good. It was nice to know Tina's experience with Sinclair's family wasn't an isolated case, and I liked Lawrence a lot just for that.

"And Miss Chavelle, I see you back there. Nothing to say to an old friend?"

"Lawrence," Tina said demurely (!), offering her hand. He bent over it but didn't quite kiss it (apparently that was a huge etiquette no-no in some circles, or in 1860). "Always a charmer."

"Not enough of one, I fear," he replied, straightening. The black suit made him seem taller than he was, and the cultivated, barely there accent made him sound like a cheerful undertaker: happy, but not *too* happy.

"That wasn't your fault," she said in a tone of mild reproach. "I think it's time you stopped punishing yourself for it."

"As always, I am at a lady's command. So lovely to see a Southern girl up here in the wild wastes of the frontier."

Okay, really really *old.*

"Please sit." Tina gestured to the love seat, couch, and chairs. "You said it was a matter of some urgency and that only the king and queen could help."

"Urgency, yes." But Lawrence grimaced and flicked a glance at Cindy. "But only according to some, like my little girl here."

"'Mnot a little girl."

He took in the sullen mumble with a fond look. "When she was younger, she called me Uncle, and so did her mama, years back."

"Lawrence," she whined.

He laid it out straight: sorry to disturb, Cindy wanted to become a vampire, like right now, like *now* now because cancer and, again, sorry to bother you with this pesky vampire stuff.

"Wait, what?"

Cindy looked at me, which was an improvement over her glaring at the yucky peach carpet. "My mom and both my aunts died of breast cancer in their forties. Both my grandmas, too. I'm gonna have to be like Angelina Jolie and get my boobs cut off and my uterus out and everything. And maybe I'll just die anyway."

Well, we all died anyway, but I was beginning to see her point. But perhaps it wasn't as bleak a picture as she was painting. I had no problem admitting this stuff wasn't my area.

Can we get Marc in on this?

Agreed.

Sinclair glanced at Tina, who simply raised her voice. "Dr. Spangler, would you join us?"

"Hmm?" Looking entirely too innocent, Marc stuck his head around the door frame. Busted! "Oh, sorry, didn't realize you were conducting business in here."

"On your way out for a jog?" I needled. "With scrubs and a stethoscope around your neck?"

He stood on his dignity and ignored me, and I had to make a real effort not to snicker. "Did you need something, Tina?"

She just quirked an eyebrow at him, and his expression— polite boredom—didn't match how he hustled into the room, almost knocking over one of the overstuffed chairs on his way to her side. "This is Dr. Spangler," she explained to Cindy, who managed a smile (and why not? Marc was a cutie anytime, but looked cute *and* competent as shit when in doctor mode), and Lawrence, who just stared. And stared. And wouldn't shake hands. And stared.

I started to bristle, when Sinclair's voice slid into my brain like a cool drink. *He knows Marc isn't a vampire but is dead. It's throwing him off. Have patience, my own; most of our kind have never seen a zombie. Lawrence is a good man and will remember his manners at any moment.*

Right, right. Sorry.

Trust me. Of all men, Lawrence will be the first to give a zombie the benefit of the doubt.

Okay. Good enough for me, let's give him a minute.

Lawrence seemed to come back to himself and reached out, lightning fast—too fast, Marc flinched—to shake his hand. "Pardon, your pardon, Dr. Spangler. It seems I've left my manners out on the street, for which there is no excuse. I— It's been a difficult week. My apologies again."

"Yeah, tell us how hard it's been for *you*," Cindy said acidly, reminding me why teenagers were terrible, and how glad I was I would never be one again. Trapped in an ever-changing adult body and the accompanying hormone tsunami, and constantly urged to act like an adult while being refused all adult privileges. Nightmare.

"Cindy has a family history of cancer," Tina explained, and brought him up to speed.

Marc thought about it, absently rubbing the stethoscope bell with his thumb. "I'm not an oncologist," he said after a minute, eyes vague while he ruminated, "but preemptive mastectomies would certainly be an option." Then he looked right at her. "You lost someone recently. Right?"

"My last aunt," came the short reply. "November."

That explains the urgency. How to explain to a teenager nothing has to be decided, much less acted on, right this minute? Answer: you can't.

What the hell, I went for it. "Cindy, I'm so sorry for your loss. But it's a little soon to decide that a lethal allergy to sunshine, a liquid diet, and permanent blackout curtains are the way to go. You've got years to—"

"No! I have to get turned *now*. If I wait too long I could be a vampire with cancer." Which was technically true. I had my appendix out when I was thirteen, and it didn't grow back when I came back as a vampire. If you had gray hairs or wrinkles or arthritis in life, you'd have them in (un)death. One of the most powerful vampires I ever met/ killed was turned in her sixties. She could overpower just about anybody, but still had permanent crow's-feet and shitty close vision. She was the vampire nation's librarian and archivist, which made the whole thing even more ironic and unsettling.

"Okay, that's a fair point, but—"

"I'm not just going to—going to chop pieces off myself to try to stay ahead of the fucking thing only to maybe end up with it anyway, *duh*!"

"*Cindy*." Lawrence's voice was like a whip (judging from her flinch, anyway). "I did not bring you here to be unforgivably rude to my sovereigns. Apologize *at once*."

I waved it away before she could open her mouth, to Sinclair's vague annoyance. "'Sfine. Look, you're not even a legal adult yet. Even if we were on board with Plan Outwit/ Outplay/Outlast Cancer, we couldn't turn you. There are laws about that stuff."

Kind of. More like firm guidelines, big number one being no fair turning kids, asshats. In the old days, the vampire who turned the kid *and* the kid were killed in a variety of nasty, vomit-inducing ways. Having met such a vampire—a century old but forever trapped in the body of a fifth grader; imagine the horror—I never wanted to meet one again.

To our knowledge, since we'd come to power no one had turned a child. When it happened (it was, Sinclair explained, inevitable, because there was nothing new under the sun, and assholes were everywhere) we'd tackle it, and them: the turner and the turnee. Penalties would depend on the circumstances, though our inclination was something along the lines of, *Fuck you. You don't do that to kids. Any last words before we set your lungs on fire?*

"I know. That's why we're here," she replied, and she actually stomped her foot in her impatience. Gawd, adults were soooo sloooow. "Because you guys can break that rule. You can break any rule; you're the ones in charge."

Her neck would snap like a dead branch. Sinclair's thought was more wistful than murderous; this was not a vampire king interested in, or used to, dealing with kids. He liked BabyJon, and found Jessica's weird babies fascinating, but that was about it.

Knock it off. Being sixteen sucks.

In my day . . .

When you do that? It's not sexy. At all. Besides, give her props just for having the courage to come. And there's something else going on with her. It's not just making an end run around cancer . . .

"I'm sorry, Cindy, but the answer is no. You're too young, you haven't adequately researched all your options, and you're too young." I turned to Lawrence, who looked like the least surprised person ever. "But it was kind of you to bring her here, and I'm always glad to meet a friend of Sinclair's." Had I ever? My husband was not a warm, welcoming man to people who weren't me, Marc, Jessica, Dick, their weird babies, BabyJon, my mom, or Tina. No, I could honestly say I'd never met a friend of his.

"No, come on!" Another foot stomp, this one more frantic. She was wearing the wrong shoes if she wanted to draw attention that way; two-inch heels would have been better and, against the thick carpet, spikes would have been best. "What do you care if one more vamp gets made? Lawrence will bite me and take care of me and teach me everything and you'll never see me again. Or you'll see me all the time! Whichever one you want."

I do not want to see this child all the time.

Simmer down, your inner old fogey is showing. I cleared my throat and said aloud, "What does your dad—"

"Don't talk about my dad! He doesn't know *anything*. Too busy scribbling his stupid local color stories that no one ever reads."

"The reason I ask—"

"He wrote for the *Pioneer Press*, but not even online," she sneered. "The *paper* part of the newspaper no one ever

reads. Until he took a leave of absence to pretend to be
sad my mom died."

"Uh—" Getting a little far afield of the topic here.
"Look, the fact that you think it'll be as easy as just getting chomped and waking up dead and then darting off
into the sunset—except sunsets would have to be avoided
at all costs—proves you haven't thought this through. For
starters, when you come back, you'll be crazy."

Cindy made an impatient noise without opening her
mouth: ggnnn! "I already said. Lawrence will take care of me."

"No, *I* already said. You're not listening. You'll be
crazy. Literally a drooling psychopath with an unholy lust
for blood. I know that sounds like something out of a bad
horror movie, but that's what you'll be dealing with. And
that particular phase of the festivities tends to last about
a decade. The lucky ones, they come back to themselves
in maybe seven years."

"That's not true, Lawrence told me all about Sinclair,
how he was born strong—"

Sinclair's eyebrows arched and Lawrence made an apologetic half shrug. "When she was younger, I would tell
her stories about my, ah, misspent youth at Snelling, and
your granddaddy."

Understandable. But he left the really nasty stuff out.
Also understandable, but only talking up the good and
never mentioning the bad was why we were trapped in
the Peach Parlor with a pissy cheerleader who kept stomp-
ing for attention in soft-soled sneakers that made no noise.

"That's very rare, dear," Tina put in smoothly. "It's one
of the reasons the king is the king."

"*How* rare?"

She didn't blink at the demand. "Perhaps one in ten
thousand."

"So there's a chance."

"*That's* what you got out of one in ten thousand?" I

asked, incredulous. "There's a chance? You've got a better chance of dying in an earthquake! Or—or—"

"Being electrocuted," Marc prompted.

"Yes!" ER doctors really came in handy sometimes. "That!"

"What about you? You look about my age," Cindy said, gesturing to Tina's youthful hotness. "How old were you when you got turned?"

Tina hesitated a moment, then apparently decided to let her have that one, likely because of Lawrence. "Seventeen."

"See! That was allowed, and you turned out—"

"He didn't ask to turn me." Tina managed a very sour smile. "He just did it. He was sorry, though. Afterward."

THAT IS ENTIRELY TINA'S BUSINESS AND HER PERSONAL STRUGGLE IS NOTHING THIS SPOILED CHILD WILL UNDERSTAND HOW DARE SHE HOW DARE SHE HOW—

I swallowed a groan and elbowed Sinclair in the ribs. Then plunged ahead because there are few things I hate more than an awkward silence. "Cindy. Listen: you'll be insane for a decade, just plan for it; any other assumption isn't realistic. I mean, someone always wins the lottery, but buying a ticket is no guarantee, so just assume you'll lose. You'll be an animal, your only instinct will be to chase down blood from *any* source *all* the time. You won't be picky, Cindy. Babies, puppies, your dad, possibly while he's writing an article you don't think anyone will read because it's not online. You'll go for Lawrence, too, though you'll hate how he tastes."

She looked at the carpet and mumbled something I didn't quite catch: "Nmmmddtt." It almost sounded like . . . hmm.

"And like I said, that's just phase one."

"I thought phase one was bleeding out and dying," Marc put in, eyes wide and interested.

"Okay, that's phase two, then. Either way, you're not

ready. And may never be. Come see us again in ten years,"
I said. "We can talk about this then, see if there's anything
to be done."

"I could be dead in ten years!"

"If we let Lawrence turn you, you'll be dead by morning," I warned. "This isn't *Twilight*, get it? It's not even a
little bit romantic. Or fun. It's not a chaste kiss and then
off to la-la land followed by a leisurely return from the
grave where nothing's changed and everyone's happy to
see you. It's not any of that. It's terrifying and it'll sweep
you up and there won't be a damned thing you can do.
About any of it. I'm sorry, the answer is no."

"Well, you . . ." Her eyes squinched up as she fought to
say something that would change my mind, or at least make
me as mad and disappointed as she was. "You're just a *bitch*.
You don't care about anyone and . . . and you're mean. You're
a mean fucking bitch, and what kind of a name is Betsy for
a queen?"

"Ouch," I replied, flicking a *calm down* glance at Tina,
who'd gotten to her feet at *bitch* and looked ready to
rumble. "You realize you're just making my case stronger
with the name-calling, right?"

"This is my fault," Lawrence muttered.

Yep.

Well. Yes.

"Filling your head with all that nonsense from the
cradle." He sighed. "But your mama and grandmama
never seemed to mind those stories . . ."

"Besides, do you *really* want to be stuck with that look
for the next several centuries? I mean, the color's cute—I
love the blue—but you don't really see Miley Cyrus as an
icon of classical beauty, do you?"

"I'm not copying that dumbass," she snapped back.
"I'm copying Rihanna!"

"Again: you're kind of making my argument for me.

Look." I pointed to myself, showed her my hands. "I was lucky enough to die when my haircut and color were only a couple of weeks old and my manicure was only one day old. How often does that happen? I mean, what are the odds? You don't want to spend eternity hating your trendy hairstyle, which is doomed to fall out of fashion, right? It'd be like—like always having to do the thong whale-tail thing for centuries: uncomfortable and unnecessary."

"You think that's a good look on you?" From the size of Cindy's sneer, I guessed she disagreed. "Your bangs are too short and nobody does red lowlights anymore."

"Wrong on both counts. People will do—or want, at least—red lowlights until the planet cracks. Now, I'm sorry we had to turn you down, but our word on this is final. You and Lawrence are welcome to stay," I lied, "but for all intents and purposes—"

"And your shoes are ugly."

I had a brief Homer Simpson moment

("Why, you little—" Cue strangling noises.)

and by the time I shook it off Tina was hustling them out the door.

"Wait! It's okay, let go of her." With deepest reluctance—I don't think I had *ever* seen her so reluctant—she did. "I want to talk to her for a minute. Sinclair, maybe take Lawrence and get him a cognac or something?"

Marc smiled. "The *g* is silent."

"Yeah, yeah. Listen, Tina and Cindy and I need a minute of girl talk. You guys head out."

I trust you're up to something, beloved. I expect to be regaled.

We'll find out. Might be nothing.

Never discount feminine intuition.

Ugh. Fogey.

"Hellooo? Are you in there?" Marc asked as the other men walked out. "You've got that blank look you get when you're telepathing."

"That's a verb now?" I asked, amused. "Scram, I said this is girl talk."

"But I'm your gay BFF! Or I would be, if anyone used 'BFF' anymore. And whatever it is you're gonna talk about, I bet it'll be good."

"I can't believe I'm telling a doctor this, but gay men don't have vaginas and thus don't qualify for girl talk. Go away."

Grumbling, he (finally) left. When he did, I turned to Cindy, who had sunk into the love seat once Tina let go of her.

"What? D'you want me to apologize? Fine. Sorry you're a bitch."

"Gosh, thanks! Appreciate it! That's the most heartfelt apology ever! Everything's fixed and now we'll be super-good friends!" I rolled my eyes; did this teen twit think she could outsarcasm me? *Me?* Easier to outswim or outdrink Michael Phelps. "What's really going on, Cindy?"

I got a shrug for an answer, which wasn't surprising. But I was undeterred. I had a shit memory for names. I was in over my head in Hell. Jessica had been doing my taxes for me since I was eighteen (and now Tina did). I insisted on wearing purple even though I was a summer. I was a bitchy wife and a selfish friend. But I knew what a girl with a crush looked like. Hell, I'd had a Ryan Reynolds poster in my bedroom. When I was twenty-nine.

"Knock it off. You're not fooling us. Is it him?" I jerked my head toward the door Lawrence had just used. "That's the reason behind the reason. Isn't it?"

Cindy's head came up, startled, and her wide eyes were answer enough. "It's not like that," she mumbled, except I remembered how he'd mentioned she used to call him "Uncle" Lawrence when she was small. And how she didn't do that anymore. She'd corrected him when he called her his little girl, too. And not in a fond "come on, obviously I'm not a little girl anymore, you sentimental old softie, you" way. More like, "Don't think of me that way. I love you. I love you. Please see me as a woman."

"Sure it is. Look, I get it. I'm married to a guy who, if he lived in Iowa, would have to renew his driver's license every two years *and* take a vision exam each time, that's how old he is. He could be king of the AARP *and* the vampires. You think I can't relate to—" I started to say "crushing on," but nothing turned off a teen in love faster than that stupid, insignificant word. "Crush," like it was some silly, immature thing, a passing fancy. Best way to get a teenager to close off? Imply that what they're feeling isn't real because they're younger than Google.[12] "You think I don't know what it's like to love an older man?"

She took that in and sort of unscrunched herself from the miserable ball she'd curled herself into, then leaned forward. "His wife's been dead forever, he's been alone forever, it's why he spent so much time with our family because he was so lonesome and I know he loves me I mean he loved my mom and grandma but he wasn't *in* love with them and besides they never loved him back like I do and you have to turn me into a vampire because I need to stay young I can't get old and cut off my tits and expect him to love me please don't you understand?"

Aw, jeez. I waited a few seconds, sort of hoping Tina might have something wonderfully insightful and wise to say to somehow fix how much messier the situation had just gotten, but she just looked at Cindy, her face creased in an expression of profound pity.

"I'm sorry," I said, and I'd rarely meant anything more. "Love sucks. And I still can't help you."

---

[12] Google was founded in 1998, which, ironically, I found out by Googling.

"Won't," she said, animation leaking away, scrunching back into a dejected lump.

"Well. Yeah. I won't help you. I know you think I'm a stupid, uncaring bitch, and I am, but in this one thing my method of handling it is for the best."

"I hate you. All of you. And him the most."

No, she didn't. Which, of course, was the problem. Tina and I looked at each other and she lifted one of her shoulders in a slight, apologetic shrug. My sentiments exactly; never had a shrug

(the whole situation is so unfortunate but there's really nothing we can do; perhaps best to let time be the great teacher)

been more elegant.

So that was that.

CHAPTER
NINETEEN

Except not. Because the next time I saw Cindy, she was trying to rip Marc to shreds. And not doing too bad a job, either.

I'd suspected nothing; I'd been working on the new and improved Ten Commandments because kindly, encouraging Father Markus was a fucking slave driver. Sinclair was off with his rediscovered bestie, Lawrence; Jessica and Dick were both home and awake and playing with their weird babies; Tina was somewhere in the house doing whatever it was she did; ditto Marc. Only I had the self-discipline and work ethic to be hard at it this time of night.

So when the crash came just after nine p.m., I was on board to check it out. Overzealous paperboy? Marc throwing another Rubik's Cube out the window in a fit of zombie? An overenthusiastic neighbor returning a cup of sugar?

Man, if only. It wasn't any of those things, it was

(Lawrence is dead the wretched child nowhere to be found take all precautions I am coming)

a lot worse. I barely had time to register who our un-invited guest had to be when Marc started screaming.

God knows how she managed to corner him without anyone in the house knowing about it until she'd drawn blood, though later Sinclair pointed out that ordinary human insane people were capable of great stealth and cunning, insane vampires even more so. However she'd pulled it off, there was a locked door between Marc and (relative) safety, but not for long. I had just enough time to hear Dick's shout, also from behind a locked door—it sounded like he'd

("We're all fine, go!")

barricaded himself and Jess and the babies in their reinforced closet—and then I was there.

Here's the thing no one tells you about kicking in a door: even if you have supernatural strength, you can't just kick it anywhere as depicted by every movie ever. You have to kick the weak spot, usually the frame or the lock. If you don't, your momentum will simply propel your leg through the middle of the door and you'll be stuck

"Ow-ow-ow! *Fuck!*"

like a trout on a hook. An angry, flailing, blond trout hung up on an oak hook.

Tina, who'd been right behind me as we'd roared down the hall, simply seized me by the elbows and yanked back. I howled as my (previously shapely) leg was dragged out, gathering about a million toothpick-sized splinters on the way. Then she kicked the door (hitting the right spot on the first try, the insufferable show-off) and it fairly flew off its hinges before hitting the carpet

(phwump!)

hard enough to raise dust. Which was pretty hard,

since Marc vacuumed every other day (like all doctors, he was constantly waging a war on germs).

Cindy had looked much better alive, but who didn't, present company excluded? I didn't think she'd been buried and clawed her way free of the grave, but only because I'd seen people who'd done that and they were much muddier and stinkier.

Not that Cindy didn't stink; she reeked of old and new blood, of fury and fear, of dried piss and garbage. Blood streaked her face, her hands; her hair had more red in it than blue. It had dripped and dried all over her clothes: black miniskirt and tights in a nod to the freezing weather (Minnesota girls wore tights when everyone else wore snow pants), white and black leopard-print shirt, short white (well, not anymore) denim jacket. Hair that probably started out sprayed and smoothed and was now wild and streaked with gore. No shoes—they'd been torn off. Or kicked off when she . . . came back.

Clubbing clothes.

Trolling-for-vampire clothes.

Marc was kicking up an admirable fuss

(*"Stop with the biting! You don't even like how I taste, ow, Goddammit!"*)

and I saw defensive marks on his hands and forearms. His neck was slashed and bitten, but the sluggish black trickle couldn't really be defined as bleeding. I reached out, got a handful of Cindy's matted, snarled hair, and yanked.

The dead cheerleader flew away from him like she'd been shot out of a cannon. I'd whipped my arm, hard, like I was back-tossing a Frisbee; Tina's reflexes were excellent and she hopped out of the way. Cindy smacked into the wall and slowly slid down

("We just sponge-painted that wall, aw, come on!"

"Yes, but you needed a change, Marc, dear, and we can fix it.")

and I was on her before she could get up.

Now what? I could indulge my earlier urge to Homer Simpson her, but strangling didn't bother a vampire too much. Stupid me, I'd run straight to Marc but hadn't thought to grab a weapon.

"I need—"

Tina slapped something in my hand; the heft was excellent and, as I discovered when I tightened my grip and swung hard, the blade was nice and sharp. Cindy had time to start a shriek—of hunger? rage? despair? general pissed-offedness?—that was cut off pretty much immediately. Just like her head, which flew a good six feet before thudding to the floor and (nightmare fuel) rolling under Marc's bed.

"I am not," he announced, straightening from his defensive crouch, "fetching that."

"Christ!" I exclaimed, immediately followed by, "Sorry, Tina, but holy crap! I mean, it's great that you had the presence of mind to grab a knife—"

"I was in the kitchen checking on the puppies."

"—but I had no idea that thing was so sharp." We had a buttload of Cutco knives for one reason only: Sinclair could stand sunlight. He'd been walking Fur and Burr, his puppies (not our puppies; never, ever our puppies), in the neighborhood and had run across a college kid selling knives door-to-door. Sinclair bought everything in the kid's catalog on the spot, which made it doubly funny when he came home with the puppies *and* a buttload of knives. ("The rest are on back order," he'd hastened to inform me, like I was going to be annoyed he didn't come home with the entire set.)

"Gotta give it to them," Marc said, staring at Cindy's headless corpse. "They make a good product."

"I didn't even know what you grabbed— I'm not sure I would have tried to behead her on the spot like that." Maybe we could have, I dunno, subdued her and locked her up somewhere? We used to keep the Fiends out at a compound, but they'd either recovered or died for good and the place was empty now. If I'd had time to sit down and think about it, I don't think I would have advocated immediate execution.

Too late now.

"Never mind, Tina, it's not your fault. Everything was so fast! It's been less than a minute since Marc first screamed."

"Yelled," he corrected. "Hollered. Shouted."

"Screamed," I teased, "like a whiney little girly-girl."

"Come over here so I can bleed icky black zombie blood all over you."

"Pass."

"You didn't know what I gave you?" Tina had walked over to the corpse and carefully nudged it onto its back, then bent to examine it, but took a moment to glance up at me, a curious expression on her face. "Why did you swing at all?"

"I knew you had it covered, figured whatever you'd handed me would do the trick."

Only Tina could look up from examining a corpse she'd helped me decapitate with such a touched expression and say warmly, "That may be the greatest compliment I've ever been paid."

"Yeah, well, your hair is stupid. Pigtails? Really?"

"I'm going hunting tonight," was the absent reply. Would-be rapists and muggers beware! Tina literally ate them for lunch. Then: "Yes, as I suspected—as we all did. She's newly risen. Killed by one of us a few days ago."

"Lawrence is dead," I said suddenly, remembering Sinclair's urgent mental holler. I took a second

(we're all fine Cindy's dead so don't crash your car in a reckless headlong rush to get back here we're fine everything's fine)

(I'm coming I'm coming)

to soothe my husband. For all the good it did. Fine, ignore my strict instruction not to crash his dumb electric-shaver car, see if I care. Oh, who was I kidding? I *did* care, the big stupid vampire lug.

(Seriously, be careful!)

Tina was shaking her head. "Dreadful. The king will take this hard."

"Well, yeah." Marc had squatted beside Tina and was also looking over the corpse. "Lawrence was his pal."

"Yes, a good man and a responsible vampire. We need more like him, frankly. Too many of us think being among the ranks of the undead is a signal to jettison all signs of humanity: empathy, remorse, sentiment."

"You don't think he turned her, do you?"

An emphatic shake of the head. "Absolutely not."

"I think Tina's right: look how she's dressed. She went looking to get jumped. Took matters into her own hands and now she's deader than shit." I resisted the urge to berate the corpse. "What a waste. So now what?"

Marc cleared his throat. "Um, this is pretty awful, and I totally get why you'd say no—"

"You want to examine her."

"Well, yeah." He shrugged. "It'll keep my brain occupied, and, frankly, living with you guys? I need to know everything I can about vamp physiology. And since you won't let me examine you anymore—"

"We waited three hours for my knee reflex to kick in," I practically shouted. "Who has time for that?"

"Majesty, I think you should allow this. The body is rather ideal for that purpose," Tina pointed out. "No one alive will know to come here looking for her. Her family may not even know she's dead yet. If she wasn't spotted breaking into the mansion, we likely have a few days before we must dispose of her."

"Just once. Just once I'd like to have a quiet Friday night at home and not have to worry about where we'll dispose of a body."

I heard the front door being thrown open and the thunder of feet on the stairs. "Honey, I'm home," I murmured, stepping away from the doorway so Sinclair wouldn't run me over in his rush to get into the room and save me. Even with the precaution, it was a near thing.

"You're all safe." It wasn't a question, but Sinclair liked to make obvious statements when under stress. No, wait. That was me . . . "Thank God. I beg your pardon, Tina."

"Under the circumstances," she said and waved away his apology.

"Beloved," he said, pulling me into his arms and pressing a kiss to the top of my head.

"Toldja. We had it covered. Tell me you didn't mow down some poor unsuspecting dog walker to get back here."

"I'm almost certain I did not." He took in Marc's injuries. "Do you require assistance, my friend?"

"Huh?" I could tell Marc was knocked sideways by "my friend." He knew Sinclair was fond of him, but my taciturn husband had never said so in so many words. The reappearance of Lawrence in his life must have reminded him how valuable our roommates were. "No, don't think so. I mean, normally I'd need about a hundred stitches, and there's some tendon damage . . ." He was inspecting his arms as he diagnosed himself. "But it doesn't hurt anymore. And the bleeding's minimal." He smiled a little. "Never thought I'd be so glad to be a zombie. If I'd been alive—"

"You'd be dead," I finished.

"Yep. That about covers it."

"I am glad the hurt wasn't worse," Sinclair said fervently. "I do not— I have always had difficulty—cultivating and maintaining friendships."

"Maybe because you make friendship sound like a garden you have to prune and fertilize?" Marc suggested.

"And I have always found friends to be a mixed blessing," he finished, raising an eyebrow at Marc.

"Aw, you know you're our favorite vampire king," Marc said and threw his bloody zombie arms around him in a spontaneous hug. He was so quick, and Sinclair was so surprised, it was like my husband had been attacked by a blizzard of elbows.

"Ah. Thank you. There now." He carefully extricated Marc's limbs from his and patted his shoulder. "Thank you." It was awkward beyond belief, but the slow, silly smile spreading across his face made it worth seeing. "Well. I admired Lawrence greatly for his accomplishments, his open mind, his fair dealings with the Indians—"

We all winced at the non-PC term.

"—and his devotion to duty. And it was good to see him again." Remembering he likely never would again, Sinclair looked down at the body and his mouth went thin. "What a waste."

"That's what I said."

"Stupid, willful child."

"Thaaaat's a little harsh. She fucked up, but . . ." I prodded her little foot. "She paid for it."

"As did Lawrence. She found him first."

"How could a newborn take out someone like your friend? He's powerful; he's gotta know his way around a fight. Y'know, because of his background."

"What?"

Marc looked at me. "The guy was the go-between between the Native Americans and the guys at Fort Snelling way back when." At our stares, Marc added defensively, "What? I looked him up. That's what I do around here these days, research. Well, that and the newsletter. And vodka runs. But anyway, this guy was pretty cool. The natives called him 'No-Sugar-in-Your-Mouth' because he always dealt straight with them. And he was looking out for Cindy's family all that time, too. How can he be dead by some newly risen baby vamp?"

"He loved her too much to fight for his life," Sinclair said at the exact same time I said, "Because love, duh."

We glanced at each other and I continued. "He fought, sure—I can figure that out without seeing his body—"

You do not want to see his body.

I'm so sorry, sweetie.

"—but he wouldn't kill her to save himself."

"Fortunately the same could not be said of you, my friends." He turned to me. "Nor you, my queen."

"Didja know, the head cheerleader beat me out for first runner-up in the Miss Burnsville pageant?"

"Er," was all my husband came up with as he eyed the corpse.

"Not that I internalize these things for years and then lash out or anything." That was *my* crown and sash, dammit!

CHAPTER
TWENTY

"Because I am a petty, petty woman," I finished.

"Um, what?" Cindy, who'd been sobbing on my shoulder, looked up.

Oh, nothing. Just reminiscing about your beheading. "Nothing," I assured her. "C'mere, sit down." I'd walked her to my office, which in the real MoA was the security office/dispatch center, and had her sit down in front of the bank of blank screens. "Thank you for asking to see me, and for apologizing."

She'd started to tense up as soon as her butt hit the seat, but relaxed a bit when I didn't instantly start berating her or jabbing her with a pitchfork. She slumped back and sighed. "Well, since you were right about everything and I ruined my life by not listening, then killed the love of my life and broke into your house and tried to kill your friend, it was the least I could do."

"Oh." I coughed. "That takes care of my 'do you remember what happened?' question."

There was a beat and then we both laughed, followed by Cindy clapping a hand over her mouth. Her eyes were so big I half expected them to pop out of her skull and dangle from the ends of her optic nerves. "Srry," she mumbled against her palm, "'M srry nt fnny."

"Sometimes you have to laugh. It's either that or go screaming foaming crazy. I've done both, and believe me, inappropriate laughter is better. So I take it getting chomped by a vamp was part of your plan? Remind me to talk to you about the shoes you wore, by the way."

"Yes." She blinked at the shoes remark, then continued. "I remember most of that night, but some of it's hazy. I remember the high points, though." She shivered. "Low points, I mean. Anyway. Lawrence told us so many stories, I could spot a vampire by the time I was twelve. And he—you know. He wouldn't do it. Turn me."

"Had you talked to him about this before?"

"No. He asked what I wanted for my sweet sixteen and I told him: to be like you. So I wouldn't die of cancer but also because . . . Well. You know."

"Suddenly girls asking for nose jobs for their sixteenth seems much less terrible. Although it is still terrible. So he wouldn't turn you, and you got him to go over his head by taking a meeting with us . . ."

"And when you wouldn't—which I totally get now, by the way—I just . . . You know."

I shouldn't keep prying, but Cindy had proven herself to have a formidable will. I could probably use someone like that for . . . I dunno. Something. "You rose—"

"Yeah, the woman who killed me got me to go with her—"

I snorted. "Like that was a challenge. You were a fish looking for a net."

She nodded. "She did it in one of those empty warehouses on First."

I nodded encouragement and made a mental note. *Get a*

thorough description of the vampire and her lair—argh, who has lairs?—so Sinclair and I can find her and burn her alive. Burn her alive sooo much. "Totally deserted so nobody found me. And when I came back, I was—so thirsty. So—everything. All I could think about was feeding. I didn't— It was the only thing that mattered. It was the world. Like Lawrence used to be my world and I—" She shook her head and didn't finish the sentence.

"Okay, so you went to his place—"

"He just . . . let me. He didn't fight hard enough to— I mean, he tried to keep me off him but he couldn't make himself hurt me." She shivered like a gale had blown through the office. Poor, poor idiot. Both of them.

"And then you came to the mansion? For what, belated revenge?"

"No!" The cheerleader I'd beheaded seemed genuinely shocked by the idea. "I just figured since you'd invited me in, I could go there."

I shook my head. "Old wives' tale."

"Well, yeah, I know that now. But it was a lot closer than my dad's house." She closed her eyes. "Oh, God. My dad. Thank God I didn't go there."

I kept up with the questions, trying to distract her from that thought. "Did you hurt anyone else?"

"I can't remember. Most of that night is a bloody blur. Oh! Your friend. Is he going to be all right?"

"Oh, sure." Marc's injuries had completely healed by morning. Which made *no* sense. The theory was if he kept close to me, my unconscious zombie-raising powers would keep him whole. Around me, he was never more than a minute dead: body still warm, no rigor, etc. "He bitched half the night—understandably, but he insisted we binge-watch season two of *Sherlock* while he healed. I mean, he really milked it. He's fine now." Relatively speaking.

"I'm glad. I don't think I had time to hurt anyone else.

I mean . . . you know." Her lower lip started to tremble but she made a visible effort and her mouth firmed. I could practically read her mind: *Crying won't do shit. Own it already and get on with your death.* "Besides Lawrence."

"Okay. Did you— Have you seen Lawrence?"

She gasped, then shook her head. "There's so many people . . . I've been too scared to really ask around."

"I can summon him if you—"

"Please don't. Please. I'm not— I can't handle that right now. Please don't."

"All right."

She slumped in her chair a little, relieved. "I'm glad I didn't hurt you."

I raised an eyebrow. "Or my husband. Right?"

"Er." She looked down. "I'm scared of the king."

"That is a sensible mind-set to have." In fact, the body count would have been a lot lower over the decades if Sinclair's enemies had adopted such a mind-set.

"Lawrence told me—I mean, he and the king were friends before the king was the king. But he was super happy when he found out you guys were in charge now. He said that the old king was all that was bad about vamps, and that Sinclair—and you, too—was all that was good."

I smiled. "Well, he was right."

"He was." Her small, round face crumpled in sorrow again. "About everything. You were, too. I should've listened."

Don't beat yourself up, I started to say. Except: Hell. That was precisely what you were supposed to do here.

"How come you waited to reach out to me?"

"It took me a while to work up the nerve to ask for you. And I wasn't sure what was— It's just, when I got here, there seemed to be some confusion about who was in charge."

"Yeah, I'll bet. Well, I'll end the suspense: it's me."

"I figured. But I have to say, for Hell? This place isn't so bad. They don't have Mountain Dew or Doritos here, but I'm not being flayed alive over and over again, either. Mostly I've been exploring, but there's so much I don't— Y'know, I've only been here a little over a month. There are people here who've been here a thousand years or more who know lots."

"Yesssss . . . hmm." There it was. A blinding new idea. "I want Jennifer Palmer right now."

And then she was there, pulled by my will in the act of handing someone a terrible Orange Julius. She took both of us in, set the drink on a nearby table, and said, "Some things you never get used to. It's so *weird* to be in one place one moment and then somewhere else before you can blink."

Tell me about it. "Jennifer Palmer, this is Cindy Tinsman. Cindy, this is your buddy from Hell. She'll take you around, introduce you, show you the ropes—pick your cliché." This might be one of those "why didn't I think of that?" ideas, except for once it would be *my* idea everyone was wishing they'd thought of. Ha!

"Buddy," Jennifer repeated, looking as though she was wondering if her ears had fallen off or something. I could almost read her mind: *Did she really just say . . . ?* "Buddy?"

"Yep. It's a new initiative." *Real* new. "You're the test case. Or patient zero. Whatever you want to call it." This could work. Or blow up in my face. But neither of them were in Hell because they'd gone on a killing spree or were serial pedophiles. They were there because they'd made one huge, life-altering, death-causing mistake and thought they should be punished.

"If *test case* and *patient zero* are my options, I'll take *test case*."

I grinned at Jennifer. "Smart choice."

CHAPTER

TWENTY-ONE

"You're not even going to believe who I saw in Hell today."

"Cindy Tinsman."

"Nope! It— Wait. You're right." Dammit. "How'd you know?"

Sinclair had been working at the desk in the corner of our bedroom (one of three in a series: *From the Desk of Sinclair*; he had one in his office downstairs and a little one in the kitchen so he could play with Fur and Burr while he worked). God, Fur and Burr. The two most indulged dogs in the history of the domesticated canine. They adored me because all dogs did, but they loved Sinclair for himself, there was nothing supernatural about it. He baked them homemade dog biscuits, for crying out loud. And why was I thinking about the pampered pups right now?

Sinclair had looked up from whatever it was he was concentrating on. "You don't talk about Hell overmuch, at least not to me, so whomever you saw would be of interest to both of us, or you would never have brought it up. Given that we've had recent dealings with that willful child, it made sense you would see her in your new capacity as the . . ." I mentally groaned; here came another one. ". . . Mistress of Hell."

"Nope." Sinclair (and occasionally Marc) kept trying out new titles for me. They were all terrible.

TWENTY-TWO

TERRIBLE NICKNAMES FOR HELL'S NEW BOSS LADY

1. *Queen of the Damned.* No. Anne Rice had that one pretty well covered.
2. *Chieftess of Demons.* Barf.
3. *The Devourer.* Not flattering. "Hey, look, here comes the Devourer! Hide the bacon."
4. *The Loud One.* Oh, just shut up, Marc. Shut up already. No.
5. *Princess of Darkness.* Sounded like a bad porn. Or bad Dungeons & Dragons.
6. *Princess of the Power of the Air.* Too long. And what did it even mean?
7. *The Accuser.* That just makes me sound shrill.
8. *The Beast.* That just makes me sound fat.

9. *God of This Age.* Too self-important.
10. *Queen of the Bottomless Pit.* Too depressing.
11. *Power of Darkness.* Too Magic: The Gathering.
12. *Ruler of This World.* Too . . . hmm. I'd think about that one.

TWENTY-THREE

"Anyway, she was really nice about the whole decapitat-ing thing. She even apologized."

Nothing. Sinclair's back was to me and his head was bent over his work again. He'd been pretty quiet lately, even for him. Like most working women, I had to juggle a demanding spouse with a demanding job(s), and my man was feeling neglected. Tell you what, though, *Cosmo* never covered *this*.

"So . . . looks like I've got the time problem figured. I've just got to make sure I've got a way to track Minnesota time when I'm there, so it doesn't get away from me again, and my handy-dandy Hell watch is taking care of that for me."

"Very good."

"Soooo." I toed off my shoes (Beverly Feldman ballet flats in pixie red) and killed a minute wiping them down and putting them away in the walk-in. But eventually I had to come out and resume my conversation with Sinclair's shoulder blades. "What'd I miss?"

"Oh, just the tedium of running your kingdom."

Kingdoms, plural, and I've noticed it's only my kingdom when you're pissed, I thought but didn't say, then thought, *Agh! Did he hear that?*

Apparently not. So, deliberately not listening or, worse, shutting me out. I resisted the urge to fidget. As an uncouth extrovert, my knee-jerk reaction to someone being quiet was to get louder. That was a terrible reaction to have to someone being quiet, because they got quieter. And thus I got still louder. It was a perfect storm of argh.

He put down his pen (he used paper! and pens! for notes! soooo old-fashioned, and also cute), twisted around in his chair, and looked right at me. He looked amazing as always: black wool trousers, black leather belt with a small shiny buckle, navy blue tailored button-down, black dress socks. Dark brown hair casually brushed back from his forehead, sleeves rolled to his elbows. This was Sinclair's version of sweatpants and a *South Park* T-shirt.

Umm, those *forearms.* I didn't even know I had a thing for forearms before I met him.

"I would like to go to Hell and speak with Lawrence."

I blinked. "Oh. Uh, just give me a message and I'll tell him."

"I would like to go to Hell and speak with Lawrence."

Aaaand here we go. Well, I'd known it was coming. I was so dreading this conversation I actually wished for a new Big Bad to suddenly show up and try to kill us, just to get out of having it. When we were in mortal danger, Sinclair often forgot to be pissed at me.

"I don't think that's a good idea."

"Why not?" Hmm. No *beloved* or *my queen* or *darling* or *my own.* Strictly business. If he called me Mrs. Sinclair I would lose my shit.

"Because I'd rather you stayed here and took care of vampire business."

He stood. He went up and up. Normally I didn't find his height intimidating. "What is going on?"

"Nothing!" It was true. C'mon, Big Bad, where are you already? Come try to kill us already! "Look, Hell is my burden, okay? And do you really think it's smart for the king *and* the queen to be in Hell at the same time?"

"No," he replied, "I think we should take turns."

And there it was. *Yeah, I'll bet you think we should take turns. When you're there, Hell is yours. When I'm there, it's ours.* "The vampire kingdom is ours. Hell is mine."

"How long?"

"What?"

"How long have you mistrusted me?"

"*Mistrust* is a strong word," I managed. Jeez, where had he been? I've mistrusted him from pretty much the moment we met. It didn't mean I didn't love him. It meant he was sneaky. He knew this. I knew this. Normally it wasn't a problem.

"And now you're outright lying."

"*Outright* is a strong word."

His dark eyes went narrow with anger and, I think, some pain. *No! Force an immunity to the puppy eyes! This is no time to back down.*

"When you're ready to have an adult conversation with your husband and king, I'll be in the kitchen baking gluten-free pupcakes for the girls."

"Well, don't hold your breath!" I shouted as he gently closed the door as he left (Sinclair was never uncouth enough to slam doors shut). And sure, I was now having an argument with a closed door, but I was never one to stand on my dignity. "I'm in no rush to have an adult conversation with my husband and king so get ready to wait a looooong time!"

Fuck.

CHAPTER
TWENTY-FOUR

I stomped into the kitchen right on Sinclair's heels. Not literally. Which was too bad. I was also thinking about kicking his shins, but I'd have to get in front of him first, and he was a speedy sucker. "I can't believe you're pulling this Fred Flintstone shit *again*."

"I cannot believe you insist on comparing real-life problems to cartoons created for elementary school children."

"Again with the snobbery!"

"Refusing to see parallels between our lives and *The Flintstones* is not snobbery. It is the function of a rational mind."

Well, he might have a point. Too bad! The best defense was a good whatever-the-saying-is. "It's 2015—that chauvinist thing doesn't play so well. Bad enough you're regressing decades, but you're pulling attitude after you tricked me into marrying you? Yeah, that's right, I said it, *tricked*—"[13]

"I deny nothing."

"—bamboozled me into a crooked vampire marriage and then tried to pull that 'no wife of mine will leave the kitchen' crapola, which was just as asinine then as it is now." It took a few seconds for his response to sink in. "And—and you deny nothing!"

Scowling, Sinclair was tying on his apron (twill, knee length, red and white striped, gift from Tina), then turning to the cupboards and getting out the whole wheat flour, the peanut butter (Dick was happy with Jif; the puppies got the gourmet stuff from Trader Joe's), free-range eggs, Madagascar vanilla, organic bananas. Goddamned dogs ate better than most of the city.

"That apron looks stupid."

"There is no need to malign the good people at Williams-Sonoma simply because you're angry with me." He was hauling bowls out of the cupboard and slamming them on the counter, so thank God for stainless steel.

"I'll malign whoever I want! And you're denting the shit out of those bowls," I added, and I definitely wasn't spiteful about it.

"They'll still work," he snapped back, setting one on a dent so it was on its side, looking like a small stainless steel cave. "Again, when you are prepared to have an adult discussion— Quiet!"

The puppies, who had been enjoying one of their eighteen daily naps, had heard Sinclair and sent up a racket from the mudroom. If yelps and barks could be translated, we'd hear, "Let us out! We aren't licking your face!

---

[13] The trickery was on display in *Undead and Unemployed*.

You're just standing there, unlicked! This will not stand! Freeeeedom!"

Since Sinclair didn't raise his voice at them when they desecrated his Italian loafers and the backseats of two of his cars (in the same week!), it was a pretty good indicator of how angry he was. But before I could say anything, we heard the back door slam, and then the mudroom door popped open.

"All right, jeez, we'll go into the kitchen, settle already, what, you smell peanut butter? Or Sinclair? Oh." Marc was looking at us as Fur and Burr made a beeline for Sinclair's knees. They were babies, but they knew what it meant when the apron, stainless steel bowls, and peanut butter came out.

"Complain as you will about how our marriage began—"

"Yeah, I was. Keep up."

"—you did eventually come to embrace it, figuratively and literally, and must admit that all I did for you—"

"To me, Sinclair. *To* me."

"—worked out for the best."

"Oh, spoken like a true Martian!"

"I insist you stop reading that book."[14]

"I don't! Marc reads it to me and then explains the tricky parts!"

"Whoa." Marc's hands were up and he was edging toward the swinging kitchen door, keeping his distance. "Leave me out of it."

"And that's another thing, I didn't embrace anything! I was tricked. Into all of it. You tricked me into being the vampire queen—"

"That's not true!" Marc cried, stopping in midsidle.

---

[14] *Men Are from Mars, Women Are from Venus*, John Gray.

"You were always going to be queen; it was your destiny! Sinclair just tricked you into making him king."

"Thank you," Sinclair replied. Then, pinching the bridge of his nose: "Please run along and stop defending me, and do those things in no particular order."

"Yes! Exactly!" I was so stuffed with triumph I was almost giddy. Marc had a great point! Which I had kind of forgotten! But now could hammer into the dirt! "And you're all mystified: Jeepers, why doesn't Betsy want me in Hell? What in our shared history would make her so wary? Why, it's a puzzler! It's not like I've slimed my way into every other aspect of her life with or without her consent."

I heard myself. But it was too late. *Never has a man in an apron looked so sexy or terrifying,* I thought.

"Never has a woman been granted so much power for so little reason! Before we met, you stumbled your way through your tedious superficial life complaining about a series of first-world problems you were lucky to have. Then you died because you didn't recall what any five-year-old is taught: to look both ways before crossing the street!"[15]

Marc gasped an oh-no-you-didn't! gasp, which perfectly summed up my feelings.

"Then you stumbled through the city, maimed any number of the innocent and the guilty, and managed to whine your way into defeating one of the most powerful vampires ever to walk the earth! All the while complaining about your stepmother's shoes and the job the mortician did on your makeup as opposed to concentrating on your new role. I had to force you to 'step up,' as you insist on recalling it, because *you* refused to 'step up.' You would have been beheaded years ago if not for me."

---

[15] It's true. *Undead and Unwed.*

"Oh, sure, tricking me was all about helping me and not at all about helping yourself to the throne! So to speak, because we don't actually have thrones!"

"Ah yes, here comes the litany of how difficult your wonderful life is. You're powerful, wealthy, loved, even worshipped by some. Legions of the undead bend to your will."

"When they're not trying to kill me! Besides, you're forgetting— What the hell?"

There had been a low rumbling getting louder and louder in pitch, a sound I'd never heard before. It took me a moment to place the source: Fur and Burr.

The small bundles of black fluff were bristling so much that they looked like irked hedgehogs. Their tiny puppy milk teeth were all showing, and wrathful growling bubbled out of them like . . . like . . . I dunno . . . evil soda pop?

And they were growling at Sinclair.

Never had I seen my husband so astonished—and this was a man who'd seen me pull off all sorts of impossible weirdness. Burr and Fur looked ready to make the alpha male their bitch. He'd kill them, of course, but they'd still go for it. They *wanted* to go for it.

Sinclair took a tentative step closer to me and both puppies lunged exactly as far as his step had taken him, then stopped.

"No . . . bad dogs," I said faintly, glad for once not to be in heels, because not falling down in surprise in socks was difficult enough. "Don't. Don't do that. You love him and he loves you. It's not right that you're on my side—I don't even like you!" Well, I did. Just hadn't realized how much until now. "You—stop it!"

They stopped growling and hurried to me, crouching miserably against my ankles and glaring at Sinclair.

My husband finally found his voice. "As you find my company so unendurable—all three of you—I shall retire."

He managed to pull that off with stiff dignity while untying his apron and hanging it next to his other two aprons.

"Oh no, you don't! *I'm* walking out on *you*! You can just stay here and think about what you've done." *Think about what you've done? Did I just get the king of the vampires mixed up with a third grader sent to the corner?* "And it'll be a cold day in Hell before I let you back into Hell, mister! The minute I turn my back you'll be running the show—"

"Which, if your continual bitching is accurate, is what you desired from the beginning."

"Quit pretending you're a power-hungry megalomaniac for my own good!"

"But I am a power-hungry megalomaniac for your own good," he replied, having the complete balls to sound genuinely puzzled.

Which, of course, was the problem, and always had been.

CHAPTER
TWENTY-FIVE

"So the new and improved Ten Commandments are up and out," the Ant was saying, "and we're pairing newbies with, ahem, 'buddies' to show them the ropes."

Silence. It occurred to me that I should probably say something, what with it being my committee and all. "Okay, sounds good," I managed while in my head I was kicking Sinclair's shins with the relentless fury of—of—something that kicked a lot. A rabid kangaroo, I dunno, something.

"And may I add what a pleasant surprise it is to see you show up early for a meeting," Father Markus added, small eyes twinkling.

I shrugged and Marc hid a smirk. He knew I'd grabbed him and popped into Hell to get away from Sinclair, and had no clue there was a meeting scheduled. Luckily he'd never rat me out, he'd just needle me about it non-stop until I begged him to cut the shit already.

"This may fall under the heading of new business. There are other priests here," Father Markus said, "and we're all holding mass. There are ministers and preachers and reverends, patriarchs and bishops and popes, lamas and imams and rabbis, too; and those who want to have been holding services for—"

"I thought Jews didn't believe in Hell," Cathie interrupted.

"That doesn't mean anything," Marc said. "Atheists don't believe in Hell, either, but there are plenty of them here."

"Jews do believe in Hell," Father Markus said, "but not as Christians understand it. It's more a spiritual holding cell than an eternal prison."

"Geheinie," I said, then pretended not to be weirded out when they all gaped at me again.

"Gehenna," Father Markus said carefully. "Yes. That's what— How did you—"

"I research," I said, and I definitely didn't sound defensive. (Maybe a little defensive.) "I read. I had to in order to redo the Ten Commandments. I didn't just pull that stuff out of my ass. Well, not all of it." Actually, learning about Gehenna had given me my big "change the face of Hell" idea a month ago and I'd been polishing it ever since. And since I was in no rush to go home anytime soon

(fuck you very much, Sinclair)

perhaps the time had come to bring it to the table, literally and figuratively. It wouldn't be easy—and not just because the table in question was made of Lego pieces—which was why I'd been putting it off. I hadn't run it by Sinclair, either (and had no plans to run anything Hellish by the Fred Flintstone of vampires ever again). And not a single one of them would be on board; they'd have to be won over one at a time. Yes, my word was law, but if they didn't agree with me, I wasn't going to force them. This was something we'd all have to be determined to make happen and, if that didn't happen, then I'd have to do it alone.

"Gehenna is where people go to sort of mull over their sins. You're not judged there, but you do become fully aware of how shitty you were in life. It's kind of like Purgatory that way. It's—it's like a waiting room for souls. And when you've been there long enough and are repentant enough, then your soul can move on to something better. In other words—"

"Gehenna is a holding cell," Cathie said, "and Hell is the long-term maximum-security prison from which there is no parole."

"Yup."

Father Markus was having a terrible time wiping the astonished expression off his face. Cathie was nodding and paying me the compliment of not looking astonished. The Ant was busy taking notes, and also nodding.

"Well. Thank you, Betsy, that was very—uh—"

"Weird? Startling? Unexpected? Out of character?"

"I'll take 'unexpected,' wiseass," I told Marc.

"As I was saying, several of us are holding religious services here. Anyone can come and, I have to say, attendance has been excellent. A few people misunderstood and thought having to attend mass was their eternal punishment—"

I laughed; I couldn't help it.

"—and, curiously, remained when they found out it wasn't mandatory."

"Speaking of mandatory, I have an idea." It wasn't my best segue, but whatever. "Something I've been working on for a few weeks."

They were all attentive, but Markus and the Ant looked tense. Their body language pretty much screamed, *Oh, God, what idiocy is she springing on us now?* Or I may have been projecting.

"I think Hell should be a maximum-security prison from which there is, eventually, parole."

Nothing.

"So, after you've served your sentence, you can move on. To reincarnation or Heaven or whatever floats your boat."

Silence.

"Is this thing on?" I made like I was tapping an imaginary microphone. "You guys are acting like I haven't brought this up before."

"The general consensus was that you had thought it through and dropped it," the Ant said with a shrug.

"Well, I didn't. Because we've all noticed people here who have been punished far longer or harder than their offense warranted. We've all seen children tortured because they thought accidentally drowning their puppy warranted an eternity in Hell. And—and I don't agree." Damn, who knew silence had weight? I could actually feel it pressing down on me. "And since this is my house, so to speak, it's time to change that." Maybe not my house. My horrible job, which, if I'm lucky, I'll only be doing for thousands of years.

Father Markus straightened and opened his mouth. Given how much he'd been nagging me to take more of the reins (not to mention attend all of the meetings), I was looking forward to his input. He wouldn't be totally on board, but he'd have to acknowledge I'd given this some real thought.

"You've lost your mind," was the flat response. Tina's eyes went narrow at that—she probably thought the same thing, but respected my office(s) too much to cough it up like that. "Completely. What mind you had is gone. It has taken flight."

"Oh, probably, but that doesn't mean it's a bad idea."

"Yes, that's exactly what it means," the priest continued. I noticed his hands had snapped into fists. "You're messing with a system that's been in place for millions of years. *Millions.* You don't have to change a thing if you don't want to. As you yourself pointed out a few weeks ago, the place runs itself, more or less."

"So why am I here?"

"Exactly," he snapped.

"Whoa!" Marc said, hands out like he was trying to stop traffic. "Uncalled for, dude."

Tina was watching me and, observing that I hadn't burst into tears or made an "off with his head" motion, simply sat back and folded her arms across her perfect perky boobs (hidden behind another navy blue designer suit, Chanel this time). Sinclair could take a lesson from her. (In restraint, not suits. Nobody wore a suit better than the king of the vampires, who got that body from farming.) Meanwhile, Cathie was studying Markus like he was a bug she'd never seen before, and the Ant kept taking notes.

"We've had this discussion before," I said pleasantly. "If you've got a problem with the new regime—"

"It's 'ruh-jheem,' not 'ree-gime.'"

"—then you know where the Lego door is."

"But why?" In addition to being horrified, the priest seemed honestly mystified. "Why make so many changes in less than a month? You've only just started here and you're ripping up the foundation this dimension was built on: a place for the damned to be punished."

"And it still is. Hell will always be Hell. But c'mon, Markus, back in the day people got the death penalty if they sang the wrong song."

"In China," was the instant comeback (damn, the man knew his history).

"Okay, well, in Tudor England it was treason to say the king would eventually die. It was punishable by death! Some of those people are still here, still being stuffed into a big wheel lined with spikes and rolled down a hill again and again, and why? Because they told the truth: a mortal man would eventually die; and they convinced themselves it was a sin worthy of eternal punishment. Which it isn't! How is that okay?" (Thank you, Showtime and Jonathan Rhys Meyers!)

Father Markus was visibly trying to calm down. His hands kept spreading open like flowers, snapping back into fists, then opening again. But at least he was keeping his fists away from my face, which was crucial for meaningful debate. "You make some fair points. But I think you're too young to make changes of this magnitude. And I think you're rushing things."

Wow, this guy was seriously hung up on punishment. "Your opinion is noted. But some of these people have been tortured far too long already. What, you want me to ask them, say to them, 'Hey, sorry you've been burning alive for three hundred years because you were gay; the good news is, we're looking into springing you, but the bad is, it's going to take a couple of years while we do the research, no problem, right?'"

"You don't ask them anything! You're their lord, they're the damned, your word is law."

"Yes," I replied, pleased he'd fallen into my little trap. "It is. And my word is now changing the law. Look, I get that I'm probably not qualified for this—" I ignored the snort at "probably." "But tough nuts, because I'm the only one doing it. The Antichrist couldn't be bothered, the devil is dead, and that leaves me." And Sinclair, if I allowed it. But Markus's response to my new plan reminded me, again, why that would be a bad idea.

"I think it's brilliant."

"Thanks, T—" Whoa. Tina hadn't said a thing. "Um. Thank you, Ant—Antonia." God, had I ever used my stepmother's full name to her face before?

At least the pressure was off me, because now they were

staring at the Ant. "What?" she snapped, shifting in her seat. As always, her body moved but her tall hair stayed perfectly still. "It's an idea whose time has come. Hell needs to be modernized just like any other long-term system of levying punishment. We don't still do things the way they did them during the Salem witch trials. Why should we do the same thing in Hell for millions of years? People change and times change, too. Betsy's right. And she's right to not want to argue it to death, either, rather than make changes that will end agony for so many *now*."

"I expected more from you, Antonia," Father Markus said coldly.

"Why?" The Ant had a puzzled frown on her face. (She may have been a Botoxed mannequin lady in life, but in Hell she could make facial expressions.) "You don't know me. We've served on a committee together for a month." She looked around the table. "I think Betsy's onto something. I've seen things here. We all have. Some of these people absolutely do not deserve what they're enduring."

Markus had no reply to that. Instead he climbed to his feet and put his hands behind his back, I guessed to keep from throttling me. "May I have your leave to go?"

I thought about refusing him, but I'd made my point. Anything else was just me indulging in being a petty bitch. Which I'd normally be fine with, but not just now. "Sure."

He tipped his head toward me in a small nod. Looked around the Lego table, nodded at everyone else. Let himself out without another word.

Marc blew out an unnecessary breath. "Wow! I thought he was going to hit you. Who would have thought a Catholic priest would be so resistant to change?"

"I had that same thought earlier."

"He was a lot nicer when he was alive."

The Ant snorted and Tina hid a smile. Cathie remained

quiet, but wore her "too much to think about right now, can't talk" look, so I left her alone.

"He'll come around. Change is hard." My private thoughts weren't so charitable. My private thoughts, in fact, were more along the lines of: cry me a river, pal.

In the past half dozen years, I'd died, come back as a vampire, found myself the queen of the vampires, been tricked into marrying and making Sinclair king, lost a friend to cancer, cured her cancer, been snatched and rescued, rescued those who had been snatched, died, killed, lost Marc to suicide, rediscovered him as a zombie, watched my friend endure a supernatural pregnancy and then give birth to her weird babies just a few rooms away from where I regularly banged my husband, and tolerated those same weird babies when they were five and sixteen and two years and four weeks, and currently I wasn't speaking to my husband, who was sulking because I wasn't letting him trick me into letting him take over Hell.

Change is hard, Father Markus, but it's also inevitable: I suggest you suck it up.

I looked at my stepmother. "Thanks. For your support. I appreciate it."

She shrugged. "A good idea is a good idea, no matter who— Uh, you're welcome."

"It's weird, but your reflexive bitchiness really broke the tension," Marc said, and the Ant surprised me for the second time in ten minutes by laughing out loud.

I was tempted to make it snow in Hell, just to add to the general surrealness. That was a word, right? Surrealness?

CHAPTER
TWENTY-SIX

For the tenth time I checked my phone, and for the tenth time I didn't have a text from Sinclair. I doubted that was AT&T's fault; it was entirely on Sinclair. The big undead baby was no doubt still pouting because I wasn't letting him Flintstone Hell.

I was thirsty—no surprise, I always was, it was a downside to vampirism—but didn't need blood in Hell. I didn't need blood as much as any of the other vampires (queen thing), and less in Hell (Satan 2.0 thing), but still: thirsty. So I headed to the food court to slake said unnatural thirst and also to check on my project.

I started to pull out my phone again, realized what I was doing, and made myself stop. *Yes, that's right, just* stop. *He's almost as stubborn as you are; he won't be texting anytime soon unless it's an emergency. And maybe not even then.*

God, am I doing this right? Any of this? As they did now and again, my internal thoughts switched over to prayer.

Or, as I called it, bitching at my maker. *If You have a bet-ter idea, or a better candidate, You should speak up anytime. If not, could You at least smite my enemies? They're, like, legion.*

Please help me get this right, and help me figure out how to juggle Hell, the vampire kingdom, my husband, my friends, my unholy thirst for blood, my lessening hatred for the Ant, my increasing hatred for the Antichrist, and the upcoming Gucci sample sale. Thank you, amen.

"Um, hello?"

I'd been so busy praying, I hadn't realized I'd been stand-ing in front of the Orange Julius counter doing an imitation of a statue. A praying statue running low on sleep, blood, and sex.

"Hi, girls." Argh. Jennifer Palmer, despite appearances, hadn't been a girl for a long time. Cindy, who *was* a girl, didn't like being reminded. "How's the buddy system going?"

"Fine," Jennifer said quickly, already reaching for a cup. "You want the usual?"

"Please."

"Oh, don't!" Cindy said, putting a hand over the cup before Jennifer could fill it. "You won't like it; it'll taste terrible."

"Not for her," Jennifer said, gently pulling the cup away. "It'll work for her. We talked about this."

"Oh." To me: "Sorry."

"Don't apologize for that. You were trying to help me *not* suck down a cup of awful." What would the Orange Julius of the damned taste like for me? Hell was tailored; everyone's experience was different and uniquely terrible. There were probably people here who hated Orange Ju-liuses, so everything they drank tasted like something Julius. For me, an Orange Julius made with rotten bananas would have been pretty hellish.

"Um, if you don't mind my asking, what were you doing when you were just standing there? I mean, I know what it looked like, but that can't be right." Cindy asked this in a tone of voice more appropriate for "Why were you taking your clothes off and twerking?"

I ignored Jennifer's shushing motions, probably because they were aimed at Cindy. "Praying."

"But . . . why?" To Jennifer: "Stop pinching me. It's okay to ask questions."

"It's really not," she hissed back and gave Cindy another pinch for good measure. "Or at least not personal ones."

"She's right, Jennifer, it's fine." Cindy had known me (briefly) in life and hadn't been impressed (I blamed the Peach Parlor: who could come across as an authority figure when they were bathed in peach?). Small wonder she wasn't as in awe of me here. "As to why I was praying . . . why not? Have you tried it since you got here?"

"No," Cindy said, sounding shocked.

"Well, think about it. Even if you don't believe in God it can be like meditation." Marc had babbled this theory to me a while back, and it stuck with me. Like Velcro! "It can be a way to get in touch with your inner—"

"I never said I didn't believe in God!" Shocked, shocked at the very idea! While standing behind the Orange Julius counter talking to Satan 2.0 in Hell. It was kind of funny.

"—cheerleader."

"I believe in God!"

Right, right, that's why she's here. Why a lot of them are here. "Okay. So. Why not pray, then?"

"Because I'm a vampire!"

"So am I."

"I mean I was a vampire on earth—"

"Yeah, for a whole, what? Forty hours? Those two nights didn't negate the previous sixteen years."

"—when you killed me, and now I'm in Hell."

"So am I."

"No, I mean—I died. And went to Hell."

"So did I. Well, I died first; getting to Hell took a

couple of years. Look," I added, because she seemed (to be kind) deeply confused. "Just try it. It's not against the rules." Wait, was it? I made a note to check with the Ant. "And if it is, it isn't anymore."

"It isn't?" Jennifer asked.

"Wait, was that a rule? Back in the day?" Meaning, prior to a couple of months ago?

"Noooo." I could see Jennifer giving her reply careful thought. Whatever she'd been in life (accidental arsonist, eighties fashion victim), she was a cautious, troubled woman in death. "It's just—why bother? How would it help? How would *God* help? I mean . . . we're here. What's there to pray for?"

I opened my mouth to answer, then spotted Father Markus and the Ant—not a couple I'd ever seen together; ooh, could this be the start of a rom-com sitcom?—with their heads together in intimate conversation at the other end of the food court. I whistled to get their attention and waved them over. They traded glances I had no trouble interpreting and hurried over.

(*Ugh, what's she want now?*)

Though it was possible I was projecting.

"Of course prayer is allowed in Hell," the Ant said when I straight-out asked. "It'd be crazy to eliminate it."

"Oh. Well, good. That's one rule I won't have to unilaterally abolish."

"Where better?" Father Markus added, giving Jennifer and Cindy polite nods. "If anything, prayer should be encouraged. Knowing God will never hear them or help them just deepens the despair. Which is the point."

"Um." For a kindly priest, Father Markus could be kind of a hard-ass when he was inclined. Either he was kind of a dickwank in life or Hell was making him mean. I had a hunch which it was, and I didn't like it. If I was right, it didn't bode well for Sinclair coming back here anytime soon. "Well,

I happen to disagree—I think God would listen. But anyway." I turned back to the girls. Women. The damned women of the Orange Julius booth of the damned. "Pray away, ladies."

"Good to know," Jennifer replied, and she actually smiled when Cindy giggled. The Ant rolled her eyes, while Father Markus just looked disapproving. I saw Marc and Tina in animated conversation a few tables away and waved (what, was it break time?), and when they spotted me they got up and came right over.

"Hi," Marc said to Cindy. "Do you remember me?"

"I'm sorry," she said at once in a small voice, looking anywhere but his face.

"So, that'd be a yes?" He smiled, trying to put her at ease. "Hey, don't sweat it. No permanent damage. See?" He rolled up his sleeves and bared his arms. Not a mark. "It's a perk when you live with what's-her-face, here."

"Having you in my life is the ultimate mixed blessing." I sighed. *What's-her-face? Really?*

"What *are* you?" Cindy asked, staring at him. "I remember you tasted all wrong. It just made me . . . madder and—and hungrier."

"It's a long story," he replied just as my hip vibrated. Text! Ah, here came the sweet anticipated apology from Sinclair, whom I would eventually forgive because I loved him and also because he liked to express remorse via oral sex. "And I come off really zombie-ish in it . . . What? Betsy? 'S'matter?"

I gulped and reread it.

Remain in your solitary kingdom if you will, but know that the Antichrist and I will be locked in a battle to the death by the end of the week.

"Holy shit!" Marc practically screamed, rudely reading over my shoulder *again*.

And we require ice and strawberries.

"What the zombie said," I replied grimly, and I looked up at my friends. "Time to go."

CHAPTER
TWENTY-SEVEN

"They are here. They move among you. They hunt *among* you. All the old stories we were told as children to frighten us into behaving are true: there are monsters. They exist whether we behave or not. I should know: the queen of the vampires is my half sister, a blight on my life and a danger to all of you."

"Notice she left out her own title," Tina pointed out.

"And her own blight-eyness," Jessica added.

Of course she did. The Antichrist is the biggest hypocrite I've ever known. Not that I could say any of that out loud. I was pretty much rendered speechless.

"This is everywhere?" Jessica asked with wide eyes. We had gathered in the kitchen and everyone was awake, and most of us were even alert. She had one of her as-yet-unnamed babies slung over one shoulder and was rubbing his/her back, while Dick was feeding his/her sibling, cradling her/him in his arms while he watched the level in the bottle go steadily down. A baby glutted on milk was hilariously cute.

"Yes, she's made several YouTube presentations, started a Facebook page with over two hundred thousand Likes and rising, and #vampiresarereal is trending."

At last I found my voice. "That alone is enough to make me throw up in my mouth a little." I looked at Sinclair. "Thanks for texting me."

"As my queen commands," was the chilly response, and I managed not to roll my eyes (I was trying to cut back on that).

"People don't actually believe this—this campaign to expose us," Tina asked, looking like someone had nailed her with a punch between the eyes. "Do they? Surely not."

"Never underestimate the stupidity of herd animals," was my husband's grim retort. "There have been times we were nearly exposed, and that was before the plague that is social media. The more man embraces science over spirit, the harder it is for us to hide."

"Oh, come on. This is just the latest Internet thing, the supernatural version of 'is this dress blue or gold,' right? In a month no one will care. They'll be on to, I dunno, reillegalizing marijuana or something."

"Not so fast." The kitchen door swung in and Marc entered, lugging an armful of junk. He put everything down on the counter, turned, and said, "Ah, excellent. You're probably all wondering why I've called you here."

"You didn't call us here," I replied, eyeing the poster boards and the tripod with more than a little trepidation. "We were just here. Where'd you disappear to?"

"We have a tripod?" Jessica asked.

"All right, this is your resident research geek speaking, so everyone put your petty woes—"

"Petty?" Sinclair asked, and I was not to be outdone: "Woes? Who *says* that?"

He ignored our interruptions, pulled an old wooden pointer from somewhere (the same place he got the tripod?), and thwacked the first poster.

"Reasons why the Antichrist's YouTube crap will probably go viral if it hasn't already," he said, and damn if that wasn't the title of the poster. He pulled the top page away, exposing the second. Another *thwack!*

"She's hot." *Hot* was right at the top of the page in big red letters and with, if I may say so, a ridiculous number of exclamation marks. "I know it's dumb—"

"She's not *that* hot," I mumbled, probably fooling no one. That was normally Sinclair's cue to say something reassuringly sexy, but . . . nope. Not today, it seemed.

"—but people want to believe beautiful people are telling the truth and are intrinsically good. It's dumb, but hotties get the benefit of the doubt all the time."

Thwack!

"Er . . . surely there is a quicker way to do this," Sinclair began, but Marc was well into lecture mode.

Legions was next, this time in black, and with only two exclamation marks, thank goodness. "She's got hordes of Satan worshippers who will do anything, literally anything, she asks."

This was true, though I often forgot about it, because Laura found her followers extremely embarrassing, didn't talk about them, and didn't let them come around. Hard to pretend to have the moral high ground when people were constantly tracking her down (something to do with astrology and the Bible helping them find her, don't ask me how it works) and pledging to do her evil will. Which in this case was . . .

"She wants to expose vampires and she's got an army of asshats to help her."

"This is the most organized I've ever seen you," I commented. Hey, it kept him busy, it wasn't gross, no dead

animals were harmed and later stored in our freezer—I had
no complaints. Well, I did, but not about Marc's process.

"Yes, well, to continue: Her minions shouldn't be dis-
counted. They're not just helping her with the YouTube
stuff, they're spreading this stuff all over social media.
And plenty of them are coming across as credible, because
she's keeping mum about that whole Antichrist thing,
and she's not letting them sacrifice babies or otherwise be
evil when the cameras are on. She's got lawyers and cops
and politicians on her side."

"So do we," Tina said.

"Dead lawyers," he explained, "dead politicians. You
can't point to one of them and be all, 'See? That thing
about vampires being real is a hoax—just ask this vampire lawyer, who will sue you *and* suck your blood if you
slander us.'"

Another poster. This one was a still shot of the "Leave
Britney *alone*!" guy. *Crazy hot* was in green, sans exclamation points. "She's just the right amount of crazy: she's
not a foaming-at-the-mouth psychopath and she's not
boring, like someone with a phobia. So you're scared of
spiders or can't handle small spaces, big deal. But Laura?
She's just crazy enough to be intriguing. And she's got a
fuckload of charisma to back it up. People want to hear
what she's got to say. And they keep coming back to hear
what *else* she's got to say. And then they tell their friends
and forward links."

"But . . . come on." Jess looked around at all of us.
"Vampires? Other than goths, who'd be willing to sus-
pend their disbelief?"

"Plenty," Marc replied grimly. "Take a stroll through
a bookstore sometime. Don't shout at me, I know you're
a new mom and I can't possibly understand your exhaus-
tion and how you barely have time to breathe, much less
go book shopping, blah-blah—"

Jessica, who had in fact opened her mouth, had to grin.

"—but vampires are everywhere. And don't forget about the Undersea Folk."

"The what?" I asked blankly.

"Mermaids."

"Oh, that whole thing." Apparently mermaids were real. Or an offshoot of humanity mutated into people who looked like mermaids. Or it was a hoax. There were roughly a billion schools of thought on the subject and I had my own problems. Case in point!

Sinclair was frowning at me, big surprise. "You've met one," he reminded me. "And not long ago, either. How can you not remember?"

Oh, now you want to talk? You couldn't pass up a chance to needle me about forgetting something, could you?

He turned his head away and flicked his fingers in a "shoo, fly" gesture. *Fine. As you will.*

"Guys? *Guys? GUYS!* Really need you to pay attention. Look, whether you think the whole Undersea Folk thing is real or some YouTube stunt—"

"Real," Tina said at once.

"Stunt," Dick replied.

"—it still got plenty of attention and it's only been, what? A year? Because plenty of people now believe in mermaids, they'll be as likely to decide vampires are real, too."

"Illogical," Tina pointed out. "The existence of one doesn't prove the existence of another. It's like saying because there are zebras, there must be unicorns."

"You're looking for logic from the teeming masses?"

"Point," she admitted.

"Look, even ten years ago Laura's plan might not have worked, but these days everyone walks around with a camera on their phone. Social media reigns supreme and people *want* to believe this stuff. I think you'd be surprised how many people want to believe in vampires."

"And kill them," Tina pointed out. "Which is, of course, the real danger of exposure."

"Yeah." Marc paused and gave us an expectant look. When we just stared back, he said, "That's it. That's all I've got."

"And if you had to sum up your presentation in one sentence?" Sinclair asked.

"We might be fucked."

"Terrific," I moaned. I was so upset, the thought of a smoothie was nauseating. Probably should stop drinking it, then; I set my glass down and buried my face in my hands. "I'm not sure how, but this is probably my fault."

"Yes."

I jerked my head up and glared at my undead skunk hubby. "What? Why? I mean, specifically?"

"You told her to do so at church. You practically dared her."

"The hell I did! I've only talked to her once in the last three weeks and I did not dare her to expose us!"

(*"They wouldn't be so pleased to see him if they knew what he was!"*

"Like I give a shit! Like he does! Tell anyone you want who he is, who any of us are, and enjoy the three-day psych hold that results.")

"It wasn't a dare, it was a stupid argument! I didn't think she'd take me up on it. And I sure as shit didn't think people would believe her."

Dick's daughter/son had pretty much passed out, drunk and lolling on milk, and he carefully lifted her/him to his shoulder and started to pat. "All this because you wouldn't help her with Project Prove God's Real?"

I rubbed my temples, ignoring the urge to bite something. In the face. Okay, some*one*. In the face. Her beautiful, lying, holier-than-thou face. "Apparently."

"With respect, my king, I think you're being a bit hard on Her Majesty."

Yeah! I resisted the urge to stick my tongue out and gave Tina my full, hopeful attention.

"This might have been the original plan," Tina continued. "She may have picked a fight—proposed a project you would have little to no interest in, at a time when she knew you were overwhelmed with your new duties—so she could then go about exposing you with a clear conscience."

Made sense. The Antichrist was her mother's daughter that way: she had no qualms about tricking people to make herself look better. Definitely an ends-justify-the-means mind-set.

"Well, Hell, I'd better call her. Or go see her. Right now."

"No need." Oooh, Sinclair was as cool as Fur and Burr sitting on ice cubes. "She's currently holding a press conference in our front yard."

Because of course she is.

TWENTY-EIGHT

"Seriously with this?" I'd stepped out on our porch to see over a dozen people standing in our front yard, and two— no, three—news vans. Most of them had microphones or cameras and they were all pointed in my direction. Laura, standing beside a grim-looking fellow holding an old-fashioned notebook and pen, helpfully volunteered, "That's her. That's Elizabeth Taylor, the vampire queen."

I shot her an incredulous look just as the pack swarmed. Startled, I automatically took a step backward; I did *not* need these guys getting within smacking distance, or even barely touching distance. I groped and grabbed the closest thing to hand. "Back. Get back! I mean it!" I jabbed at the media and then realized what I was jabbing with: one of the pitchforks my asshole roommates kept leaving around. I groaned and tossed the pitchfork into the corner of the porch. Laura must have been thrilled: I'd just given her great footage for the "my sister's evil and must be exposed" campaign.

"Don't let my lack of pitchfork make you think you can swarm again. I mean it! Back. *Off.* D'you think the whole private property thing, it's—what?" This time I stepped back into Sinclair's chest and only then realized he'd followed me. His hands steadied me as I continued. "You think it's not so much the law as a guideline?"

The response I got was a babble of questions, all along the lines of "So apparently you're a vampire: can you confirm that and how do you feel about that?" I pulled myself free of Sinclair's steady hands so he wouldn't have to keep pretending we weren't furious with each other.

Man, that was nice. His hands on my hips. I'd missed that; I'd missed him. We'd been freezing each other for three days, and it felt like three decades. Could there be any fixing this? I still felt the same way, that Sinclair + Hell = Armageddon, and not the good kind. It was—

"Ms. Taylor? Ma'am? You have a death certificate on file; can you explain that?"

Oh. Right. Throng of journalists currently trying to interview me. "It was a joke . . . obviously, since I'm standing here in front of you. And again: seriously? C'mon, guys." I took a step forward and looked up at the frigid sky; it was late winter but the sun was shining. "Shouldn't I be going up in flames about now?" I pointed to my husband, who was po-faced. "Shouldn't he?"

Excellent, Elizabeth. Keep avoiding the questions and manufacturing scorn. Later, if it matters, it can be argued you did not lie.

Oh. Right. Yes, that was definitely part of my plan and not at all because I was honestly flustered and incredulous and had no fucking idea how to handle this.

More babble, broken by the man standing next to Laura:

"Bring out the other one. Your assistant. Prove ordinary vampires can tolerate sunlight. Not just the king and queen."

Whoa. Okay, I knew Laura's obnoxious campaign included snippets about our lives that were none of the public's business. Those snippets included everything that came out of her mouth while on camera. But these people were actually paying attention to the details! They knew Sinclair and I were special; they knew regular vampires were vulnerable to sunlight and fire. For the first time I was more frightened than pissed. Did today's media really have nothing better to do than troll YouTube videos put up by gorgeous blondes?

Don't answer that.

"I don't have to prove anything, pal. That's on you guys. Do *not* take that as a dare! Besides, you— Sorry, what's your name?"

"Ronald Tinsman."

"Right, Ronald Tinsman. Do you really not have anything better to do than stand in my yard babbling about vampires and freezing your ass off?"

"No," he replied quietly.

"Oh." Well, *that* took the wind out of my sails. "Well. Okay, then."

Tinsman. I knew that name. I'd heard it in recent, unpleasant circumstances. He didn't look or sound familiar and was dressed in midwinter casual: jeans, boots, a partially unzipped parka revealing a green and black flannel shirt. He was pale and puffy, with thinning brown hair and an exhausted gaze. But there was something about his eyes . . . dammit, where'd I know this guy from?

Sinclair must have caught the stray thought, because . . .

I doubt Mr. Tinsman is interested in our condolences on the loss of his daughter to vampirism and beheading.

"Oh, *fuck*!" I managed, and the shriek of microphone feedback nearly deafened me. "Argh, sorry!" I shook my head like a dog at a whistle to clear the ringing. "Wait, I'm not sorry. You're all trespassing and this is a stupid story. Isn't there a war going on somewhere? I'm almost positive there's a war somewhere. It's not the war on drugs, we've pretty much given up on that one . . ."

"What do you have to say about your father giving sworn affidavits testifying to the fact that vampires exist?"

"My *father?*" Tilt! Too much to process. For the first time ever, I longed to be back in Hell. "You mean the asshat who faked his death to get out of spending time with his family because he didn't care for the paperwork that comes with divorce proceedings?" I glared at Laura, who just shrugged. Suddenly this was making a lot more awful, awful sense. The Antichrist, in her continuing efforts to find the adult equivalent of a Daddy and Me class, had teamed up with my dad to expose me and mine to the world. And for what?

Revenge for imagined slights. Both of them. Pathetic. Both of them.

"My father and my half sister have at least one thing in common," I said shortly. "They're both liars." This was technically true, though more so in my dad's case than Laura's. The Antichrist was a huge fan of lying by omission, then convincing herself it wasn't like that.

"But what about the allegations of—"

"This unscheduled interview with you pack of trespassers is over. And this is private property. All of you get out. Not *you*, Laura. We need to talk."

Understatement.

CHAPTER
TWENTY-NINE

"What the fuck is wrong with you?" I was so pissed, so shocked by what had just happened, I couldn't get any volume or inflection. My outraged question came out like a little flat statement.

Laura shrugged and leaned against the back of the love seat. We were in the Peach Parlor, the first room I could drag her into once the front door closed. Sinclair hadn't tried to follow us in, which was confusing. Still mad at me? Assuming he wasn't invited to the ass chewing because he wasn't a blood relative? Didn't dare be in the same room with her because of the overwhelming urge to strangle? I could relate to the last one at least.

"Laura! Answer the question, what's wrong with you?"

"Nothing's wrong with *me*. Besides, I'm just doing what you told me."

"God, you're an *infant* sometimes, you know that? It wasn't a dare and you damned well know it!"

"It was a taunt," she replied. "You were taunting me. You're always taunting me."

"Taunting, huh? That word-a-day toilet paper is really working out for you."

"See?"

I was pacing back and forth in front of her, trying not to rip my own hair out. Harshing my highlights would help no one; looking less attractive would help *no one*. "And how the hell do you know Cindy Tinsman's dad?"

"We both volunteer at Fairview."

"Of course you do."

Of course they did. My entire postdeath life consisted of huge, life-changing pieces of luck: sometimes good, sometimes bad. This time it was definitely the latter.

"And don't get any ideas," she warned, looking far too comfortable for the trouble she was in. "My people have instructions on what to do if I mysteriously disappear. You can't do anything to me while the world is looking over your shoulder."

"You're definitely watching too much television." I rubbed my forehead and added, "Walk me through this insanity of yours. You and Cindy's dad know each other, and somehow you found out what happened to his daughter—"

"Happened to?" She snorted. "You're making it sound like she was caught in a thunderstorm. You decapitated her after turning her."

"I didn't turn her! And Sinclair didn't, either, and neither did Tina—"

"One of your filth," she said with a flick of her fingers. "It's on you."

I ground my teeth. She had a point. With great blah-blah came great blah-blah.

"I was the only one who would listen to him. And together we decided to expose you. He's got media contacts, and I've got plenty of—"

"Satan-worshipping staff," I interrupted. "I'll bet you didn't mention to Mr. Tinsman that you're the Antichrist."

"I did, actually," was the calm reply, and I nearly walked into the wall (probably should slow down my pacing).

"You did? Really?"

"Of course. We can't be partners without transparency."

"And you think him being numb means he's fine with that."

For the first time, she faltered. "He's not— I mean, yes, he's grieving. But he knows I'm a force for good, despite my birthright, like he knows you're a force for evil, despite yours."

I stopped pacing and stood in front of her. "No," I said bluntly. "He's lost his wife and daughter in a very short time. His wife died of cancer while he was helpless and could only watch, and his daughter was recently murdered in a particularly nasty way, because a lifelong friend of his family happened to be a vampire. You could have set yourself on fire and waltzed with a grizzly bear and he'd have had the same reaction: 'Yeah, okay, sounds good, I don't care.'"

"I don't—"

"Yeah, that's just right. You don't. Oh, say, where's our dear old daddy-o?"

"He—" She realized she didn't know, and closed her mouth. I was too irked to feel much triumph. *God, what an idiot. Both of them. Must be a genetic thing. Curse. Whatever.*

"You didn't even notice he wasn't here, did you? Too busy preening for the cameras. He ditched you. And that, little sister, is our father in a nutshell. All talk, no follow-up. He's made a career out of terrible choices that he can't stick with."

"He's scared of you! And he's right to be scared. I said I'd protect him—"

I almost giggled.

"—and when I told him my plan he thought it was a wonderful idea. He *wanted* to help. He helped finance the operation."

"With his ill-gotten gains. But hey, the ends justify the et cetera, right, Laura?"

"You just can't stand that he wants to help me expose you. He had to fake his death just to get any peace."

I sighed. Laura had an amazing ability to interpret all my actions as evil, and all our evil dad's actions as good. And her own intentions were, in her mind, always golden. "Yeah, he committed fraud for the greater good. Except not really."

"And why do you suppose he did that?" she asked in an exaggerated let's-find-the-answer-together tone.

"Because he's a raging coward who thrives on ducking familial responsibility?"

She glared. "That's our father you're speaking of."

"I know." I could feel my shoulders slump. Exhausted and it was barely noon. "That's why it's so awful."

"He did it because he was afraid of you."

"Oh, Jesus-please-us." I rolled my eyes hard enough to hurt. "He can't think I'd ever hurt him."

"You threatened to kill him!"

"Mmm . . . doesn't sound like me. No, I'm pretty sure I never— Oh. Wait. Huh." It was all coming back to me, like those nightmares where you're naked and tardy and haven't studied for the test and everyone's throwing tomatoes at you. "Fine, I did threaten him. Don't look at me like that; it was a stressful couple of days, took me a second to remember. Do *you* remember every conversation you've had in the last two months?"

She took a breath and put her hands behind her back. I grinned; in her mind she was throttling me. I've been seeing that look on people's faces for decades. "So you admit it. You know he doesn't trust you!"

"Wait, the guy who *faked* his own *death* is the one having trust issues? Jeepers, who'd have thought?"

"He still wanted to help me. He was so happy to see me," she babbled, lost in the happy memory of our father pretending he cared. "He was on board from the start—he thought telling the truth about you was a wonderful idea."

"He thought revealing he'd faked his death and committed insurance fraud was a wonderful idea?"

"He— What?"

"Moron!" I'd leaned down and shouted it into her face, and watching her flinch was deeply satisfying. "He broke the law! It's a felony, dumbass! He'll be lucky if he's *only* sued. They could slam his ass into Stillwater for—for—"

"Up to twenty years and a fine of up to one hundred thousand dollars in the state of Minnesota," the doorway said, except not really.

"Oh, you might as well get in here," I said, resuming my pacing.

To my surprise, Dick led the charge: "You're pathetic." Tina stretched on her tiptoes to peek over his shoulder and nodded in agreement. The others were crammed in behind them (narrow doorway).

Laura said nothing, just raised her eyebrows.

"She's only ever welcomed you," he continued, presumably referring to me, "and occasionally called you on your shit." Definitely referring to me.

"Not her job," Laura snapped back.

"It by God ought to be someone's job! Sorry, Tina."

"It's fine." The rest had come in and were glaring en masse at Laura, who should have been less irritated and more afraid. "Understandable."

"I can't wait until someone catches you flinching at the Lord's name on camera," Laura said.

"You underestimate our resources," was Sinclair's cool reply. "And you underestimate our queen, as ever." In small rooms he always seemed taller than he was, and if Laura wasn't exactly cowering (she got points for that, if nothing else) she was definitely in his shadow. In *all* ways. "You think you're the only person in ten thousand years to try to expose us? This is nothing new. You're nothing new. There's not one original thing about you, not a unique thought in your head. Everything about you is a cliché, including this childish resentment you have for your older sister. I'd pity you, Laura, if you warranted it."

Whoa.

That one must have hurt, because she didn't engage. Just stared at him for a long moment, then turned to me. "They can't help you," she hissed, her mouth turning down, her eyes going narrow. "You like to flaunt your friends—"

"I really don't." Where was *this* coming from? "Having friends isn't the same as flaunting them."

"—and pride yourself on complaining you have to do things you don't like, then shoving those things off on friends and complaining *more*, for some reason."

Okay, that *did* sound like me. But c'mon. Was all this really happening because the Antichrist thought I had a lousy attitude?

"They can't help you this time; they've all got secrets, they've all got too much to lose. Didn't you notice how they didn't all rush out into the yard with you? Just the one you've—the vampire you've enslaved with your—your—"

I cut her off, amused in spite of myself. She was neck-deep in a plot to expose and betray me, and she couldn't say the words. "Are you trying to infer Sinclair's pussy-whipped?"

"I imply; *you* infer."

"Yeah, like I said."

"Shut up! Don't you understand what's happening?"

"Kind of?" Okay, even I wasn't this dim, but it was doing interesting things to Laura's blood pressure and, for that reason alone, was worth pursuing. And the others were mercifully silent, except for Marc's muffled snort (cut short by Tina's elbow to his ribs).

Laura puffed a hank of perfectly golden hair out of her face with a frustrated blast: *pfffttt!* "Dick's a cop, for heaven's sake; he could have run them off in thirty seconds. But he stayed inside. I out-and-out told Jessica what I was up to; I even offered her and her husband shelter so they could avoid the fallout—they're only guilty by association, they're not undead—and she couldn't be bothered to pass it on. If she had, you wouldn't be so shocked." *Wait, what? Don't turn around and glare at Jess, don't turn around and glare at—* "None of them came to your aid; they just cowered inside, hoping you'd fix this and knowing you couldn't."

"I'm having trouble following your villain rant. Are you doing this because you think I'm inherently evil, because I have a lousy attitude, because you resent my friends, because you don't like my friends, because you don't like your brother-in-law, because you hate your birthright, because you regret tricking me into taking your birthright, or because you think this will win you Daddy's love?" At her furious silence, I added, "It's at least one of those, though, right?"

She stood and smoothed her (immaculate) jeans, ready to leave now that she'd ruined my week/month/decade. "You've got a nasty way of making morals sound ridiculous."

I laughed at her. (It was either that or burst into furious tears.) "It's hilarious that the *Antichrist* used 'morals' and 'ridiculous' in the same sentence."

She was halfway to the door by then but checked and turned at my words. "They'll see you for what you are, you know. Everyone will. Then they'll destroy you. Your friends can't help you. Your father won't help you. You'll just have to go to Hell. And stay there forever."

She left.

We let her.

CHAPTER
THIRTY

*Marc's comment broke the difficult silence: "The Anti-*christ miiiight be crazy in addition to evil."

"It's worse," Jessica said glumly. "It's so much worse. The Antichrist isn't evil and/or crazy because she's the spawn of Satan. She's evil and/or crazy because she's a fundamentalist the-Bible-is-literal-and-I'll-kill-you-to-save-you nutjob. She's determined to be good and she'll destroy anyone she has to in order to prove it."

We'd adjourned to the kitchen, too depressed and freaked to even consider pulping fruit, ice, and yogurt into a delicious drink to be ardently slurped through straws. And I figured now was the best time to tackle the primary issue on my mind, while we were still reeling from what the Antichrist had visited upon us, but I didn't yet have a plan.

I cleared my throat, and they looked at me hopefully, but that was where I was stuck. I wanted to glare and shout, but didn't dare. Jessica and I had been friends since our training-bra days (cue jokes about how Jessica could *still* wear training bras, then cue me breaking your nose). I couldn't bear it if she was scared of me after everything she'd seen me through. If she was afraid of me, this time I didn't have the excuse of having read the Book of the Dead and turning evil (temporarily).[16]

But what other explanation was there?

"Jessica, how— Laura said she told you. Um, so . . . I was wondering. Just, y'know, out of curiosity. Simply to pass the time while we come up with a plan. Just as a way to keep the conversation going . . ."

Marc had buried his face in his hands. "Oh, just spit it out and *ask*," he groaned into his palms. "This is too painful."

I glared but kept my tone mild. "Why didn't you—"

She turned her head toward me so fast I heard the tendons in her neck creak. "You think I kept this to myself? That your jackass sister confided her sinister plan and I decided silence was the best option? Why would I do that? For fun? For spite? To see what would happen?"

Tina leaned over and carefully relieved Jessica of one of her babies, then backed out of the line of fire. This freed Jessica to jump to her feet and sort of loom over me, since I was sitting at the counter. I tried not to cower. I failed.

"I'm not mad," I said delicately, "but it's important that you understand, we could be in a lot of—"

"Now you shut your mouth and listen to me, Elizabeth Anne Taylor."

Whoa. Full name. Abort, abort! My hands were instantly up, placating. Now Dick *and* Tina were backing away with babies. "No, really, I'm not m—"

---

[16] Betsy turned evil and raped Sinclair in *Undead and Unreturnable*. Sinclair was too delighted to notice he was being forced. It was a whole thing.

"I have no recollection of that conversation, partly because I don't pay much attention to your judgmental bitch-cow sister—"

Bitch-cow! The gloves were off!

"—but mostly because I've been averaging twenty minutes of sleep a night for weeks! Which is why I didn't mention it to you! Because I promptly forgot it! I don't know if she called or came by or meant to tell me or just blurted it out, and I don't give a shit! What*ever* her reason, why*ever* she told me, if I'd been well rested and in my right mind I would have told you right goddamned away! Because the Antichrist offering shelter to me and mine while she exposed you and your husband to the world is something I would have felt you needed to know! Okay?"

I nodded so hard I almost fell over. We were all nodding. "Yep. Makes perfect sense. Thanks for clearing that up. Never doubted you—"

"Oh, shut up," she said, but a smile broke through the scowl.

"—for a second. A nanosecond. That's less than a second, right?"

"That said," Jessica added, thankfully out of shout mode, "this is not good. For any of us."

"Got that right." Marc looked as glum as I'd ever seen him. "Not to belittle your sister's deep insecurity and instability, but I can't help wondering if maybe she should just get laid."

"The only thing I want to discuss less than being exposed is my sister's virginity. I can't believe this is happening. Any of it."

Tina was still cradling a baby, but came over and rested a cool hand on top of mine. Her voice was a lull. The babies loved her. She could hum about four notes and they were out like teeny lightbulbs. "Majesty, the king was right when he said this isn't the first time humans have tried to expose us. We've fought this before and won before. And that was without the queen on our side."

"Thanks for the entirely misplaced vote of confidence. And yeah, obviously Laura's sinister plan is a rerun; other people knew about vampires in the past and tried to blow their cover. But this is the first time it'll probably work if we don't think of something. The world's a lot smaller than it was a thousand years ago."

No one said anything, which was a real shame. I was hoping to be refuted. Soundly, even.

"This— It's—" I broke off and shook my head. I couldn't find the words. Maybe because there weren't any. "I'm . . . I'm so sorry, you guys. I've put you all in danger. More so than usual, I mean." I couldn't stand their expressions. They were upset, but not with me. They were mad . . . but not at me. They were concerned . . . *for* me. Concern I knew I didn't deserve. "I'm very, very sorry."

I fled.

CHAPTER
THIRTY-ONE

I heard the door open and knew it was either Tina or Sinclair, the only ones who could have kept up with me. Probably Sinclair, preparing to explain at length how my idiocy had ruined his (after)life.

The bed dipped as he sat beside me. I was facedown on my pillow in the middle of a half-assed suicide attempt. Even if I needed to breathe, suffocation via pillow would still take too long. Stupid memory foam!

"My father and my sister have teamed up to destroy me," I said into the foam, which Sinclair probably heard as "Mmm ffmmm sssmmmm hvvv mmmm mm."

No response, which made sense. He had to be pretty annoyed, and was likely thinking up the best way to explain the depths of my fuckuppery. Constantly blowing Laura off, denying her Hell after she tricked me into taking Hell, threatening to kill her father, constantly questioning her choice of footwear . . . my unsisterly behavior had piled up to endanger every one of us.

I felt it then. Sinclair's hand on the small of my back, warm(ish) and steady.

I am so sorry, my own, my dearest. You're worth ten of them.

I perked up a little. "Only ten?" (Which came out, "Nnn ttnn?")

"A hundred. A thousand. A centillion."

Damn, that sounded like a lot. I rolled over and blinked up at him. His dear face was creased with concern, but his fist was clenched. He wanted to beat Laura to death as much as he wanted to make me feel better. I could relate.

I took a deep breath, let it out. "I'm sorry. About before."

"No, the offense is mine. You were correct to be wary of my objectives. I truly have no intention of—er—"

"Glomming on to Hell?"

He quirked an eyebrow at me, dark eyes gleaming. "Yes. But then, I had no intention of falling in love with you, or tolerating our many roommates, or being a pet owner, or participating in the Winter Carnival, and all those things have happened." He stroked my bangs away from my face. "To my unending delight."

I sighed and snuggled into his palm.

"All that to say," he continued, "I may not have intended to take over Hell, but perhaps it would have come to pass regardless of my intent and your wishes. It's— You're so young and sweet. You have too many burdens as it is. I want to relieve you of them, but perhaps that isn't my place."

I made a mighty effort and didn't snort at "young and sweet." *Wrong on both counts, pal.* And for one of the few times in our marriage, I felt every year of the age gap between us. He thought I was a spoiled child and I thought he was a controlling chauvinist, and sometimes we were at least partially right about each other.

"The thing about Hell." I reached out and caught his other hand, linking our fingers. "It's not just me trying to prove something to myself, that I can do this thing on my own. Well, on my own with a committee. Every suggestion you've made has been a good idea and I've implemented almost all of them. No," I rushed ahead as he opened his mouth, "I am not implementing a Black Labrador Appreciation Day in Hell; you've just got to accept that. Fur and Burr aren't going anywhere near Hell."

"Of course not," he said, offended. "Labs we don't love would go to Hell."

"You're a monster!" I almost shouted, then got a grip. "Anyway. It's not happening. But the thing about Hell, the real reason I don't want you down there, so to speak . . ."

"Yes?" His face was calm, he was stroking my cheek, but his gaze was riveted to mine and I could see the tense line of his shoulders. He was expecting something bratty or hateful or both. Was bracing himself for it. Was telling himself it was my choice, not his! Christ, I did not deserve this man.

"It's turning Father Markus mean," I said in a small voice.

His eyebrows shot up. "What?"

"He's getting mean. I think it's being there—I think Hell's corrupting him. Maybe even being on the committee is corrupting him; I'll have to watch the others. How would I be able to tell if Hell made the Ant a bitch? She was already a bitch when she got there. So was I."

"You're not . . . always . . ." he began loyally.

"And Tina—well, she's been around the block a few times; I'm not worried about her. She's used to the assistant role; she likes helping behind the scenes and hates being onstage. I can't imagine ever having a power struggle with her. And Marc doesn't seem any different—well, that's not entirely true. Being in Hell makes him lonely.

I don't know why. I mean, he's always lonesome. He needs someone in the worst way, and I can't help him. Maybe—"

"My love, I don't understand."

I wriggled until I was propped up on my elbows. "Hell is changing Father Markus. He's not as quick to forgive, and he's much quicker to judge. He's not very interested in decreasing anyone's suffering. He's fighting me on every major change, and I'm pretty sure he's undermining my efforts when I'm not there. And since I refuse to be in Hell twenty-four/seven, he's got lots of opportunities. And I don't want that to happen to you. Some people would say you're already mean. But they don't know you like I do.

"You're not mean, you're driven. And ruthless, when you have to be. But you don't enjoy it any more than I do. And I'm not downing you for any of that; your nature is the reason you existed long enough for us to meet."

"Existed," he murmured, but he seemed pleased. "Yes. The perfect word."

"You've taken lives, like me, but you've saved plenty along the way, also like me. But . . . come on. Father Markus was right out of central casting for the 'kindly priest who wants everybody to love their neighbors and their enemies' trope. This was a guy who wouldn't set actual mousetraps in his church, just those awful humane ones so he could release disease-carrying rodents into the wild where they could go into *other* houses. You remember, you met him in life."

Sinclair was nodding. "He was compassionate and open-minded. I found him to be a good man. He certainly grieved when he thought you had died, and he'd only known you a few days."

"Right. All that and then some. But these days? He's pretty cold." I reached for Sinclair's hand again. "So I started to wonder. What would Hell do to you? You're tricky and ruthless and brilliant when you *aren't* corrupted. What if Hell changed you like it's changing Markus?"

"I don't understand. Are you saying—?"

"But me? I don't take anything seriously. I'm not brilliant and I'm not especially tricky. And I'm not so ruthless I've lost my humanity . . . yet. But I want people to get along. I want to decrease what I see as meaningless suffering. And I have people who love me to retreat to when Hell is overwhelming. I think that's why I can handle it down there. I think that's why I'm *supposed* to handle it down there."

He nodded. "I understand, my own. And I regret doubting you, and my unkind words. You've been a fine queen for our kind; I've no doubt you'll be one in Hell, too."

I sighed and flopped back. "Any other time and I'd be tempted to believe you. But now we've got our regular problems, plus Hell, plus the Antichrist and my useless father plotting to expose us. And they'll probably succeed. I mean, we can't kill them." I paused. "Can we?"

"Likely not. I don't doubt your sister has taken steps to ensure still more exposure for us if she were to disappear."

It's also morally wrong, I thought but didn't say.

He smiled. "And it's also morally wrong."

"Cheater! You picked that answer out of my brain."

"Oh, I often do. As to your father, he's hardly worth the effort of killing."

I giggled, which was probably the wrong reaction, but fuck it. "That's him in a nutshell." But the laugh stuck in my throat. Sure, we were joking about killing him, but we were doing so because he was in the middle of betraying me, putting me and mine in the worst danger of our lives, and for what? Because he didn't like how our last meeting went.

"Y'know, if he'd loved me a tenth as much as he loved himself, that would have been enough." I could feel my mouth trying to tremble and pressed my lips together. "More than enough. More than he ever gave me in life and a shitload more than he's given me in death. I don't— Was it one particular thing I did, d'you think, that made him not like me?"

Elizabeth . . . He wasn't speaking out loud, but I could feel the pain behind my name.

"Or was it just my basic personality? I'd blame it on being a vampire, but honestly, he was like this pretty much the whole time I was alive, too. Except this time . . ." I paused, then forced the rest of the words out. "This time he's putting everyone I love in danger, too. For spite. You're in the worst danger of your life because my dad never loved me."

And that was it. I clapped both hands over my eyes in a gesture I knew was childish

(if I can't see them they can't see me)

but was too upset to care, and burst into tears. I hadn't cried so hard since my dad faked his death to get away from me. There was probably a lesson there, but I couldn't get to it. So I just wept and let Sinclair offer what comfort he could, and in a while I fell into an exhausted sleep.

CHAPTER
THIRTY-TWO

Jessica's twins, who were about a month old, were just getting home from kindergarten when I walked into the kitchen a few hours after my breakdown.

(This will take some explaining.)

Though life was currently stressful and shitty, I knew everyone was working on the problem. The reporters hadn't come back, though we expected more press tomorrow . . . I'd given them a few sound bites while processing my sister's betrayal. Don't even get me started on the horror of Mr. Tinsman's grief being a contributing factor to this . . . fucking . . . mess.

The one bright spot: I'd popped into Hell for an hour, almost sad I'd fixed the time problem (how great would it have been to come back a year later, when Sinclair and Tina had fixed everything?). To my surprised pleasure, things were running smoothly. Operation Hell Buddy was still going strong, and Cathie and the Ant had started reviewing cases/souls that were eligible for parole, as it were.

I was beginning to realize that running Hell was like the old saying about one person eating a bear by herself. It seemed impossible when you thought about the whole job, but the trick was to do it one bite at a time, however long it took.

Hell was my dead bear.

Meanwhile, there was *this* to deal with.

"H'lo, Onnie Bets."

"Hi, kiddo. Sorry, plural." Jessica's twins—a boy and a girl who reminded me of Poe's Raven ("Nameless here for evermore") due to Jessica's hatred of government paperwork—were seated on bar stools pulled up to the big butcher block that dominated the kitchen. They had identical expressions of "well, we're politely waiting, how about you move your butt and get us a snack already?" on their teeny cute faces.

"Aw, c'mon." I tried not to whine. "You guys will get me in trouble with your mom again. And she was super pissed at me just a few hours ago. I'm not stirring that pot again."

"Nuh-uh! We won't say anything."

"You can stir, you can stir! And even if she knew—"

"Not from us!"

"She'd forgive you 'cuz you're best friends."

"That's true," I admitted, because Jessica had overlooked worse crimes (borrowing her eyeliner without asking, coming back from the dead, temporarily wondering if she was in cahoots with the Antichrist), "but there'll be hours of shouting first."

"And also, you have the most prettiest shoes in the world."

"Well, one cookie won't hurt." I smiled at them. Dammit, they were *adorable.* "Besides, you should be rewarded for being so smart."

In unison (which should have been creepy but was just cute): "We know!"

I opened the snack cupboard and stretched to reach the Thin Mints, which Marc still obsessively bought and hoarded even though he didn't eat anymore. The cookies-on-the-top-shelf ploy worked except when Jessica's weird babies were in their late teens. Then it was like a pair of wolverines had been released into the cookie cupboard; the mess was right out of *I am become death, destroyer of worlds.*

"Here." I gave them each two, then poured milk and watched carefully as they drank. In *this* universe, Jessica and Dick's babies were still newborns; we had no sippie cups on hand, and so kept an eye on the kids as they drank. Two weeks ago one of them (I forget which) lost his or her grip and sloshed chocolate milk on my Nicholas Kirkwood prism ankle boots. They took turns comforting me as I collapsed in a heap on the floor and sobbed for five minutes (I'd have cried a lot longer if the boots hadn't been black).

A sweet, high-voiced chorus of two: "Thank you!"

"Welcome. Now keep your lips zipped. If your mom kills me, I'll kill you."

A chime of giggles. "Nuh-uh! Not even if someone tried to make you."

"Not even if we took your Blanks!"

I grinned; I couldn't help it. "Blahniks. Manolo Blahniks, you little savages."

They were dressed in what I liked to call future toddler fabric: shiny overalls, his green and hers blue. No idea what the material was, but nothing stuck to it. *Nothing.* Frankly, I could have used a few outfits made out of whatever it was. They had dark blue long-sleeved T-shirts beneath the overalls, and their sturdy little feet were clad in fuzzy red socks.

Jessica and Dick's gorgeous biracial kids were Exhibit

A for Proving Bigots Wrong: races should mix *constantly* because I'd never seen more gorgeous kids.

Their skin was pale with rosy gold undertones, and their hair was deep black and kinky. The girl wore hers pulled back into braids that reminded me of Jessica's killer-tight ponytail; the boy's was clipped short. Their enormous dark eyes were their mother's, too. And they were precocious, and not just because they were continent newborns sitting up and feeding themselves and going to kindergarten. They were *smart.* Whip-smart. Marc was always fascinated when other iterations of the twins popped in, and he did IQ tests on them disguised as games. Which they immediately figured out and called him on. Which made him want to test them more. Which they tolerated, what with the blatant Rice Krispies bar bribery that always ensued.

Of course, not everybody was enchanted by their, um, special gifts. Parenting newborns was relentless and stressful enough (at least, judging from Dick's and Jessica's permanent state of exhausted confusion). Newborns who were sometimes a month old and sometimes in elementary school and sometimes old enough to drive . . . that was trickier. Jessica had explained it like so: "I don't know the five-year-olds, so how can I love them? Understanding intellectually that those are my children years from now doesn't help me *feel* it. I love the babies. I don't know the others."

I didn't have a clue about parenting, not really, and made the rare decision to nod and keep my mouth shut. My half brother/son BabyJon spent more time with my mother than he did here. It was better that way. Safer.

And speaking of safety, how would the recent unpleasant developments affect Jessica's family? Dick was beyond tolerant of our supernatural shenanigans, but if reporters were going to be poking around—or, worse, goth kids searching for real vampires—how were they going to handle that?

"You're our best most favorite aunt," the girl told me approvingly, draining her milk and handing me the cup like I was a goddamned waitress. (What the hell. I took the cup and rinsed it. She got me off an unpleasant train of thought, after all.)

"Your only aunt," I reminded them.

"Nuh-uh! There's Tina and Grandma Taylor."

"Grandma Taylor is *Grandma* Taylor, not aunt," the boy corrected. (Argh, when was Jessica going to name these things? We all agreed asking the twins would be cheating, and the kids never addressed each other by name, preferring "No, *you* shut up!") "And Tina's a friend in the family. Right, Onnie Betsy? Friend in the family?"

"Of the family," I corrected, taking his empty cup. I could see him making a mental note so he'd use the phrase correctly next time. He would, too. These guys never forgot anything, except that they weren't supposed to have too many cookies after school.

"D'you know where Mommy is?" The girl had glanced at the calendar on the wall and then outside, figured it was daylight and business hours, and assumed Dick was at work so no point in asking after him. All correct. Cripes, when I was five I sometimes forgot how to open the fridge.

("No, honey, *pull*. Don't push."

"But I'm so hungry!")

Dick hadn't wanted to go back to work—well, he had, but he hadn't wanted to admit it, and he'd both dreaded and anticipated getting the hell out of the house. Jessica had insisted, pointing out there were few things scarier than a man legally required to carry a gun who was over-tired and shaking from too much caffeine. He was on a part-time schedule for now, trying to figure out his official cop stance on Operation Expose Vamps. He felt bad about hiding in the house during my inadvertent press conference that morning and was determined not to do so again. But how to explain to the brass? "Of course it's not true. I'm definitely not exposing myself, my wife, and my helpless infants to vampires and a zombie. Well, time for my gun and me to patrol the streets—hope I don't run into any reporters, ho-ho-ho!"

The good news was, he didn't have to work at all—he had almost as much money as Jessica did—but he loved his job. We loved it, too. If not for his job, he and Jess never would have met.[17] Sinclair had taken him aside and asked him not to make any permanent decisions for the next few days. He'd agreed.

All that to say he wasn't home right now, which the twins figured out immediately.

"Onnie Betsy?"

"Sorry; thinking. Your mom's coming now." I started pulling smoothie ingredients from the fridge, because I knew my pal would need one. The kitchen door swung in and, as we both were prone to do, she was in midfret and didn't bother with social niceties like "hello" or "get your big white butt off the counter—we *eat* there!"

"I can't find the babies again, will you please help me I— Oh." She saw her newborns, who were on either side of me and chewing like piranhas to get rid of the cookie evidence. "Oh." She managed a smile and put the big Barnes and Noble bag she had with her on the counter. That was a little odd; I knew she hadn't left the mansion all day. Probably full of clothes for Goodwill. Or even books. "There you are."

I sympathized. Could *not* imagine what parenting these darling weirdos was like. Well, I could, because I saw a lot of it, but stressful didn't begin to cover it.

---

[17] Poor Dick was assigned to Betsy's assault, and investigated her death as well, in *Undead and Unwed*.

Jessica and Dick were unique in our house: they were run-of-the-mill normals in a house of the undead. But somehow, when Jessica got pregnant, her proximity to me as I was learning how to navigate other dimensions (Hell) and time travel backward (Salem during the witch hunts, also known as Hell) and forward (Minnesota in the future was a winter wasteland, twenty feet of snow in July, also known as Hell) affected her unborn twins.

Jessica's twins were drawn to this mansion, this time-line, and to me. *Any* of her twins. From any reality out there. In one universe, she'd had her babies a few years earlier, thus: the kindergarten newborns sucking down Thin Mints. In another, she and Dick had known each other in high school and she'd gotten pregnant on gradu-ation night: the twins who had driver's licenses.

We should have been tipped off during her pregnancy, except anyone in the house (where Jessica and I spent most of our time) either wouldn't notice something was very, very odd, or we'd notice but didn't find it alarming. My mother eventually figured it out, and that only because she *didn't* live here. One day Jess wasn't showing, the next she'd look eleven months pregnant, then later that week she'd barely be showing again. Jessica's weird babies were weird even in the womb.[18]

Without exception, the twins always knew who we were and where they were. They were never alarmed to find themselves in an entirely different universe. And they would disappear as mysteriously as they'd arrived. It took some getting used to—we still weren't, not really—but most of the time it was jarring but also kind of cool.

Most of the time.

---

[18] The weirdness was on display in *Undead and Unwary*.

"What's this?" Jessica asked, bending down to peer at her daughter's mouth. The girl gave an elaborate, overly innocent shrug. "Hon? What are you eating?"

A head shake. Big wide innocent eyes got bigger and wider and innocenter.

"Answer me, please."

"She has linjinitis," the boy suggested, lightly spraying his mother with Thin Mint crumbs.

I snickered. "Laryngitis." Everybody was always correcting me. It was nice being the one to do the correcting. I figured I should enjoy the twins until they were smarter than me in another four, maybe five years. "When you can't talk? That's what she's got."

"Sure she does." I got a Defcon 2–level glare and pretended not to be terrified. "Betsy, hand me those baby wipes."

I obeyed at once.

"Aw, Mommy, those are for babies. We're not babies because, look! We're big kids. And mmpphh!"

"Don't fight it," I advised the boy.

"Shush."

We all obeyed her. I watched my friend scrub away all traces of Thin Mint crime and wondered how long this iteration would hang out. It was never for very long—I think a half hour or so was the max—but again, this had only been going on for a few weeks. We'd never seen them leave. They just walked through a door—usually the mudroom—and vanished.

Once they didn't know who Dick was. At all. They were in fourth grade, they were both wearing dresses for some reason, purple for him and orange for her (the future must have a more enlightened view of gender roles and clothing for same), they both thought I was the greatest thing since sling-backs, and they had no idea who their dad was. And not in a "Dad died last year, so sad" way.

A "we never knew our dad, Mom never talks about him and we've given up asking" way.

Once only the boy came. Sinclair and I were getting cozy while slugging down the dregs of a fantastic banana strawberry smoothie and while Marc made shooing motions with his hands—"Jeez, you have a room for that shit, go *away*"— and we were starting to make out solely to piss him off, groaning into each other's mouths and groping at each other with smoothie-sticky hands, we sensed something and turned.

Where no one had been sitting (Tina had mumbled something about tax season and abandoned her chair when the make-out session started), there was, suddenly, Jessica's son, about age ten.

He said nothing. He didn't even look at us. We kept asking where his sister was and he kept shaking his head while fat tears rolled down his cheeks. He didn't want food. Didn't want to talk. Ignored Marc's gentle coaxing and my increasingly worried questions and Sinclair's furrowed brow

(Perhaps it's best not to push, my love.)

and we were following him into the mudroom when he disappeared. It had been a thirty-second encounter that rattled the shit out of us. Sinclair, who had lost a twin to an ugly death, said what we were thinking: "My suggestion is we not mention this particular iteration to Jessica or Dick."

And we haven't.

"Now what's this?" Jessica said, gently turning her son's arm to get a better look at a long scrape, a red line standing out against his golden skin. What is it about the undersides of kids' chubby arms that makes you just want to devour them? "What happened, baby?"

"The cat we don't have yet scratched me," came the cheerful reply. "It was turr'ble."

"He cried," the girl added.

"I did not! But I need more cookies, Mommy; it makes me upset to talk about it."

"Oh, nice try," I said with pure admiration. "But you have no idea how heartless your mother—"

"*One* more, and that's it," Jessica warned.

"—can be in her ruthless determination to— What?" A chorus of yays.

"Dammit, Jess, you're poaching on my territory," I argued. "I'm the fun aunt who hands out cookies and you're the hard-ass mom who's no fun at all but they'll appreciate it when they get older while secretly loving me more!"

"*Two* cookies," Jessica said with total bitchy malicious intent, and beamed at the stereo cheers. I was marshaling my arguments ("No, *you* shut up!") when the twins slipped down from their stools and went into the mudroom to play with Fur and Burr. (That was another thing: they always knew who Fur and Burr were as well. A psycho-paranormal-ologist (if there was such a thing) would have a field day.

"And furthermore, as reigning Cool Aunt, it's my God-given right to ignore your fascist toddler rules in order to—"

"Betsy."

"Dammit!" They'd slipped away again, without us noticing again. Again! The only things in the mudroom were Fur and Burr, the washer and dryer, and two wrinkled newborns.

Until this started happening, the puppies had had the run of the mudroom, their own place to nap, play, and poop in the rare moments when there wasn't someone around to spend time with them. After an eternity of bitching, Sinclair had blocked off a portion of it for the Amazing Disappearing Reappearing Babies. Sometimes when the babies reappeared, Fur's and Burr's shrill yaps would alert the household.

"God, it's like living with tiny twin Batmans."

"Yes. Well. No one said being an honorary aunt would be easy." Jessica had picked up Thing One and I'd grabbed Thing Two, and now she turned to face me head-on. "We have to talk."

Shit.

THIRTY-THREE

I saw at once Marc and Tina knew what was up, because they sort of swooped in, grabbed babies and puppies, and swooped out, bound for parts unknown. I looked at my closest, dearest friend and raised my eyebrows.

"Like that, is it?"

"Like what?" Dick had just walked into the kitchen, home from work. He'd stopped long enough to lock his gun in one of the safes (his weird babies had forced extensive babyproofing pretty much immediately), but hadn't changed clothes: gray slacks, white dress shirt with a brown and blue tie, chocolate-colored jacket tailored to accommodate his swimmer's shoulders and nine-millimeter Glock. His hair—short, blond, military cut—was mussed (which was amazing, given the lack of length), and his blue eyes were slightly less exhausted than usual. He gave Jessica a kiss and settled on the stool beside her.

"Do people at the Cop Shop know we've got reporters sniffing around?" I asked, honestly curious.

"First of all, we prefer 'Pig Paddy.' Second," he continued, ignoring my gasp of horror (I had great respect for the police and would no sooner refer to the good people at 367 Grove Street as pigs as I'd pair flip-flops with a formal), "a couple of the guys asked me about it but I blew it off. None of the suits were worried enough about it to want to see me." *Yet* was unspoken. "And I'm glad to keep doing that until Tina and Sinclair figure out how to thwart the Antichrist—"

"And Betsy, too," Jessica said with touching, hilarious loyalty.

"You're adorable!" I cried. No one in the history of human events had better friends than I did. Especially when you considered what I put them through, consciously and otherwise. Borrowing clothes without asking didn't begin to cover it.

"—but it's a stopgap measure at best. If this outing-the-vamps thing gains any momentum, and Marc's pretty sure it will, we'll need a new plan. I'll have to explain that, yep, I live with vampires, they're definitely real—oh, did I not mention that?"

"You're right," I said, nodding.

"Which, uh." Dick coughed into his fist and darted a glance at Jessica. "Brings us to this."

"You're moving out."

"Wait, hear us out! It's not that we don't— Yes. That's the plan."

"As it should be. No, I'm serious." I rushed ahead in the face of their astonished expressions. "You're a family now; it's not just about the two of you."

"We're all a family. Everyone here." Jessica reached out blindly, found Dick's hand, squeezed. He squeezed back. "Better than any family I had growing up."

"Yes, but now you've got your weird babies to think about. It was one thing when there wasn't any media scrutiny. If the Big Bad of the week showed up here, he'd have to get past multiple vampires, a zombie, the occasional visiting werewolf, puppies that wouldn't hesitate to pee on them, and an armed cop before he'd even *see* the babies. But who knows what'll happen now? The reporters will be back. The looky-loos will follow. Heck, Marc chased a few of them away already today. We'll have to lock it down, deny everything, maybe even disappear a few people, God forbid, or . . ." I trailed off.

"Or?" Dick prompted.

I shook off my thought; now wasn't the time. "Or not. But either way, too many unknown varieties, y'know?"

"Variables. Yes." Jessica shifted on her stool. "I have to say, I thought you'd take this a little harder." She glanced at the Barnes and Noble bag she'd brought in with her, but made no move to touch it. "I thought there'd be threats and promises and at least one tantrum, and maybe bribery."

"Don't get me wrong, Jess. I don't want you to go. I want you and Dick and your weird babies to stay here forever. But like I said—and like you two *know*: it's not just about you. It's barely about me." *Wow*, that felt weird to say. "You've got to put your as-yet-unnamed babies ahead of everything else."

"That's very—"

"It's just I love you," I continued, while Dick made a funny coughing noise, the way tough guys do when they don't want you to know they're tearing up. "It'll be hard to see you go. We've been on-and-off roomies since we were . . . what, nineteen?"

"Twenty," she said, smiling. "Since the U bounced you just before the end of sophomore year."

"They really should warn people when they register:

if you set so much as *one* measly accidental fire while drunk, suddenly it's an expellable offense."

"The early signs of living with you being a terrible idea were all there," she replied, grinning. "But, alas, ignored."

Undeterred, I went on. "I love living with you. And it's handy having a cop around, I won't lie. I shouldn't have complained all those times about having all these room-mates. I'm sorry I did that."

"You never meant it. We always knew that."

"Yeah, I gathered, what with how none of you ever left despite the power of my bitchery. I don't want you guys to go, but the weird babies come first."

"You've *got* to stop calling them that."

"The minute they stop being weird, I will."

I meant it. All of it: the smart thing would be for them to get gone, and I'd be a terrible, selfish friend to try to prevent that. Frankly I was surprised it had taken them this long to figure it out.

But I couldn't help thinking about all her other weird babies, the kindergartners and the high schoolers and all the twins in between in all their delightful strange itera-tions (the Antichrist's word of the week was *taunting*; mine was *iterations*). They were never surprised to find them-selves in the mansion kitchen. They always knew where everything was. They always knew who we were. They always had thorough, intimate knowledge of the mansion and everything and everyone in it.

So I didn't think Jessica and Dick and the babies would be gone very long. Either something or someone would drive them back or eventually they'd feel safe enough to return on their own. *Please, God, let it be the latter.*

"Are you going to hire help?" I asked. "I mean, what about when your weird babies do that weird thing your weird babies do?"

Jess looked at me for a long moment without speaking,

and Dick wouldn't look at me at all. She opened her mouth to reply, when I figured it out. "You think they won't do that if they don't live here. With me."

Identical shrugs. "It's just a theory."

I wasn't sure how I felt about that. I couldn't blame Jess and Dick for craving normality, but I sort of loved the weird thing their weird babies did. However: not my call.

"Marc's promised to come by and help us while pretending he's not in it to experiment on our children."

"Aww. That's sweet. Do you have a place picked out?" Again they wouldn't look at me. "Oh. You do. You've had this in mind for a while. It's okay, I'm not mad." Hurt, crushed, despairing, but not mad. "I was wondering that it even took you this long to decide. But it didn't take you this long."

"It's just a little house in Stillwater. Not even half an hour from here."

Usually when a multimillionaire says something faux deprecating about his place, like "aw, it's just a cottage— a glorified shack, really," after the urge to kick him in the shins passes, you find out the glorified shack is a mansion on Woolsey Lane on Lake Minnetonka. But Jess was never a fan of flaunting the millions her parents had left her. The money represented the worst of childhoods, with a sexually abusive father and an enabling mother.

Until she'd bought the mansion for all of us to live in, she and I shared a two-bedroom condo in Apple Valley. In college she lived in a studio apartment that was just a little bigger than her mother's walk-in closet. She was one of those people who never buy a luxury car, because she didn't care about how her car looked, but how it ran. If it got her from point A to point B with a minimum of fuss, she didn't care if it was a covered wagon.

"White Pine Way," Jess continued, "four bedrooms."

Which made sense; the babies needed a room and she needed an office. I knew the area a bit. White Pine Way meant new construction, not quite as big or pricey as a McMansion. Compared to the mansion she was departing, it *was* a shack.

"When—"

"End of the week."

"Oh." *Too soon! I don't like change! Can't we ditch the babies and go get pedis? Remember when our biggest problem was our neighbor borrowing kitchen stuff and never bringing it back?*

"Well, that's great. Need help moving?"

"We've got it covered." That was Marc, who had doubtless listened at the door and, when he didn't hear shrieking or the *clang!* of me braining Dick with a frying pan, had come back in, with Tina and Sinclair behind them. Sinclair's brow was adorably furrowed and he was lugging an infant; Tina had apparently forced it on him, as she had her laptop in one hand and her phone in the other.

"Tina explained."

"Wait, Tina *and* Marc *and* you guys all knew before they—" I forced myself to stop. "Never mind, not about me, totally fine." If I kept saying it wasn't about me, I might eventually believe it.

"I am sorry you feel you must leave us, dear," he told her, then turned to Dick. "But we quite understand your reasons."

"Thanks," Dick said, returning Sinclair's handshake. "We're sorry to go, but under the circumstances . . ."

"Of course."

Are you hearing this, my own?

I don't like change, Sinclair!

I know it well.

"It's not completely terrible," Jessica said, smiling and handing me the B&N bag. Because a book totally makes up for my best friend having to leave me because her family was in danger. Blech.

"Thanks," I said automatically. "I'll read it right away, maybe."

"Open it, dumbass." This said in the kindest of tones, so I obeyed. To my surprise, there were no books. The edges I'd felt were shoe boxes. Two of them! "Two of them!"

"It could be a cruel trick," Marc offered. "The boxes could be full of travel guides."

"Don't you joke about that *ever*." I pulled both boxes out, plopped them on the counter, flipped the top off one, yowled in delight. "Manolo Blahnik 'Tayler' d'Orsay pumps! I wanted these so bad, but I couldn't decide between black and . . ." On a hunch I flipped the other lid. "Bone!" I was beyond yowling. All I could manage was thrilled gurgling. At nearly eight hundred bucks a pop, this was a pretty decent reverse housewarming gift. "Oh my God, thank you! Tina, I'm sorry! But cripes, bone *and* black!"

"Totally understandable, dread queen, think nothing of it." This with an admirably straight face.

"This doesn't mean I'm not sad about you leaving," I explained, and I was doing so from the floor, because I'd promptly sat and started releasing the shoes from their prisons of box and tissue paper, while also wrenching my socks off so I could yank the new shoes on my willing feet. If feet could feel emotions and be happy, mine were. "Because I am. But this makes it slightly—*slightly*—easier to— Damn, how great do these look?" I'd slipped them on and now stretched out my legs to admire them.

"I don't get it," Dick said. "They're black high heels. I'm glad you're glad, but they're black high heels. There's a million of them. You've got at least five pairs yourself."

"Oh, Dick, you adorable moron, if I have to explain then you'll never get it. And they're black *and* bone high heels." How to tell him they'd always look great, they'd go with almost everything, that I'd wear them all the time for that reason alone, but even better, I'd wear them because every time I saw them I would remember how much my friend loved me.

"That makes sense."

"Didn't realize that was out loud." I'd clambered back to my feet with a helpful yank from Marc. "Maybe if you guys get some peace and quiet in the new place you'll be able to think up names for the babies."

"We have. Almost forgot to mention it." Dick retrieved his son/daughter from a relieved-looking Sinclair. "Jess is filing the paperwork this week."

"Well?" What would it be? They'd ignored my helpful suggestions (Salt and Pepper, Pepsi and Coke, Rocky and Bullwinkle, Batman and Robin, Frick and Frack, Polar and Bipolar . . .) and swore they'd come to a decision soon.

"Oh, sorry." Dick had been smelling his baby's head, and who could blame him? When they weren't pooping, they smelled terrific (the same could be said of all of us in the mansion). "It's Elizabeth and Eric."

"That's nice." Ugh. At least it wasn't Maeve and Mable. Or Tommy and Teeny. Or James and Jenny.

"Not even you're this dim," Marc said. "Are you?"

"Hey, I've been given a buttload to process in less than a week, so why don't you— Oh." They named their weird babies after me! (And Sinclair.) "Ohhhhh."

"An honor," Sinclair said, smiling. "Truly. Thank you."

"Don't cry," Dick warned me. "I always cry when you do. And you cry a lot: when the Antichrist betrayed you, when Macy's didn't have anything 'cute' in your shoe size that time, when Marc killed himself, when we ran out of ice . . . I've bawled more in the last year than in the last ten."

"Shut up! 'Mnot crying," I sniffled. "Allergies." That ought to fool him. "And—and I'm honored, too." I leaned over and hugged Jessica. I didn't even mind the spit-up on her shoulder.

"Who else would we name them after?" she replied,

squeezing back. "Dick and I never would have met if you hadn't become a vampire, and you wouldn't be here if you hadn't married Sinclair."

"Now that I think about it, yeah! Who else? Why'd it take you so long? It's brilliant and it makes perfect sense."

Marc shook his head over Tina's laughter. "I swear, your ego is made of Silly Putty. You have setbacks, but you always bounce back."

As a philosophy, it left a bit to be desired. But as a go-to attitude, it suited me pretty well. Betsy the Vampire Queen, Ruler of Hell and the Undead, with the footgear of a fashion goddess and an ego of Silly Putty.

Nah. Needed work.

CHAPTER
THIRTY-FOUR

"There's a werewolf on the phone for you." Marc was holding the phone out to me and literally dancing in place. "He sounds gorgeous!"

I, lounging in the TV parlor (second floor, almost directly above the Peach Parlor), was unimpressed. "Any particular werewolf, or just a random werewolf?"

"Michael Wyndham."

Ah. The big boss. I trudged to the phone, about as thrilled to have this conversation as I was to have the Sex Talk with my mom when I was in fifth grade. ("Wait, he puts his what *where*? What is wrong with you? What's wrong with every adult everywhere?") *Tell Sinclair,* I mouthed at Marc, then remembered I had a telepathic link. *Never mind.*

"Hi, Michael."

"Betsy." I knew that warm, deep voice. Michael Wyndham, Pack leader. "I've been watching some fascinating YouTube videos lately. And press coverage."

"Nothing better to do on Cape Cod in wintertime, huh?"

Oh, dear. Elizabeth, it would be lovely to keep the Wyndham werewolves on our side.

Oh, please. He likes when I give him shit.

I know how he feels.

"Yeah, yeah, you're hilarious. Anything you think I should know?"

"It's family business. I'll tell you if you really want me to. But it's a long story and I come off like a clueless asshat."

A muffled laugh. "I'd be grateful if you would. I suspect you're doing what you're best at: being too hard on yourself."

Spotting knockoffs at twenty paces was what I was best at, but I appreciated the sentiment. Man, if I hadn't met Sinclair first . . . Michael had the looks to go with the voice. And the voice was great. Like, podcast great. Guy sounded like verbal velvet. And he had golden eyes. Golden! Eyes!

"Okay, here it is. My sister, the Antichrist, is super pissed at me for not helping her prove to the world that the Christian God, and Hell, exists, thus (she expects) inspiring all non-Christians to instantly convert. So to get back at me she's trying to expose vampires to the world."

Silence, broken by, "That was a remarkably short story, actually. Er, do you require our assistance?"

Careful.

Duh. He's not offering to help, just wondering if we want it. It'll help him decide how much of a mess we're in out here. What he really wants to know is how this affects his Pack: If vampires are outed, can werewolves be far behind? Will we protect them, keep quiet about their existence? Or out them to get the pressure off?

They've already been through this with the Undersea Folk; it's understandable that they're wary about another world-shaking hidden species revelation.

Yeah, no shit.

Tell him he and his are welcome to visit, as always, but we require no assistance at this time.

Oooh, tricky. "Everything's totes fine here; we don't care if you come or not." *Playing it cooool.*

"We're fine, Michael." I studied my nails. Sounding unconcerned was easier for me if I looked unconcerned, even if the other guy couldn't see me. "Don't get me wrong, you guys are welcome anytime; I'd love to see what Jeannie's up to." Michael's mate was human and, like Tallahassee in *Zombieland*, set the standard for "not to be fucked with." She'd also helped me pick out my wedding gown a couple of years ago, and her children were terrifying in a wonderful way. "And your awesome, scary children, too."

He laughed again, sounding much less tense. "Perhaps we will. But if all is well on your end—"

"We've got it under control." Translation: I don't meddle in your business, how about you keep out of mine? "But if you change your mind, come on out."

"I will. Thanks very much for your time; I imagine you're pretty busy."

"Well, if it's not one thing, it's another." By now Sinclair had come from his office and was standing next to me after giving Marc a gentle push away to prevent the man's blatant eavesdropping. A pouting Marc was not a pretty sight. "Say hi to Jeannie and the kids for me."

"I will. Pass my regards to Sinclair and the others."

"I will. 'Bye."

Click. Well, not really, not with these modern phones. I missed the satisfaction of hanging up. Pressing the end call button wasn't nearly as satisfying.

"He's coming."

"Oh yeah." I nodded. "Definitely."

"What?" Marc came out of his pout long enough to add, "From what I could tell, you set his mind at ease and he's *not* coming."

"A visit's pretty inevitable. It's just, now he won't leave *today*. They'll watch from Massachusetts and show up, what? Within the next week or two?"

Sinclair nodded.

"Right. So that's our deadline. That's how long we've got to get this shit under control."

"Piece of cake, right?" Marc looked from Sinclair to me and back to Sinclair. "Right? You guys are making a plan?"

Not really. But there was nothing sadder than a depressed zombie. So we lied.

CHAPTER
THIRTY-FIVE

Later, Marc shooed the reporters away again. It took a few minutes because one lingered and they chatted on the lawn for a bit—what was *that* about?—until the sun was down far enough that it was too dark and too cold to comfortably continue.

Marc had been worried about going outside to deal with reporters, but after giving it some thought he changed his mind. As he put it, "No one outside the six of us knew I died, so there wasn't a death certificate or a funeral. And it's winter—lots of people feel chilly, not just mobile dead guys. And maybe they should see a friendly face—sort of, 'Look, it's not my call, but c'mon, how about you get out of our yard, sorry to be a hard-ass, my boss is a real meanie' . . . like that."

"I object to 'real meanie,'" I objected.

"It's like good cop/bad cop, when everyone else in the

house is the bad cop. So, like, there's a platoon of bad cops behind me, but I'm friendly and helpful."

"You sure seemed friendly and helpful out on the lawn. And why are you limping?"

"I'm getting to it, just give me a—"

"What were you talking to that guy about? Besides the fact that you definitely live with vampires?"

"John Cusack."

?????????

"Betsy? Did you hear me?"

"I heard you. It just took me a couple of seconds."

"His name's Will Mason and he runs the G-Spot."

"So much more than I needed to know."

"Grow up. It's the name of his website. He started out as a ghost chaser but now he covers all kinds of paranormal weirdness in the Twin Cities."

"That should keep him busy." People didn't normally associate Minneapolis–St. Paul with lots o' paranormal weirdness. But even if you didn't know vamps and weres were a thing, there were lots of people who claimed they'd seen ghosts. When I was alive I blew it off; after death, I rearranged my perceptions. A famous local French restaurant, Forepaugh's, was known as much for its killer desserts (deconstructed banana cream pie, drooool) as for the ghost who haunted it: the spirit of a maid who'd fallen for the boss, slept with him, discovered she was pregnant, and jumped out the third-story window after he broke off the affair. Management was weirdly proud that that poor sad ghost hung around the place drooping in despair, but again: deconstructed banana cream pie.

Heck, a house on this very street, Summit Avenue, was famous for being haunted: the Griggs Mansion boasted the ghosts of a maid, a gardener, a Civil War general, and a random teenager, among others (weird how a place always seems to be mostly haunted by the servants, never the rich people). The maid, like the poor girl from Forepaugh's, threw herself out a fourth-story window after a bad breakup. Warning: if you're a servant prior to 1950 and you throw yourself out the boss's window, you're apparently doomed to live in that house forevermore.

All that to say, the blogger in question—Will?—had plenty to keep him busy even if vampires weren't real.

"This led to John Cusack how?"

"Well, we got to talking about the movie *Better Off Dead*, which as you'll recall is the greatest movie of that decade, which got us talking about *One Crazy Summer*, which inevitably led to *Say Anything*, and then—"

"Well, thanks for playing good cop."

"I did more than play. One of the news vans almost clipped him when they drove off, but I—"

"Good, that's great, thanks." A window of opportunity! No reporters, Sinclair was probably ready for a break, it was relatively quiet around here for a change. I couldn't let this chance go. I had an inkling of what to do about my Father Markus problem, but I needed more info first. "Sorry, Marc, I gotta do something. Tell me more about it when I get back."

"You realize whenever you say something like that, it ends up being really important la—"

"Sinclair?" *Want to take the puppies for a walk?*

Sinclair, who'd been holed up with Tina for the last hour, answered at once. *Oh yes! You must wish to get out of here as much as I.*

Who knows when we'll have another chance? Time to carpe the diem, pal.

You know I go weak in the knees when you butcher Latin.

Please. You go weak in the knees when I change my socks.

In next to no time we were being led by the leashed furballs. It was unseasonably warm for late winter—thirties—

and the full moon shone down on us so brightly we almost didn't need streetlights. Well, with our vamp-o-vision we *didn't* need streetlights, but you know what I mean.

"So tell me about your friend Lawrence. We had that dumb fight before I got a chance to ask. How'd you two even meet?"

Sinclair brightened and I felt his pleased surprise
(????????)
as he began to talk. I paid attention to what he said, and what he didn't say. I was getting used to having an agenda below my agenda and was a little worried that it didn't bother me the way it would have five years ago. Even two years ago.

That didn't stop me from pumping Sinclair for every scrap of info about his friend, though. The price of power, I guess. If things went the way I hoped, there could be a happy ending of sorts. If I was wrong, or my plan backfired, I likely wouldn't be around to worry about the fallout.

That shouldn't have been a comforting thought.

CHAPTER
THIRTY-SIX

"There's a mermaid on the phone for you."

"Oh, there is not," I said, freshly irritated. I'd just about decided what steps to take to fix my Hell problem where both Father Markus and my husband were concerned, and I wasn't keen to start. It was one of those things where you don't want to be right and, if you *are* right, you don't want to have to take the next step. I couldn't tell if my reluctance to proceed was sensible caution or just another manifestation of my chronic procrastination. Worse, I'd have to move soon, especially before Tina and Sinclair put their awful plan into action. And that was a whole *other* thing: their awful plan.

Marc was holding the phone out. I knew he wanted to distract me—Jessica, Dick, and the babies had moved out that morning. The fact that they had to drive their moving van past several reporters camped on our sidewalk just pissed me off all over again. And Marc's new friend—Bill or Bob or whatever—the G-Spot guy, he was always the last to leave. I hoped it was for the reason I suspected, and not for the reason I feared.

He added, like it would having meaning to me, "It's a Dr. Bimm? From Boston?"

"Nope. Take a message."

"Says she's the queen of the mermaids? Or something—yes? Ow." Marc jerked the phone away from his ear, but even without vampire hearing I could hear the tinny shouts. "You should definitely take this," he added, holding the phone out to me as if offering a dead rattlesnake. "She may come up here just to kill me if you don't." More squeaking from the phone. Marc's hand started to tremble. "Jesus. She's seriously scary."

"You're a terrible gate," I told my terrible gate, snatching the phone. "Yeah? Hello?"

"Hello again, Betsy."

"Hi. What's up?"

"You're asking me? Apparently you're being outed, if the YouTube stuff my intern made me watch is any indication."

"And you care because . . . ?"

"Excellent question. Because I have firsthand knowledge of how intensely annoying you are." Dr. Bimm's tone was cool, with just the slightest trace of a Boston accent. She wasn't quite dropping her *r*'s, but only just. "Nevertheless, this isn't about you and me as individuals, it's about my people and yours. Society's already endured finding out about the Undersea Folk, and I thought you might want some advice on how to handle the sudden, unwelcome intrusion of fame."

"Who is this again?"

"Fredrika Bimm. Formerly of the New England Aquarium, currently on the phone with an idiot. You came to Boston at my intern's request, and we foiled a stereotypically evil supervillain's plot to destroy every merperson on the planet. Then you insisted we go out for smoothies, which put the surreal cherry atop the surreal sundae that was that night."

"None of this sounds right." Well, maybe that last part. The aquarium thing, though, that was ringing a faint bell. But for all I knew this was a reporter on a fishing expedition. Like those scammers who call and check your identity by making you tell them your account numbers and social security number. Like I'd fall for *that* again. "I think you've got the wrong gal."

I heard a faint creak and realized she was tightening her grip on her phone. "Are you serious?"

"Look, lady, I don't know who you are—"

"I have told you three times!"

"—but obviously you need a hobby if you've got nothing better to do than prank call and— Hey." Sinclair, doubtless prodded by Marc, had come into the kitchen.

"Hey, *what?*"

"Not hey you, hey my husband." I put my hand over the phone. "Someone named Ricky Binn says we helped her foil evil and then went out for smoothies."

Faintly, from the phone: "I cannot believe this shit!"

Sinclair smirked. "Yes, darling, we did. Our august presence was requested by a young woman who was the adopted daughter of one of our subjects. We joined Dr. Bimm in Boston, where we discovered a diabolical plot to exterminate life in the sea, which we promptly foiled, then we celebrated with smoothies and later by making love in a suite at the Marriott Long Wharf."[19]

"Oh, the suite sex! Right." Into the phone: "You should

---

[19] Spoiler alert: it's true! *Undead and Underwater.*

have just said 'suite sex,' I would have gotten it right away. So, Fred, nice to hear from you, kind of. What d'you want?"

Nothing but a low grinding—were those her teeth? Then the disgruntled response: "Jesus Christ."

"Oh, come on. Just having a little fun. The yuk-yuks have been pretty thin this month."

"No doubt. Is it true? Is your sister trying to expose your people?"

"Yes. It's her childish way of expressing her displeasure with pretty much everything I've ever said and done. You know how it is with little sisters."

"Thankfully, no." Her tone was getting less frosty, though it hadn't quite crossed over into warm and friendly. "Would you like some help? Or advice?"

"No to the former, yes to the latter."

"I'm impressed. I was sure you'd get those mixed up. Here's my advice: no matter what you do or say, some people will always assume you're lying and some will always assume you're telling the complete unvarnished truth. The trick is getting the ones in the middle to come around to your way of thinking."

"Uh-huh. And how do I make that happen?"

"Well, that depends," the mermaid replied, "on what your way of thinking is going to be."

I thought about that while Sinclair was whispering and gesturing, giving Marc the CliffsNotes version of our adventures in Boston last fall.

"Is this one of those things that seems like lame advice at the time, but later turns out to be perfect, dead-on advice?"

"That's up to you, too."

"Ugh. Got anything that isn't a platitude?"

"Yes: your shoes are ugly."

I gasped, horrified, then remembered. "Ha! Joke's on you, Bimm, you can't see me! I'm barefoot, so suck on *that*."

"God help every vampire everywhere," was the rejoinder, and then the grouchiest mermaid in the history of mermaids hung up on me. Not a moment too soon, either, because Marc was all over me.

"I can't believe you met a goddamned mermaid and didn't tell me!"

"Hey, there was a lot going on that week. Most likely."

Sinclair chuckled. "Oh, my own, tell him the real reason you've repressed conscious knowledge of Dr. Bimm and the ways of her people."

"No." I pouted.

"As you like." My traitorous husband turned to Marc. "The good doctor is, ah, volatile. And my beloved is flippant and easily distracted. At times," he added, like that made it better. "Dr. Bimm despaired of keeping her attention, so she seized an issue of *Time* and struck the queen."

Marc's mouth popped open. "She hit you?"

I nodded. "With a rolled-up magazine." I could still feel the sting. "On my nose."

"Like a dog?" I couldn't tell if he was thrilled or horrified.

"Exactly like a dog," I confirmed. "I was so flabbergasted I forgot to beat her to death."

"Dr. Bimm," Sinclair said, already headed back to his office where Operation Terrible Plan was being ironed out, "does not suffer fools gladly."

"Got that right," I muttered, and when Marc started laughing and didn't stop, I grabbed a coupon insert and smacked him on the nose. He shrieked and hit me back, and I ended up chasing a zombie all over our mansion the day my best friend moved away to guarantee her family's safety. So, a mixed day.

CHAPTER
THIRTY-SEVEN

"Dread queen, Tina and I have come up with a plan to stop the Antichrist, punish your father, and discredit the reporters covering this story. We'll need to put it into practice at once. With a little luck—which you have always brought me—this entire episode will be a thing of the past a week from now."

It was later that same day, the end of a bad week and a stressful month. And it was finally time to get down to it. We were in Sinclair's office, just down the hall from our bedroom. I'd been waiting for them forever, seemed like. There was only so much research I could lose myself in. And if my DVR got any more stuffed with shows I didn't have time to watch, it'd explode all over the TV parlor.

"Yeah, I know. Been waiting for you to bring it to me."

"Ah. Very good." They were both in their casual Friday business suits: a deep rose for Tina, black for Sinclair. No shoes: Tina was wearing black stockings, and Sinclair had black dress socks. Me? Deep brown leggings, red hip-length sweater, slouchy red and white socks. Because I (a) knew how to dress for lounging about the house, and (b) wasn't stuck in the past. I loved Sinclair and Tina, but sometimes they acted every year of their great age. Case in point: their awful plan. "Shall we walk you through it?"

"Nope. You're going to tell vampires all over the city, state, and country to snatch the reporters covering this story, work vamp mojo on them, and get them to either retract everything or 'discover' the whole thing was a hoax. You'll discredit Laura by revealing she's the Antichrist, arrange for my dad to take a long swim in the Mississippi with lead Uggs, and then stomp every inquiry into all that you did, until people have forgotten or lost interest or are too scared to poke around anymore. And all for the greater good. Right?"

They both gaped at me. Finally Sinclair cleared his throat. "Well, it's a bit more complicated than—"

"And we're not doing it. Not any of it."

"Wait—you knew?" Tina asked me, surprised.

"I guessed. C'mon, we've been hanging out for how long? I know how you both think. You're traditionalists. You still send letters snail mail, for heaven's sake. So you were going to come up with a traditional vampire solution to an old problem: Stomp the messengers. Kill the message. Sow enough fear and confusion to keep working under everyone's sightline. Then wait for things to get back to normal. And why not? Time's on our side." I paused then added, very gently, "That won't work this time. We're not doing that this time."

Tina was shaking her head. "Majesty . . . forgive me . . . but then why wait for us to decide on a course of action?"

"Because I was hoping you'd come up with something better," I replied bluntly. "You're both smarter than I am; it wasn't an unreasonable thought. Maybe you'd have a plan B that wasn't quite so Gestapo-esque that we could have gone with. But you don't. Right?"

A sharp inhale from Sinclair, which was a pretty good indication of his shock, since he didn't have to breathe. He'd lost friends, good friends, in World War II. He had so much contempt for Hitler you'd think the guy was still around causing trouble. "Do not—"

"I said Gestapo-esque," I continued, "because that's what these strong-arm tactics are. It's Nazi bullshit. Raping the brains of reporters because we don't like what they're writing?"

"If we don't, there will be no way to calculate the danger, or the damage to us."

"Except we're always in danger. It's always something. When our default is hurting people for doing their job, we deserve to be exposed."

"My own, your compassion is laudable." Sinclair was trying not to look *and* sound distressed, and failing. "But this isn't just about the danger we personally face. We have to think about what's best for the vampire nation, not just ourselves."

"Yeah, yeah, it's not just about me, there's a bigger picture to consider—apparently that's the theme this week. But c'mon. Kidnapping, scaring people? Setting a horde of vampires on the media, for God's sake? Why not just host a book burning and get it over with?" I could feel my voice rising with my temper, and forced calm. "We're better than that. The vampire nation is (as of now) better than that."

"So . . . what, then? What?"

"Well, like I was saying, I was waiting to see if you'd come up with something besides Operation Media Rape. Since you didn't—which is nothing to be ashamed of— we're going with my plan."

"Which is . . . ?"

I took a deep breath and told them.

It didn't go well.

THIRTY-EIGHT

FROM THE PRIVATE BLOG OF WILL MASON
The G-Spot
February 27

The most incredible thing. Hard to even think about, much less write down. This won't go on the website. This is something else, something for me.

Not to get too doleful, but the Freak might have found someone. Or would Marc be some*thing?* I don't know. He's not human; he can't be. But he's *real.*

He's wonderful.

Okay. The beginning: heading over to Summit, checking out the vampire thing. That gorgeous girl in all the YouTube videos from the last couple of weeks. She's on camera naming names, giving out addresses, saying the craziest shit while sounding sane and looking earnest as hell, and backed up by people who don't seem crazy, either.

I mean—these guys are getting affidavits. They're basically swearing on a Bible that what they saw was real, that vampires are real . . . it was worth checking out. Unlike most of the media, I knew there were plenty of things out in the world we didn't understand. Unlike most of the media, I wasn't at the supposed Vampire HQ because the YouTube girl was slim and blond and had wonderful boobs. I actually listened to what she had to say. And it was fascinating . . . if she was telling the truth.

I kind of forgot about her when I saw *him*. This was the next day, after the so-called vampire queen shooed us away like we were a flock of unruly chickens. Which wasn't far off, come to think of it. She hadn't seemed like the terrifying soulless dark queen of the undead described on YouTube. For one thing, she had highlights. For another, she seemed genuinely exasperated to find a bunch of reporters camped in her yard. And finally, she seemed as interested in her shoes as she was in getting rid of us.

Anyway, next time *he* came out.

God, how to describe? Taller than me by a couple of inches. Super-short black hair and the most wonderful green eyes, bright and piercing. He was probably wearing clothing; I couldn't get past his face. And he was super nice, politely but firmly telling us to fuck off. I was alternately embarrassed to be there and thrilled I'd come.

Then, the best thing, the most perfect thing, he makes a *Better Off Dead* reference. A couple of the guys there were from the *Strib* and the *Press*, so he mutters, "Four weeks, twenty papers, that's two dollars. *Plus tip!*"

When opportunity isn't just knocking but kicking my door in, I go with it. I walked right up to him and introduced myself with, "I want my two dollars!"

He grinned—God! What a smile! I said my name, first

and last, and he gave me his, just the first. Then we traded lines from the movie back and forth, and then he did a sublime impersonation of Bobcat Goldthwait, and that led us to *Say Anything* (we both agreed Cusack must have had some wondrous upper-body strength to hold up a boom box so long; impressive for a skinny guy), and before I knew it we were talking. Just talking.

He's so beautiful.

But then it was like he remembered this was business and not pleasure and sort of walked me off the lawn. I didn't care, I couldn't look away from those green eyes. I was babbling something—I don't remember what—and walking backward, and then those eyes got big and startled and he lurched forward and shoved and I went flying. And I just lay there looking up at the sky and thinking, *I knew it was too good to be true. My own fault. My own fault; how often have my sources told me I'm alone?*

And then I sat up. And I saw what Marc had done. He'd shoved me out of the way of one of the news vans. The driver, in the deepening gloom, hadn't seen me walking. (I'd been walking backward, so I couldn't really call the guy on his carelessness.)

He didn't just save me from a nasty accident. He had the nasty accident instead. I could actually see the bulge in his jeans (not like *that*, unfortunately) from the broken bone, halfway between his knee and his ankle. In the winter gloom the blood trickling through the denim looked black.

I babbled something ("Oh my God I'm so sorry are you okay I'll call an ambulance no wait I'll drive you to the ER I'm so sorry thank you thank you for saving me please let me help you oh your leg your poor leg"), and he was all "No big, I'll be fine," stands up *on his broken leg* and starts limping back to the house. Just a sprain, he says. (Gorgeous, but thinks I'm an idiot.)

"I'm coming back!" I said, grabbing at his arm. I'd been frozen, staring at him as he limped out of my life, and finally woke up enough to run after him. I caught his arm and helped him up the steps. "I'm coming back," I said again, quieter.

He was all stiff, not friendly anymore, no trace of that smile. "Don't. It's fine. Don't."

"Not about *that*," I said, waving at the mansion to indicate my sudden lack of interest in Vampiregate. Who gave a shit about vampires when *this* enticing mystery was in the same house? "I want to see you. Check on you, I mean." That sounded casual, right? "You saved me. Of course I'll come back."

"Don't," he said again, but he gave me a long look before he got the seriously heavy door open and limped inside, out of my life.

"I'll come back," I said, and it's true. It's the truest thing I've ever said in twenty-seven years.

CHAPTER
THIRTY-NINE

"I think it's time you went to Hell," I told the king of the vampires.

"Ah, darling. Is it over between us already?"

"Very funny. Just for a visit, like last time. I've got no plans for you to be there forever, any more than I plan to be there forever."

Sinclair was trying his damnedest not to look over the moon, and failing. Adorable! "As you will, my own."

"Marc, Tina, I'd like you to come, too." I've said it before and I'll say it again: everyone liking smoothies was so *handy*. We were almost always in the kitchen. Super easy to have meetings. Not like Hell, where everything was scheduled and when I wasn't pissed I was bored and when I wasn't bored I was overwhelmed. Tempting to just dump it all on Father Markus.

Yeah, right. Just a daydream. And a dangerous one.

"Of course, Majesty."

"Sure!"

"Not right this second," I added, looking at my phone, "because apparently my mom's on her way."

"Dr. Taylor is coming? Oh, dear . . ." Tina hopped off her stool and checked the fridge. She knew my mom liked a nice glass of Chardonnay now and again, and she tried to keep some on hand for the rare pop-in. "Ah! Still here."

"And I need to talk to Laura."

"Ugh," Marc said, accurately summing up everyone's feelings. "Why? Is it a ruse to get her here so you can punch her in the teeth?"

"It's a ruse to get her here so I can explain to her exactly what she's done." I grinned, and Marc flinched. "In great and terrible detail."

"Cripes, don't *look* like that."

"Like what?"

He shivered all over like Fur or Burr when Sinclair grabbed the Handi-Vac to suck up errant dog hair. "Like you could kill someone for looking at you crooked and never lose sleep over it."

"It's just to talk," I assured him.

"You think she'll come when you call, my own?"

"Sure. She feels safe—we can't disappear her."

"Not just yet," was the silky reply.

I frowned at him. "Quit it. She'll come because she'll hope to see me scared. She wants that. She wants me desperate to protect myself, desperate to keep all of you from being exposed. She's hoping I'll be sorry. She'll think I'll apologize. Trust me: she'll come running."

"Accurate assessment," Tina said at the same moment Marc added, "Depressing."

Tina and Sinclair turned their heads and I heard it, too: a car pulling around the back.

"It's like living with dogs. Blood-ravenous talking dogs," Marc bitched.

We jeered at him and I topped off his triple berry smoothie (why did we use blackberries? they were all seed!) just as my mom came in the mudroom door, exclaimed over Fur and Burr, knocked politely, and stepped into the kitchen.

"Hello, all, can the puppies come in, too?"

"Sure, Mom. Hi."

She crossed the room, shrugged out of her coat, and gave me a quick hug. Sinclair was on his feet at once, taking her coat, and she gave Marc a kiss. I looked her over; much as I hated to admit it, dating was doing her good. Weird to think of your mom dating. Weirder when your mom was *old* and dating. Weirdest that dating probably meant fucking. Annnnd time to scour that thought out of my brain . . . someone needed to invent a good brain bleach that did the job but wasn't toxic . . . permanent damage would be okay as long as it was localized.

The puppies, while excited to find themselves back in the kitchen, frisked around for a few seconds and then darted back to the mudroom. Not like them, but it certainly made things quieter. And less slobbery.

"Dr. Taylor," Tina said in a tone of great respect, "how pleased we are to see you. Would you like a glass of Chardonnay?"

"Yes, and you stop that," she scolded, "how many times do we go through this? I'm not the Queen Mum."

"Um . . . technically you are." When all I got for that was a distracted smile, I knew this wasn't a social call or, worse, the "soon you'll have a new daddy!" talk. "Time to be resigned, Mom. Heaven knows I am."

She accepted a glass from Tina and looked me over. She had always looked young for her age, despite the white hair (she'd had it since her senior year in high school), and her blue eyes were bracketed by fine laugh lines. She was dressed in Professor Casual: tweed skirt, brown tights, sensible brown shoes (despite my years of effort, she selected footgear for comfort, not style), cream-colored turtleneck, cream-and-brown cardigan. She taught at the U of M, her specialty was the Civil War, and she thought Tina was wonderful. ("What was Lincoln *really* like?")

She sipped her wine and zeroed in on me with a focus that was one of my earliest childhood memories. Nothing stood in my mother's way if she perceived an injustice to a loved one, however slight. It was why she was so stubborn about hanging on to her married name. It was why she'd fought my dad for so long before, during, and after the divorce: because "we have our daughter to think about, you cheating, creepy son of a bitch."

"I've come," she said, shaking her head at Tina's proffered plate of hors d'oeuvres (who at once dropped her gaze and took a step back, and how long have we had Havarti with dill? Sometimes I miss cheese), "to plead for the life of your idiot father."

Marc broke the short silence with an uncertain "Should we step out?" It was a mark of his respect for my mom that he didn't assume he'd be staying.

"There's no need," I said quickly. "Mom, I won't kill him."

Her shoulders relaxed. "No? Because you must know your sister wouldn't have been able to start this nonsense without his help. If nothing else, he must have financed it."

"Half sister. And you're forgetting her legions of dorks. They do anything she says. If she'd said, 'Can you float me a few hundred grand to finance a campaign to expose vampires to the world?' they'd have sprinted to the bank. No, Laura's choices are on her, and Dad's are on him, and I'm not going to kill either one of them for it."

Unless they force my hand. Unless they push me to it. Unless it's in self-defense of me or mine.

Agreed. How I cherish you, my queen. Even when you're good, you're somewhat bad.

We haven't had sex in way too long.
Hours. I agree.

"Oh. Well." She managed a smile. "I had all my argu-ments marshaled. Now I don't need them."

"All?" I teased.

"Well, one." She took my hand in hers, the only part of her that showed her age. Wrinkled and softened and cher-ished, those hands had touched me with love my entire life.

So many childhood memories centered around me being small and looking up as she extended a hand: to help me up, to bring me to a library or a museum, to show me the garden, to bring me to the banks of what looked like an ordinary river but was the site of Custer's last stand (Little Bighorn was a surprisingly peaceful spot), to clean her shot-gun at the beginning and end of every hunting season. (There were several dead ducks and geese who likely hadn't thought her hands were soft *or* cherished, but it's a duck-eat-duck world out there.) "I would have wanted you to spare him to spare *yourself*. You don't need patricide on your conscience. As someone with a less-than-loving father," she added dryly, "I understand the urge. Believe me."

I snorted. She was right; my maternal grandfather was the worst. How he'd produced a thoughtful, intelligent woman who would no sooner strike a child than she'd torch a Civil War museum was the mystery of my childhood. That, and how my dad could have preferred the Ant to her.

"Where's BabyJon?" Marc asked, correctly gauging that the tricky part of the conversation was over.

"He's with my—"

"Don't say it," I muttered. "Bad enough he can't visit for a while; knowing your boyfriend is baby-sitting my half brother/son just adds to the weird."

"Betsy called a few days ago and explained what was hap-pening. We agreed I should keep BabyJon for a bit longer."

"Prudent," Sinclair said with an approving nod.

"And awful."

"It's not your fault." That was Marc, loyal to a fault when he wasn't bitching.

"Except it is." I was missing his childhood. I was his legal guardian, but lately my mother had been more of a parent to him than I was. That was going to change. It had to. This was the only child I'd ever have.

But first things first. "Stay for supper?" I asked. "Soup and smoothies for everyone."

She laughed. "Of course. But aren't you going to ask about Jessica? She and Dick and the lovely babies had me over last night. Her new place is charming."

"Yeah, I know." I'd been invited, too, but couldn't risk any reporters following me to her new place. Now that I knew the course of action we were going to take in response to Laura's spiteful plan, I was doubly glad she and Dick were clear of it. It was going to get a lot worse before it got better. "Tell us all about it."

So she did. And for a while, it was like we were a normal family with ordinary problems. It was as nice as it was strange.

CHAPTER
FORTY

FROM THE PRIVATE BLOG OF WILL MASON
The G-Spot
February 28

I went back! And nobody killed me! And I'm going back tomorrow!

From the beginning. I couldn't sleep that night, thinking about the man who'd saved me. Not a human, not a vampire, not a ghost. What, then? What was most amazing: I didn't care. Well, I cared, but not as much as you'd think; I didn't want to classify him, I just wanted *him*. In my bed or just talking about movies, grocery shopping, or having coffee, whatever he wanted to give me, that was what I wanted to take.

But I had to be careful. I had to convince him I wasn't

after a story. And that was the tricky part. Because he didn't know what I was, either.

I'd been watching the mansion like a pathetic stalker when a car pulled in and drove around the back. I followed (no security system? odd) and saw a smart-looking older woman climb out and walk up to the door. She let herself in (key? or unlocked?) and after a minute I did, too.

Dark, except for the strip of light beneath a door at the far end of the room. It smelled like laundry, mud, and wet dog. I could faintly hear a conversation, took a step forward . . . and stopped.

Growls that managed to be shrill and menacing (and short; the dogs sounded big but couldn't have been very tall) came from nowhere, so I froze in place for a bit. After a long moment (a minute? an hour?), I took a cautious step toward the crack of light. Nothing. Another step. Nothing. Four more steps: growls.

It went on like that for a while. The dogs hiding in the dark would warn me, then get used to me and let me move forward, then warn me again. I couldn't ask about them; none of my sources were here. They were letting me approach . . . but on their timetable.

Subjectively I was in that room for a day and a half. (Later I found out it had been just over an hour.) I also found out that the old lady had come to ask Betsy not to kill her dad. But Betsy the so-called vampire queen had no interest in killing her dad, or her sister, even. Given that her sister was busy either exposing her or telling horrendous lies about her, that was a pretty decent reaction.

So, already worth the trip. They wouldn't kill me for overhearing that someone *wouldn't* kill their family, right? Someone who valued life so much he'd save a stranger wouldn't allow that.

Right?

After a while I realized the old lady was going to leave the way she came in. I realized this when she opened the door in her coat with her car keys in her hand. Before I could calm her down ("I'm not here to steal!") or explain ("I have a crush on the guy with the broken leg whose last name I don't know.") she was on me. She grabbed me by my ear (who *does* that?) and hauled me into the next room, which I discovered, as I blinked painfully to adjust to the light, was the kitchen.

"No wonder the dogs didn't want to stay in here," was the first comment.

"We can kill him, right? Breaking and entering?"

"It's just entering!" I said. Okay, squealed. "Please, I just want to see him— Ow-ow-ow!"

"See *who*?" This from the so-called vampire queen.

"Me." Marc sighed. Then: "Uh, it *is* me, right?"

"You know this man, Marc?" The old lady released the pincher grip on my ear and I groaned in relief and rubbed rubbed rubbed. Who knew something so far above my waist was so susceptible to pain?

"He's one of the reporters we keep sending on their way." This from Eric Sinclair, the husband/vampire king. His deep silky voice was terrifying. So were his height and build—he looked solid, like he worked out, and was almost a head taller than me. He had perfected the art of long-distance looming; he wasn't even close to me and I still felt crowded. His face was pale. His eyes burned. "And yes, we are well within our legal rights to kill him on sight."

"You won't, though." I coughed and tried again. *Less squeak this time, Will.* "You don't need that kind of pub-licity."

"If no one knows you were here, no one will know this was where your trail went cold." This in a voice so matter-of-fact it was terrifying. People had said "I guess I'll have fries" with more emotion.

"Knock it off, sir." Yes, hardly any squeak that time.

"If she won't kill her dad for helping her sister betray her, she's not going to let you kill a random blogger."

"Good heavens, how long were you in there?" The old lady's fingers twitched and I shied away from her.

"Not the ear again!" I shouted, then tried to calm down. My ear felt puffy and hot and I was sure it was swelling. *Please let Marc think cauliflower ear is sexy.* "Look, you've nothing to fear from me."

"Yes." This from Mr. Sinclair, who was smiling at me in a way I didn't like at all. Any other time, someone built like that giving me his full attention would be heady. Not now, though. It was just frightening. "That's true."

"Not because I'm an insignificant bug compared to a vampire king. I'm not here to write about you, any of you." I rubbed my ear and glared at the old lady. "Well, maybe you, ma'am."

"Try it, boy," she snapped back. "And it's Dr. Taylor."

"Please, he saved me." I was trying not to whine. "I just wanted to see him again. He didn't have to lift a finger but he did. He hurt himself to help me for *no reason.* And then he blew it off like it was nothing."

"It—" the pretty blonde in the corner began, the first time she'd spoken. She looked about seventeen, which she probably wasn't. "It was—"

"It *wasn't* nothing. He broke his leg for me."

Betsy, she of the vampire kingdom and blond highlights, snapped her fingers. "Son of a bitch! Your limp!" She whirled on Marc, whose dazed expression hadn't changed since Dr. Taylor dragged me into the kitchen ear-first. "Why didn't you tell me?"

Marc snapped out of his trance. *Please let it be a sex trance brought on by cauliflower ear.* "I tried! You blew it off to take the dogs for a walk and then my leg was—and then I kind of forgot about it."

"Because your broken leg got better," I said and got a

bunch of glares in reply. "Because you're not human. Any of you." I glared at Dr. Taylor. "Well, maybe you."

"Watch your mouth, boy."

"I'm not a boy," I said with the little dignity I had left. "I'm almost thirty." This prompted the little blonde and Mr. Sinclair to burst out laughing. So they were significantly older than thirty. "And you don't have to worry about me. I knew about vampires before your sister outed you."

"Oh?" The little blonde came closer. Her body language was pure deference, but her eyes missed nothing. I wondered how many people looked at her curves and her sweet face and never saw the knife. Or the fangs. "Would you like a drink while you explain yourself?"

"Please." I didn't even have to think about it. Whatever I needed to do to stay as long as I could. If she'd offered to give me a tattoo, I would have agreed just as quickly. Did they want their basement cleaned? Did the dogs need baths? Anything. "Hey, are you guys drinking smoothies? That's not very sexy-scary. You're going to ruin vampire reps everywhere."

This time Betsy laughed. "Want one?"

"Sure. Raspberry and . . . strawberry!"

"And blackberry," she added glumly.

"Uck, those things are all seeds. But I'm sure they're delicious in drinks," I added.

She beamed, which made everything weirder. Out of everything I'd done and said, dissing blackberries made her warm to me?

Who cared? Whatever it took.

In a few minutes Dr. Taylor had left, so I could relax a bit. Marc pointed out the idiocy of being afraid of a human and not the vampires, or whatever Marc was, and I replied that I couldn't explain it, it just *was*. This pleased them all, but I've no idea why.

"I don't believe in vampires because of what I overheard,

or what your sister said," I explained, sipping at the best smoothie I'd ever had in my life (the secret, the little blonde explained, was real vanilla and fresh fruit). "I always believed in them."

"Why?" Betsy asked, and though she'd warmed to me a bit, she was clearly still suspicious. So, not a *complete* idiot.

"My sources told me."

"And they are . . . ?"

"Spirits." She just blinked, so I elaborated. "Ghosts. I see dead people, pardon the line."

"See?" she cried, pointing at me, and then at them for some reason. "That's how screwed our lives are. That thing he just said? Didn't sound insane!" She stopped pointing and calmed down. "You should be careful when you say something we can actually test."

"It's true. When I found out where you lived, I went to the Griggs Mansion and checked with my sources and they confirmed you're a vampire." I looked at Marc and then looked away. It was too tempting to just stare helplessly at him. "They didn't know what you are, though."

"Well, that makes sense." Marc, who'd spent most of the time looking stunned, finally warmed to the conversation. "It's considered the most haunted house in the Twin Cities. People have seen—let me think—a maid, a gardener, a Civil War general—"

"Yeah, that's bullshit. 'Scuse me, ma'am," I added politely to the little blonde who looked like a teen but wasn't. "He's a Union soldier who deserted."

"And you know this because . . ." Tina (she'd introduced herself while pouring my smoothie) paused delicately.

"He told me himself." I looked around at all of them. "It's all on my website."

"The G-Spot," the vampire queen said and snickered. At my beleaguered sigh she added, "Simmer down, Haley

Joel Osment. If that's what you're gonna name something, you have to be resigned to getting shit for it."

"Fair enough."

"Do you know why we've been sitting here for an hour drinking smoothies instead of running you off or draining you dry?"

"No." I gulped. "I know it's not because you're worried about negative publicity."

"I could give a shit. If I thought you were a danger to anyone I loved, you'd be so much cooling meat on a slab somewhere. I haven't disappeared you because I believe you when you say you're grateful to Marc."

"I am! He didn't have to help me. And he's the only man I've ever met who has a bigger crush on John Cusack than I do." I have *no* idea why I said that. It just slipped out.

"Okay, I'm not commenting on that at all, or we'll be here all night."

"John Cusack?" Tina asked while Marc groaned and buried his face in his hands. "Really?"

"But listen, I See Dead People: if it turns out we're wrong—if the only reason you're being so friendly is because you're trying to get your scoop—"

I giggled, but stopped when she scowled. "Sorry. You know it's not 1957, right?"

"Shut up. If I find out you're using him to get info on us, unbelievably terrible things will happen to you." She topped off my smoothie. "But in the meantime." She dropped a whole strawberry on top as a garnish: plop! "Tell me about your sources."

So I did. I figured the more they knew about me, the more they'd relax and the longer I could stay. And I was showing off a little for Marc, who always looked away when I glanced at him, but whose gaze I felt when my attention was on one of the others.

I told them about having no idea that the many playmates

of my childhood were dead until school started and none of the other kids could see them. I told them about the multiple visits with the school psychologist, about never knowing my mom, at ten losing my dad to cancer, and the devastation of never seeing their ghosts. I told them about using the money Dad had left me to try to find other people who were like me, and never succeeding. I talked and talked and they didn't interrupt me once, or laugh, or even look skeptical.

At one point Betsy excused herself and came back about ten minutes later with a slim blonde (Minnesota could be a bit homogeneous) who had a ponytail and a cynical expression. Betsy didn't refer to the woman in any way, and neither did the others, so I ignored her, too.

"And then Marc pushed me out of the way of a news van, even though he had every reason to stand back and watch me get clipped, and I snuck back in to thank him."

"Thank you for explaining," Tina said.

"You really— It wasn't necessary," Marc muttered. "It was no big deal."

"Don't say that," I said. "It was a big deal to me." I took a breath and forced it out. "I think you're wonderful. I want to know all about you. I don't care that you aren't human."

"Are you?" Betsy asked. She seemed honestly curious, and the suspicion seemed to be gone. She certainly didn't have to worry about me hurting her—any of them. I was well aware that I was at their mercy; it wasn't the other way around. "Human, I mean."

"Sure. Being able to see ghosts doesn't translate to, I don't know, werewolf or something." I forced a laugh, then stopped when I saw they weren't even smiling. Oh, God. Were werewolves a thing, too? I made a mental note to ask my sources.

"If we aren't going to drink his blood until he dies of shock," Sinclair said, effortlessly terrifying me, "we *do* have business to attend to elsewhere."

"Yep, yep." Betsy got up off her stool and it looked like— Yes! They were going to leave me! With Marc! Who wasn't moving off his stool! All the dangers and ear wrenching I'd endured were worth it. But . . .

"Aren't you going to ask me about the ghost standing by the stove? About five foot five, blond ponytail, khakis, red sweater, scowling?"

"Ah," Betsy said, sounding pleased. "You *do* see her, I was starting to wonder. What's her name?"

"I don't know, she hasn't told me."

"But you definitely see her?" Tina asked, looking at me with a lot more interest.

"Of course he sees me, you Southern belle boob," the ghost said crossly. "And my name's Cathie. Betsy, you dragged me out of Hell for this? To vet the latest addition to the mansion freak show? Father Markus is undermining you all over the place and I've got more new arrivals to assign buddies to." To me: "Take my advice: run and never look back."

"Nope." I clutched my glass at the very thought. "I like it here. I like them."

She let out an inelegant snort. "Hope you like constant chaos and spending way too much time drinking pulped fruit when the Big Bad isn't trying to kill you and Betsy's not bitching about missing a shoe sale. Because that's what you're in for."

"Sounds great," I said, which was nothing but the truth. "I'm Will Mason, by the way."

"Oh, who cares?" she said and walked through the wall and disappeared.

"So." I cleared my throat and found a smile. "Do I pass?"

"You bet," Betsy said, and those were the magic words, because everyone else loosened up. "Welcome. Next time just knock and come in like my mom did. Don't skulk in the mudroom."

"Thank you." Yes! Yes! Yes! To Marc: "And thank you, again."

"I'm a zombie," he said in abrupt reply. "I'm not a sexy vampire or a mysterious ghost. It's nothing cool or fun."

"Cathie wasn't especially mysterious," I commented. A zombie! Fascinating! "I'm glad. If you'd been human you could have been hurt or killed when you helped me. That wouldn't have been fun for either of us."

He stared at me like I'd spouted Swahili. "You saw my blood. You *saw* it and it wasn't that color because it was getting dark. I have sluggish black blood because I'm a zombie."

"Sluggish is good. Cuts down on ruining clothes, and bleeding out." My sources had died in so many ways, and most of them sounded awful.

"You're glad? That's not— You're not disgusted?"

I realized they'd all left. That I was alone in that cavernous kitchen with that gorgeous man. Zombie. Gorgeous zombie. *They left me with this wonderful, beautiful zombie.* I reached out and, when he didn't flinch away, took his hand. "You feel cool," I said, squeezing slightly. "But you're not, y'know, squishy or gross or anything. And your leg's better." I tightened my grip and felt my pulse zoom when he squeezed back, just a little. "If you're a zombie, you haven't been dead very long. It's fine if you don't want to talk about it. I already said: I'm not here for work. I just wanted to see you again. I'm so glad to see you again."

He was shaking his head like he couldn't believe he was there. Or I was there. "You really don't care?"

"I care. I already told you, I'm glad you're a zombie, I'm glad you can't get hurt or die—again, I mean." Didn't he know? Everyone died. Everyone died and left me. Except for the people who lived in this house.

He took a deep breath (did he have to breathe?) and told me things. Wonderful, terrifying things. We talked for hours. I wanted to kiss him but didn't dare. But I never let go of his hand (except to go to the bathroom, and he'd loosened up enough by then to tease me about having to take a piss).

I don't know when I'll kiss him. But I will.

I can't wait. I—I hope he can't wait, either.

Who cares about vampires? Tell me more about zombies.

I found myself in my office, stepped out, and said, "I want Cathie right now." And like that, she was there.

"*God*, that's disconcerting. What?" she complained. "What d'you want?"

I grinned; I couldn't help it. In a dimension where millions were terrified of me, her snark was refreshing. "I've got a guy at the mansion who says he can see ghosts."

"What am I, a litmus test for weirdos?"

"Perfectly put. Yes. I need to bring you to the mansion for a couple of minutes, but you can come right back. And then I want you to hang out in the food court for a bit."

, She looked interested. "Something up?"

"Yes."

"Sharing deets?"

"No."

"Boo. Okay, but just for a minute. Your stepmother and I have been working on the buddy system—"

"Yes!" I cried. "That's it!" So much going on this week, and I kept forgetting to tackle something: "I want Cindy and Lawrence. Right now."

"Who are you— Oh."

And there they were, looking startled to suddenly find themselves outside my office and, when they caught sight of each other, looking crushed.

Cindy broke first, taking a tentative step forward. "Oh, Lawrence. Lawrence, I'm so—"

"Cindy, my poor child, can you forgive me?"

She stopped short. "Me forgive *you*? No, jeez, I'm the one who killed you, can you forgive *me*?"

"Nonsense. Don't be a silly g— Don't be silly. It's my fault. I filled your head with so much nonsense and when you needed me I refused to help."

"You *did* help: you tried to warn me. I was stupid and selfish—"

"Oh, ugh," Cathie muttered, looking like she'd rather be anywhere, anywhere but there. I would have giggled if it hadn't been deadly serious business for Lawrence and Cindy.

"You were your mother's daughter, determined to make your own way. I should have respected that instead of dismissing your wishes because of your youth."

"You were right to dismiss them; it was a dangerous, stupid plan and I deserved to have Betsy cut my head off."

"Oh, ugh," Cathie said again, rubbing her forehead.

"Then I shall forgive you, my dear, if you're kind enough to forgive me."

They were ignoring me completely.

It was kind of glorious. And then they were hugging, and that was kind of glorious, too.

"Can you please," Cathie asked sweetly, "get us the fuck out of here?"

"It's always so nice to see you," I said, smirking, and her wish was my command.

CHAPTER
FORTY-ONE

"Please don't construe this as criticism," the vampire king said critically, "but it's so *odd* that Hell looks exactly like the Mall of America."

"Hey, the system works." "The system" meaning Hell looked like whatever the person in charge wanted it to look like. When Lucifer was in charge, Hell was a waiting room leading to any one of a million billion doors with something awful behind each one. Dead kittens. IRS auditors. Severed heads. The Payless ShoeSource website. "And really? You're here five minutes and you're giving me crap?"

"Mostly to conceal my terror and admiration," he admitted. He glanced at me and smiled. *Thank you for allowing my return.*

Okay, so our link works in Hell if you're here, but not when you're in the real world. Interesting . . .

I don't know that the mansion is the real world anymore. Surely after all you've seen, it cannot be so.

It is to me, Sinclair.

Fair enough, beloved. For me, the real world is wherever you are.

Awwww.

"Quit it," Marc said, waving at us like we were flies. Flies with a telepathic link. "Bad enough when you gaze at each other without talking for an hour back home. I won't put up with something that annoying in Hell." When I laughed at him, he grinned. "I'd better rephrase."

"You'd rather be canoodling with Will Mason," Tina teased. She and Marc were holding hands. Not like that, of course. Sometimes I think she saw Marc as an overgrown kid and herself as his protector/honorary aunt, because often when she grabbed his hand it was to lead him toward or away from something. ("Be careful, Marc, the fire is hot and will burn you." "Tina, please stop hiding the paper clips. I promise I won't put one in my mouth and choke.") He tolerated it, because he adored her. "A shame you couldn't call on him before we left."

"Okay, first, never say 'canoodling' again. Second, we're going out tomorrow and I happen to be scared shitless. My first date since I died. My first date altogether in three years. My first—"

"It will be fine," she assured him, patting his hand. "He seems like a sweet boy."

A useful boy as well, my husband thought, and I grinned.

My thought, too. I never go looking for ghosts—the few who find me never leave me alone until I do whatever chore they left behind when they died. But it'd be pretty handy to have someone around who could see and hear them. Think of all the good gossip he could tell us!

Intelligence, my darling.

Dress it up how you like, pal, it's still gossip. It's talking about people behind their backs about things they don't want you talking about.

. . .

Ha. Got him.

We were entering the food court, which was teeming with the damned. Funny how people often stuck to a schedule—it was 12:32 p.m. HST (Hellish standard time), so that meant it was time to hang in the food court and stand in line, choke down something you were allergic to, be offered drinks you couldn't stand, or get stuck talking to people you cordially loathed.

Speaking of cordial loathing, the Ant was at one of the larger tables with Cathie and Father Markus. She saw us and kept talking. Cathie turned, spotted us, rolled her eyes, and jerked her head in a "come on over" gesture. The Ant's surliness made Cathie seem like Miss Congeniality (and I should know).[20]

A path magically cleared for us and we started toward them. I could see Cindy and Lawrence sharing a table and talking, Cindy with her hands while she gabbled at him, Lawrence leaning forward and listening intently, smiling every once in a while. Good; that was settled, then. One less thing to worry about.

I could sense Sinclair's surprise and pleasure at the deference, and . . . yep, there it was. Pride, too, that I could command that kind of respect. He knew they had no idea who he was, knew they weren't parting like the Red Sea for him or Marc or Tina. Seeing so clearly into his emotional state made me ashamed it had taken me so long to let him come back to Hell. Our link working here was no excuse; the link worked fine in the real world, too. I could have seen his pride in me if I'd bothered to look. Instead, the only things I looked for were reasons to exclude him.

---

[20] We found out Betsy is a recovering Miss Congeniality (Burnsville High School) in *Undead and Unwed*.

The Ant's eyebrows were arching, but not quite high enough to disappear beneath her hard shiny bangs. "Hello again, Betsy's husband." She wasn't kidding. She'd never bothered to learn his name. "Hi, Marc!" Whoa. Actual warmth.

"You know you missed me," Marc replied, smiling. She giggled
(!!!!!!!!!!!!)
I know! My thought exactly: !!!!!!!!!!!!!
and ducked her head.

"Father Markus was just explaining why the buddy system should be dismantled."

"I didn't use the term 'dismantled,'" he said mildly. He turned to me. "I understand you're trying to lighten your own workload by getting the souls here to take on some of the burden. But you're laboring under the same misunderstanding you always have: it's not your job to make things easier for them."

"Actually, I'll be the one who decides what my job is." I kept my tone mild, too. "We've had this discussion already. The buddy system stays. The new and improved Ten Commandments stay. Which reminds me, it's time for me to work on the new and improved Seven Deadly Sins. Being jealous because your neighbor got backstage passes to Jim Gaffigan is no reason to be damned for eternity."

"That is *enough.*" Father Markus was on his feet, face flushed. "With all respect, Betsy, that's idiotic."

Don't, I thought as Sinclair's fist clenched. *Seriously: you keep the fuck out of this. I mean it.*

As you will.

Thank you.

If he touches you, I may have to disobey. Punish me as you will. His thought was serious and unwavering, like a five-hundred-watt flashlight in a dark basement: this is what will happen, I'm sorry to disobey, I will accept the consequences. There were some things a chivalrous man in his nineties couldn't tolerate, I guess.

It didn't matter, it wasn't going to come to that. But I made a mental note to give the old duffer a serious scolding when we were back at the mansion. After I'd fucked him.

"You know, Markus, I've about had it with your attitude. For a guy who's never been out of Minnesota, you're pretty surly."

"Minnesota Nice is a lie," he replied, so I punched him.

Ohhh, did I punch him. My hand snapped into a fist and I belted him in the face as hard as I could. That punch, which had been trying to escape for at least a week, came up from my heels and knocked him twenty feet through the air until his momentum was stopped by a helpful cement pillar.

Total, complete silence—no one gasped, no one stirred, it was just a sea of open mouths and eyes everywhere—broken by Markus groaning and trying to sit up. Once he sat up he tried to stand. Took a few tries, and I was bitchy enough to take pride in that.

I actually heard the click as he pushed his dislocated jaw back into place and Marc hissed in sympathy behind me. "That usually requires big-time anesthesia," he muttered to Tina, who murmured agreement. They were still holding hands, looking less like an elderly auntie watching out for her boy, and more like Hansel and Gretel wondering when the witch was going to make her move.

????????

Wait.

Excellent punch, beloved. Anything that flies that far and fast usually has wings.

Shut up. I'm working.

"Nnn fffrrr," Markus said, limping toward me. He'd broken an ankle or a leg when he hit the pillar, too.

"You should put some ice on that," I suggested, smiling. "Or a cast."

He shook his head again, spraying blood in fat drops. He opened his mouth but this time I cut him off.

"Who are you?"

He just looked at me.

"There's this nifty thing called the Directory of the Archdiocese of Saint Paul and Minneapolis," I told him. "It's online, and free. It lists all the priests and their backgrounds. Father Markus was born in Connecticut and ordained in Boston. He only got to Minnesota a decade ago." I reached out, seized him by his fake collar, and hauled him toward me until we were nose to nose. "Who are you?"

Those bright brown eyes, which I'd often thought were sparkling with compassion and humor, were gleaming with what I now knew was scorn. "You know," he whispered, kissing-close. "Don't you?"

I dropped him and he fell to his knees, scrambled back, and then made the painful climb to his feet again. Except he was moving quicker, easier. The blood was drying, disappearing. The broken bones were reknitting. The black suit and collar were fading. He was shrinking into something else. No. Someone else.

I turned to my family, who'd been watching in stunned and fascinated silence. "You guys remember Lucifer, right?"

And there she was, looking as Satan always had to me: like Lena Olin in a wonderful black suit, sheer black stockings, and black Christian Louboutin Pagalle pumps.

One eyelid dropped in a small wink. "Miss me, sweetie?"

CHAPTER
FORTY-TWO

"Oh my God," Marc managed. He looked around. "I might need to sit down. Possibly forever. You killed her!" He said that to me like I'd fallen down on the job, or lied. "It's the whole reason you're stuck running Hell! It's the only reason we're in Hell with you!"

"Well, there's killed," the devil replied, still absurdly cheerful, "and then there's killed."

"I always maintained she let me win," I replied, because it was true. The devil and I had fought to the death, and we'd gone at it hard, but somewhere in there I'd gotten the sense that she wanted out, wanted to be gone, wanted away. Why else do me a favor as she was leaving? Why else grant me a wish, and let Sinclair bear the light of God's love again?

"How'd you know?" Satan seemed honestly curious. "Checking the directory was a neat trick, but how'd you even get suspicious enough to do that?"

Sinclair's thoughts were so stunned, they seemed to come from far away. *She was a fool to underestimate you.*

Yeah, maybe. But I'm not going to make the same mistake. She's the Lady of Lies, you know.

The Ant coughed into her fist. "I'd like to know that, too. Because I—" She left it unspoken, but I knew her. She meant: *I knew Satan better than any of you—we were friends, kind of—and if I didn't suspect; how the bleeding hell did you?*

"There were lots of hints," I said.

"Oh?" Satan smirked, because she was a bitch. "Enlighten me."

"When you said that thing, 'Behold, evil's coming forth' or whatever . . ."

"'Behold, evil is going forth from nation to nation,' *that* tipped you off?"

"I looked it up when I got home. It's from the Old Testament. Catholics in general and priests in particular tend to stick with the New Testament. And you knew who that Civil War guy was—David? Davis? Not Jefferson Davis—most Americans have heard of him. You knew about the *other* Davis, the one who murdered his CO and never went to trial, the Davis almost no one has heard of. I remember being surprised you were a Civil War buff when it had never come up before. When you'd never asked Tina about anything Civil War related, though you knew she lived through it. That seemed out of character. My mom's doctorate is all about the Civil War and she practically stalks Tina. Why didn't you?"

"Perhaps because I could speak with any number of people who lived through it here?" she suggested.

"That's another thing. You knew so many backstories of the damned, but you were never seen interviewing anyone. You just knew what they'd done in life to deserve their punishment in death. I put it down to efficiency, but after a while I realized nobody was *that* efficient. You knew their stories because you know everyone here. Because you're *you*. And even in disguise, you're so fucking vain you couldn't resist sticking up for yourself."

She'd been listening to me with what looked like fond attention, head tipped to one side as she smiled. The smile dropped off at that. "Explain yourself."

"Don't you remember? We were in one of our meetings—one of the many meetings *you* scheduled—and got to wondering where you—Satan you, not Father Markus you—had gone to. Someone suggested Heaven, and you were pretty quick to point out that the devil wouldn't set foot in Heaven for anything. And not because the devil was sulking—except you were, Satan, just admit it already: you've been in a billion-year sulk, a sulk for the ages.

"You said it was more complicated than that—except it wasn't. You said even if God could forgive, 'who's to say the Morningstar would want forgiveness'? You were supposed to be a kindly priest, but couldn't resist defending your childish bullshit. It's hilarious when you think about it."

Any pretense of being interested in how she'd given herself away, how this was just too cute and my goodness wasn't Betsy adorable, dropped away. Satan was scowling, and I'd like to say it wasn't a pretty sight, except she looked like Lena Olin, so it was.

She gestured to the masses of souls behind her. "No need to do this in front of everyone."

"Oh, sure, *now* you need privacy."

She gritted her teeth. "All of you: disperse."

NOBODY FUCKING MOVE.

I hadn't said it. I'd thought it the way I did with Sinclair. And I fired that thought like a bullet into every soul in Hell.

Nobody moved.

"Where's the real Father Markus?"

"How should I know?" she cried, recovering quickly. Had to give it to her, Satan was like those stand-alone punching bags with sand in their base. You could punch them, but they bopped right back up. "Not here, that's for sure! He's in Heaven with my Father, I suppose, or haunting a rectory somewhere. I needed to be someone you'd trust, so he was it."

Well. I guess it was good that the real Father Markus wasn't condemned to Hell. Still, it made me sad for some reason, because I should have been happy for him. But now wasn't the time.

"You're here, you're 'alive,' whatever that means anymore. But you're not as strong as you were, because Hell is mine now. They"—nodding to the souls who hadn't budged—"listen to me now. So tell me: why couldn't I make it rain in the conference room? Why do some things here bend to my will, and some don't?"

"Because you didn't really want it to rain, you were clutching at a straw. When you really needed a watch, Hell provided. When you're just bitching, Hell's got nothing to fix on."

"That sounds completely made up."

She shrugged. "Mouthing words with nothing behind them isn't bending Hell to your will. It's just babbling, for which I assume you could take the gold."

I smirked. "Yes, I babbled and I'm so stupid and, by the way, I saw through you in less than a week. So how about you choke on that for a while, you hateful tricky twat?"

Ever wonder what Satan would look like if she tried to swallow her own face? I don't, because I know. It's pretty funny. And like all mistresses of deflection, she didn't directly respond. She just turned to the Ant (who was wearing a distinct "ulp!" expression) and said, "I expected better of you, Antonia."

"Me?" she gasped. "Why, what was I supposed to do?"

"Prevent some of her sillier changes from going through! Rewriting the Ten? *Buddies?* And now she's rewriting the Seven? What shit!"

"Well, I expected better of you," the Ant replied, drawing herself up, her big, shellacked hair making her seem taller than she was. "You let her kill you, for what? So you could sneak back in and try to slow down any changes to your precious regime? That's not worthy of you, Lucifer. Stay or go, but don't do this cowardly in-between nonsense."

"I know nobody says this anymore," Marc murmured to Tina, "but oh, snap!"

"Shut *up!*" Satan snapped.

Marc gulped. "Yes, ma'am."

"Oh, you're disappointed in me?" the devil taunted. "You think I should have confided in you? Did you think we were friends?"

"No." That was it, just "no." My stepmother stood on her dignity, which I would have thought was impossible.

"Good. We were never friends." She ignored the Ant's flinch and continued. "I allowed you to be the Vessel for the Antichrist, and when you left your tiresome dull life by way of your tiresome dull death, I put you to work so you'd feel wanted. That's all you were to me: a worker bee. And I would have thought that you'd know a real leader from the false moron who's been pretending to be in charge."

"She might be a moron, but she's doing a pretty good job so far. And as she pointed out, she figured you out pretty quick."

"A fluke from a flake."

"Ladies." I cleared my throat. "I'm right here. Well within earshot." Also, this was further proof (like I needed it) that this was all happening in Hell: the Ant was sticking up for me. And appeared to be sincere! Soon: the three horses of the Apocalypse. Wait. Four horses. Right? Red, white, black, and pink. No. Pale. Right? Argh.

I shook off thoughts of pink horses. "But why?" I asked. "Why do any of it? Why let me kill you and then sneak back and try to help, kind of, when not trying to undermine me? Because you *were* helpful, some of the time. But how come?"

"I wanted to see how you'd do at the helm. I couldn't give you on-the-job training unless I came back disguised like someone you'd trust. If you sucked at this too much," Satan said with aggravating cheer—I'd never known anyone to get so mad and then recover so quickly—"you'd have been replaced. My daughter might have been stuck with it. I went to too much trouble to prevent that, so I wasn't going to just stay gone and risk that my sacrifice was for nothing."

"God forbid," I muttered. Blech: even after dealing with Satan, I still had to go back and deal with her rotten kid. Well, one thing at a time. Meanwhile, the devil was still pontificating.

"I might not have had control over how that went, or what happened after. *You,* though. You're almost trainable, and occasionally close to being bright. And you know what they say." One eye closed in a slow wink. "The devil you know, right?"

"Ugh." Overdone, but it was all I could think of to say. Then: "So all those times you said you were praying on one of my ideas, you were never praying."

"Duh."

"We're done," I decided. I turned to check with my friends. "Unless you guys had anything to add?"

I never saw so many heads shake so quickly: no, nope, definitely not, we're good, carry on.

"I'll leave when I'm damned good—"

"You were never good." I took a deep (unnecessary) breath. It helped. Kept my knees from shaking, anyway. I'd half wondered if at this point in the festivities, we'd be fighting to the death again, or if the devil would have just tossed me out of Hell on my toned butt. "I want you gone. I want you away forever."

"You can't—"

The archdiocese directory wasn't the only thing I'd studied. "I command you, demon. Get you gone from here. Leave Hell behind, now and forever."

"Don't. Don't do that."

I drew myself up and, unlike the Ant, didn't need pineapple-colored hair to look imposing. "You are cast out. *Get you gone!*"

It wasn't at all dramatic. She'd didn't explode, or vanish in a flash of light or a puff of brimstone, or let loose with a cackle like Maleficent and stay right where she was. She just faded. She got lighter and paler and her expression went from pissed to surprised to astonished to frightened and she just faded away.

You know the saying "you could have heard a pin drop"? Not this time; at least a thousand people were murmuring and gasping. You couldn't have heard a platoon of pins dropping.

"Oh, good," I managed. I turned so my back was to the damned, so I was facing my family and could let my expression relax. "I was kind of afraid that wouldn't work."

"What *was* that?" Marc managed. "Did you look up some kind of spell book?"

"No. It's from *The Eyes of the Dragon*. You know, Stephen King?" At their combined incredulous gazes I added, "What? I don't do magic. And it's not about the words, anyway. It's about the will. *My* will. Which reminds me." I turned to the king of the vampires, who looked equal parts staggered and proud. "About Hell: I got this. Okay?"

"Yes, dread queen."

"Okeydokey, then." I turned back to the damned. "Lawrence, could you come over here for a second?"

He was on his feet at once, and if he was nervous about Satan 2.0 calling him out in front of everyone, he didn't show it. He looked as he had when he was one of mine (although he still was, but this time not as a vampire): dark suit, carefully groomed, immaculate. When he got close he dropped to one knee. "Majesty," he murmured at the floor.

"None of that," I said and stepped forward to seize him by the armpits and ungracefully haul him up. "Sinclair, you were asking about Lawrence. Here he is."

"My king," he said, smiling.

"My old friend," Sinclair replied. They clasped hands in a vigorous handshake, the way older men did when what they wanted to do was hug.

"Lawrence, Sinclair was telling me all about you—your old nickname was Never-Tells-a-Lie or something—"

"No-Sugar-in-Your-Mouth."

"Right. You were really good at going back and forth between the Native Americans and the army."

"That was my duty and my honor, my queen."

"Well, as it happens I've got a spot on my committee, and I could use someone with your skills. Interested?"

He bowed. Man, these guys knew how to class it up. "My duty is again my honor, good lady. I thank you."

"Welcome." Then: *Now, don't sulk, Sinclair. I don't need you on the committee. I need you in the real world, our world.*

Of course, my own.

Oh, sure, "of course." All I had to do was outwit the devil— again—to earn your respect?

You've always had it, my own. But now you have my unshakable confidence. It goes hard with me, letting the woman I love fight her own battles. But, like you, I am learning.

All I can ask. I smiled at him, but the smile morphed into a scowl when Marc whispered to Lawrence, "They do that a lot. Stare at each other silently while sending vampire vibes back and forth. It's beyond creepy."

I rounded on him. "You know, I *did* just thoroughly defeat evil *again*. Would a teensy bit of deference be out of the question?"

"That's exactly the amount of deference we give you," he replied. "A teensy bit."

"Oh. Well." I looked at the Ant. "Thanks for sticking up for me."

"Let's not talk about it."

I laughed; I couldn't help it. "Agreed. It'll never be spoken of again." And to my great surprise, I got a real smile out of Antonia Taylor for the first time ever.

CHAPTER
FORTY-THREE

The last thing. Well, the second-to-last thing. Laura was fretting impatiently in the Peach Parlor (she was no longer welcome in the kitchen and was forever barred from Smoothie Time). "Finally," she complained, which for some reason she thought was an acceptable greeting. "I've been here five minutes."

"Yeah, yeah. It's been a busy day. Thanks for coming."

"Yes, well. I imagine you have some things to say to me."

I just looked at her. She was earnest and smug, and a little nervous. She looked beautiful, as she always did. She'd taken some care with her appearance; I'd never seen her in a sweater dress before. Deep blue, knee length, with ribbed tights in the same shade. Scuffed flats from Payless, which I heroically decided to ignore. Long hair held back from her face with a wide black headband. No makeup; the lucky bitch didn't need it.

"It doesn't matter what you say," she said, clearly anxious to get on with her agenda. "I'm going forward with this. You think the media was bad this week? More and more cities are picking up the story. People who've been attacked by your vampires are speaking up, since they realize there's a good chance they'll be believed. None of your denials will—"

"We're not denying it."

"—do any— What?"

"We're not. Denying it. Oh, the first plan was to kidnap and rape a bunch of brains, specifically media brains, you know, the usual. But we're not doing that this time. We're not denying anything; we're not fighting you on this. At all."

"That— You're lying."

"Nope."

"You are."

"Nope. And I've got you to thank for it."

"Now you *are* lying."

"Are you as deaf as you are outmatched? Pay attention: I've made some changes in Hell and they're going pretty great." That might be an exaggeration, but Laura didn't need to know that. "Sometimes old, outdated rules are old and outdated, so they've gotta be pitched. Or at least reworked. Doing the job *you* tricked me into is what gave me the idea, so thanks for that."

"You would never. It's too dangerous. You'd never risk *your people.*" That last was spit out; oooh, jealous much? *The mindless worshipping minions not really doing it for you, Laura? It's not much good without friends, is it?* "It's too risky."

I laughed. "Risky. That's funny. What isn't these days? You used to know that, before you turned traitor. Oh, and you might have doomed the planet, too."

"I— No!" She was on her feet, but I didn't move. I was nice and comfy on the love seat across from her and would remain relaxed while she lost her shit. I have to say: I was really looking forward to it. "That's *you*; that's your people, your vampire nation. That's why you have to stay in the shadows; that's why you're lying about coming forward—"

"And that's exactly my point: we can't stay in the shadows anymore. Time to embrace the twenty-first century and the sooner the better. We probably would have come to this decision on our own, just not this soon. But . . ." I shrugged. "Since you're bringing it about, why fight it? But that's the least of your problems because, again, you might have screwed the world. Good trick for a virgin!"

"Why are you lying?" This in a whisper, and I had to grit my teeth

(stay strong stay strong she's her mother's daughter but you are too)

at her sad, overwhelmed expression. Poor kid. No fucking idea what she'd unleashed—as usual.

"Betsy, just tell me the truth. Okay? Stop saying these lies and trying to get me upset and just be honest."

"Okay." I pinched the bridge of my nose and had sympathy for anyone who'd had to deal with me when I did something deliberately, awfully stupid. "Here's the truth: you're such a numb-cunt sometimes." I hated that word, I almost never used it. It was so cruel and misogynistic and filthy. But it had to be said. The Antichrist was a cunt.

Shocked, she had no response, but her knuckles whitened. Since she wasn't clutching anything, it was kind of impressive.

"You remember Ancient Me in the future, right? That particular detail hasn't vacated your brain while you've been running around implementing phase one of Getting Daddy to Love You, right?"

She reddened. "That's not—"

"And you remember how I'd— How shall I put this? How in the future I *took over the fucking planet and ruled over a desolate winter wasteland*, right?[21] You recall that? Vaguely?"

"But that's— We fixed it. When we came back the timeline was changed so that could never—"

"Maybe one of the reasons Crone Betsy took over was because somebody outed vampires and she had to take on the world, you oblivious shithead! Did you ever once think of that?"

She hadn't. I could see it on her face. She rallied pretty quickly, though, and I saw some of my own "this has caught me off guard but I'm surging ahead anyway, so fuck it" attitude come to the fore. "That won't happen. The tyrant Betsy made Marc a vampire . . . *you* made him a zombie."

"No, fuckwit, Ancient Me made him a zombie!" Somehow Old Me had gone back in time, raised recently suicided Marc as a zombie, and disappeared back to her own timeline, never to be seen again. "How can you forget this really important shit when you were there? Oh, but I know how." I stood, because I was kicking her out. "You don't give a shit about saving the world. Outing us isn't about protecting people, it's about proving you're good and I'm not. So, prove it. Actually *help people* instead of stirring up shit. And did it never occur to you that I might tell the world you're the Antichrist?" I wouldn't. I had no interest in speeding up anything that would make her embrace her birthright and drag the planet into her sad-ass idea of a necessary war between good and evil.

"Yes." She'd slumped back into her seat, which was too bad because, like I said: time to go, bitch! "But who'd believe you?"

I just looked at her. "So. Many. People. Now get out."

"What?"

---

[21] It's true. *Undead and Unfinished.* Ancient Betsy was awful.

"I said get out. You've abused my good nature for the last time, Laura."

"Good nature!" She was on her feet again—excellent—and practically choking on the words. "You've never been—"

"Oh, shut up. I genuinely don't care. Go away now. Forever, if you like. Oh, and tell Dad that I haven't forgotten about him. Well, I have, in that I'm not tracking his ass down anytime soon, but he— Oh my God, he left." I could see it at once. Laura had the worst poker face ever. "He's gone! Isn't he? He helped you make a mess and then he snuck out of town and left you with the broom." I laughed again. "That is so like him! That's exactly like him. He's not anything like you'd hoped, is he? Oh, God, that's hilarious." Chuckling, I shooed her toward the door. "And speaking of terrible parents who continually disappoint, your mom says hi."

Oooh, that got her. She'd been stumbling toward the door, fending off my "shoo, shoo!" motions, and now turned so quickly she nearly fell. "What? When did you see my mother?"

"In Hell, just before I kicked her ass out. Again. And that time I did lie: she didn't say hi. She didn't say anything about you at all. Makes you wonder, doesn't it?" We were at the front door by now, and I was pretending not to notice my roommates scrambling out of the entryway, like I hadn't heard them sneaking close to eavesdrop the minute I entered the parlor. "If you ever needed a reason to turn your back on your parents and live by your own code, you've got it now. You don't owe either of them a thing: you can be true to yourself.

"But you won't. You're locked into showing everyone you're good. But you can't do that by just being good. No, you have to show them someone who's *bad* and force a comparison. You picked the wrong girl for that one. *Again.*"

"Stop pushing," she snapped. "I'm going!"

"Well, finally." I wrenched the door open. "If I see you again—"

"Yes, yes, you'll kill me, that'll definitely show how good you are."

"—I'll slap the shit out of you, probably in front of witnesses. It'll be hilarious!" I giggled at the thought, gave her one last shove, and slammed the door in her furious confused beautiful red face.

Then I leaned against it and blew out a breath. Whew! Stressful, but satisfying.

Which was the perfect description of my life, come to think of it.

EPILOGUE

I walked onstage, already blinking despite the sunglasses.
It had nothing to do with my sensitive vamp vision and
everything to do with all the lights trained on me. Already
this whole thing was a pain. At least Tina knew how to
call a press conference; I'd had no idea.

I stepped up to the podium and faced a dozen microphones that looked like big black ice cream cones (lico-
rice? Earl Grey?).

I cleared my throat (note to self: break that unnecessary
habit) and said, "Hi, my name is Betsy Taylor, and I'm
the queen of the vampires. Yes, vampires are real.

"Any questions?"